Forever's Fight

FOREVER CREEK SHIFTERS: BOOK ONE

MARISSA DOBSON

Published by Dobson Ink
Printed in the United States of America
ISBN-13: 978-1-939978-65-3

Dedication

To my readers, who have loved the Alaskan Tigers series. I hope you enjoy the Forever Creek Shifters.

To my husband, who took Pup Cameron out of my office and played with him when I needed to work. For Pup Cameron who eventually realized Mommy couldn't play all the time.

Thank you, Teresa Riley, for your feedback on *Forever's Fight* and for all the work you've done so I could focus on this book. To Allyson Brann, for putting together amazing release parties and everything else you do behind the scenes. I would also like to thank Rosa Sophia and Laura Hampton. Without all these amazing people behind me, I'd never have gotten this far.

Chapter One

The law said shifters were lesser beings.

They were to be captured and imprisoned in one of the camps scattered across the country. Resistance meant death. American citizens could kill anyone who showed signs of being a shifter, and it *wasn't* considered a crime.

The past year had been rife with change, and the ones affected most of all were shifters. The whole world knew about them now, and they were being hunted down like the animals they shifted into. Mobs used it as an excuse to hunt, and murderers were turning to shifters to get their thrills— *if* they could catch them.

Patrick O'Reilly stood by the window and remembered what had brought them to the abandoned ski resort deep in the woods. Though the new home was beautiful and safe, it was nothing like the world they'd left behind. Forever Creek Resort wasn't just any ski resort, it was a *castle*. It even had a moat, though half the time it was frozen over. Since they were so high in the mountains, the moat had once been used as a place for guests to ice skate. He could almost picture people skating around the castle while others gathered at one of the fire pits now hidden under all the snow. From the window, the shadow of the five floors of the castle was spread across the ground before him. There was plenty of room for them to train, or bring others into their fold to keep them safe. There would come a time when they would have to recruit the best of the best in order to survive.

He stepped away from the window and back to his desk, looking at the computer screen to check on his siblings. Once they'd taken up residence in the castle, one of the first things he'd done was enhance the security system. Whatever areas were lacking, they updated, and now he could make sure they were safe. There on the screen, he could see each of his sibling going about their normal routines. Despite this, he couldn't stop the rush of memories from before they had gone into hiding.

He pulled the door to his small medical practice shut and stepped out into the freezing temperatures. He should have been home hours before, but a string of last minute patients had kept him late. A clatter caught his attention. It was coming from the alley next to his building. His beast sniffed the air and was met with the rancid odor of blood. Lots of it. The sane part of him told him to turn and continue on his way, to not enter the alley, but he couldn't stop his feet from moving forward toward the noise.

He had just stepped into the entrance, and not more than twenty feet before him were two police officers. Blood seeped from a man lying against the alley wall. "Shifter. I won't let you contaminate our world any longer. We'll kill every one of you. Gun you down and bathe in your blood."

That night, he'd realized how dangerous things were. It had been the final straw that sent them into hiding. *We're safe now.* He could take some comfort in the fact that even if someone were looking for the castle, it was difficult to find, so there was little chance anyone could stumble upon them. It wasn't the way they had lived before, but at least they were together and alive. None of them were stuck in some camp, or worse, being used for experiments.

They had put their skills together and started Shifters Underground. It had started out as an online forum letting others know of safe places they could seek refuge and places to avoid at all costs. Now, it had expanded. The siblings went out to rescue those who were in dangerous situations. Any shifter could send a cry for help, and the O'Reilly family would do what they could. They planned rescue missions, mapped out a safe route of travel with safe houses, reunited families, and whatever else they could to keep shifters safe, under the radar and out of the camps. Each of them were putting their skills to good use, trying to do what they could to save their species.

There would be a day shifters would take no more, and they'd stand together and fight back, but that wasn't the case *yet*. There were little bands that had tried to fight back but for the most part, the government swept into action, making examples out of them. Torturing shifters before finally killing them. Many were killed in public for others to see. It had started on the streets where the townsfolk would gather, and recently it was being broadcasted on television. For those who weren't killed, their fate was worse for their rebellion. They were sent to labs for the scientists to experiment on as they searched for a way to control shifters, to make them less of a threat. There had been some shifters spread around the country willing to help the O'Reillys on a large scale, but for the most part shifters were trying to stay under the radar. They'd hide someone in their homes, but that was as big of a risk as they were willing to take.

It sickened him to think of what happened to shifters, and through it all he had little doubt that things would only get worse before they were better. If they ever got better. There had already been rumors of experimental tracking chips being placed in shifters in order to control their movements and to possibly control their ability to shift. To take away the capability to shift was worse than locking them away in cells like animals in a zoo. The beast would fight within the body, trying to free itself until eventually the mind collapsed. Shifters wouldn't last if that were their fate.

Instead of standing there staring out at the woods that surrounded their home, his lion clawed within him, demanding something be done before it was too late. Shifters were dying as he stood there watching the trees blow in the wind, and there was nothing he could do about it *yet*. He needed to gather other shifters to stand together and fight against what was happening to them. To petition the government to leave them in peace.

It was one thing to kill rogue shifters, those who went on a rampage and started this disaster, but it was another to kill their entire species because of the actions of a few. That was like eliminating humans because of murderers. This was no different, and it made the government no better than the rogues.

"Patrick." Jade, the youngest, and only sister of the O'Reilly siblings, stepped into his office appearing pensive, her arms wrapped around her body as if she was hugging herself. "I emailed you a document. You should take a look at it now."

He stepped away from the window and back to his desk. "What's it concerning?"

"The government is rolling out an injection that hospitals and emergency personnel can use to test for shifters. It can be administered by a needle or through a dart gun. If the person is a shifter, it will force them to shift. If they're human, they're saying the only side effect is nausea. It should be in their hands by the beginning of the week and all hospital staff, emergency workers, military, and government employees will be forced to undergo the test in order to keep their jobs."

"Shit." He leaned over his office chair and pressed a few buttons until her email displayed on the screen.

"As if that's not bad enough, within three months' time they're expected to make it available to the general public. It will be uncontrollable then, and it'll be even harder for us." She rubbed her hands on the outside of her arms.

"We'll overcome." He quickly scanned the announcement and found no further information than what she had already told him. He caught the name of the drug—Lycan Ultra Neuro Acid, also referred to as LUNA— and committed it to memory, in case he caught that word anywhere else in his research. "There's got to be something we can do to counteract it. If I could just get a sample of the compound they're using to bring forth the beast, I might be able to find a way to bypass the reaction."

Austin, the next oldest O'Reilly stepped around the corner with only his workout shorts slung low on his hips and a towel in hand. "I can help with that." When they both turned to look at him, as if wondering where he had come from, he held up his hand. "When Jade passed the gym, she looked agitated so I followed to see what happened."

"What do you mean you can help with getting a sample of the compound?" Patrick took a seat behind the desk and pushed the chair back to recline slightly.

"If they're going to distribute it to every hospital, police station, and firehouse, they're going to go through the military. I still have friends in the service. I'll call them and see if they can get me a couple vials."

"Good, then I can go through the compounds and figure out what we can do to make the playing field even." It wasn't what he went to medical school for but at least he could put his skills to use. Since they'd been forced to give up everything and move to the woods, he lost his position as the town's doctor. Now, his medical training was being wasted. "If any of your friends are shifters, you'd better tell them to get the hell out before testing begins."

Austin nodded distractedly, confirming he'd already been thinking the same thing. Like Patrick, Austin had to give up his career. As a former Army Ranger, turned police officer, it was hard for him to not have the daily activity. "Just my buddy, Nolan. I'm going to try to convince him that

Shifters Underground needs him. He's a good soldier and we could use men like him when things get worse."

Patrick quirked his eyebrow upward. "We should begin recruiting our troops *before* things get more menacing. We're going to need the best if we're going to stand a fighting chance."

"Wait a minute, both of you. Are we talking about going to war?" She stared at them both, her eyes wide, letting them know she was appalled by the idea.

"Jade—" Austin started before Patrick cleared his throat.

"We won't have much choice." He tried to soothe the youngest of the pride because he knew just how much she hated the idea. "One day things are going to get so bad we're not going to have any other options. It will be time for us to take up arms and stand together against this, or we'll all die."

"Not just in some distant future," Austin said. "It's going to be soon. Can't you feel it?" When no one answered, he continued, "With every step the government makes to crush our species, we're starting to rise up. Right now, there are just small groups like us but eventually we'll all stand together. You can see the changes on the Shifters Underground website."

"We understand the thought of going to battle against them scares you, but we'll do whatever we can to protect you." Patrick watched as his sister hugged herself tighter. If anyone understood what the government was capable of, it was her. Things got nasty when the government caught a shifter. Jade had personal experience; she *knew*. He did his best to set those thoughts aside. There was no need to relive the nightmare now that she was safe in their forest retreat.

"That's the thing." Her voice trembled. "You *can't* stop these people. No one can. We should run, leave the country. We should go home to Ireland." Her fear permeated the room like a toxic gas.

"Don't be stupid," Austin snapped.

"Austin!" Patrick scolded him.

"Come on, she needs to wake up and realize this is going to go worldwide before long. There will be nowhere to hide."

"You're right, but she doesn't need that right now." He tried to calm the situation, but she had already stormed out the office. "Damn it, Austin."

"Patrick, it's time she realizes what we're up against."

"Don't you think she understands? The scars she has from those experiments they did on her before we could get to her, are daily reminders of what the future might hold. How can you be so heartless? She's terrified, damn it, and comments like that aren't helping anything."

Austin slung the towel over his shoulder and nodded. "You're right. I'll go apologize."

"Later. I'll smooth things over for now." Knowing she had most likely taken refuge outside, he grabbed the jacket he'd tossed over the back of his office chair and came around the desk. "Before her capture she was a take-no-shit type of girl, but what they did to her broke something deep within her. She's just beginning to find her way back to the person she was, and she needs our support. She's safe here, for now, but that might not always be the case. We need to get her back to the person she was, so fight alongside us."

"What did they do to her?" Austin asked, sounding hesitant, as if uncertain he wanted to know. "In the middle of the night when she has a nightmare, you're the one who goes to her. Has she told you anything?"

"Only bits and pieces. For the most part, she doesn't want to talk about it." He slipped the jacket on and tried not to picture her huddled in that tiny cage, the electrodes and machines attached to her. She had been so drugged when he found her, she'd fought him even as he tried to rescue her.

To discover his baby sister in that condition still haunted him every time he closed his eyes. Worse was the knowledge that others were suffering the same fate and there was nothing they could do about it *yet*. They needed to locate the labs conducting the experiments in order to attack and close them down. The longer they were operating, the longer people suffered inside them. From what he could gather, they were worse than the camps.

He strolled from his office, leaving Austin in his wake to go back to his daily workout routine. In the distance, he could hear Luke and Blake in a heated discussion about something, and Chase's lion purrs as he tried to add his opinion to the conversation. He didn't want to get involved with whatever they were bickering about, so he snuck out the side door. He'd go around the castle, back to the creek that ran a little distance from the building. Jade would have sought her refuge there, letting the sounds of water tinkling over the river rocks soothe her.

Even with the snow on the ground, she sat there next to the creek. She was too lost in her thoughts to notice the cold and wind beating against her. Her long blonde hair whipped around her from the breeze and she didn't bat it out of her face like she normally would.

"Jade." He called to her as he neared, but still she didn't acknowledge him. *My dear sister, what can we do to help you?*

During medical school, he had studied cases of trauma and depression, and during his time as a family doctor he'd had to treat it, but when it came to his sister, he hesitated. He wanted to do whatever he could to help her return to the woman she had once been, but there were dangers. If he pushed too much, he could send her retreating further into herself. It was a lose-lose situation, but he was the only one there who could help her in a medical way. Besides being her brother, it was his job as her Alpha to heal her. The best way for her to move past the trauma was to talk about it. It didn't have to be with him, it could be any of the brothers, but she had to talk to someone or she'd continue to relive it night after night in her dreams. He could only hope she'd find the courage.

"Jade." He called to her again as he stood above her.

"I really just want to be alone." She ran her hands down her jean clad legs and pulled them tighter against her chest.

"I know, but that's not always good for you." He sat down next to her, the snow soaking the bottom of his jeans. It was better than hovering above her. "Austin's an ass."

"But he's right," she said. "Eventually this will be worldwide. What are we going to do?" Tears welled in her eyes.

"We're not going to let that happen. With every lead that comes through Shifters Underground, we follow up on it, destroy labs, and rescue those who need us." He tugged off his jacket and wrapped it around her shoulders. "We're going to make it through this."

"Maybe Austin is right, though. Maybe we need to start building our team and prepare to fight if we have to."

"I know none of this is easy for you, and I know you're scared, but he is right on this. The time is coming when we're going to need to fight in order to stay alive and free." The terror that radiated from her permeated the air until it was almost palpable. He forced air into his lungs and added, "I'd rather have you here where we can keep you safe, but if you want, Dad's family will welcome you in Ireland."

"I'm not leaving without everyone. I've never deserted the family and I'm not going to now." She turned to him. "Do you think Dad's still out there? In one of those camps or a lab?"

He wanted to lie to her, to tell her their father could take care of himself, but she'd have smelled it. A lie wouldn't bring her comfort, it would only piss her off. It was time the whole family faced up to what had happened to their father the night he'd walked out for some air, only hours before the family went into hiding. "I don't know. If he were free, he'd have found us by now, but I don't know if it's better to wish he was captured and imprisoned in one of the camps, or hope he was killed on sight."

"I can't help but fear he might have ended up in one of the labs." A single tear rolled down her cheek before she wiped it away. He wrapped his arm around her shoulder, knowing she was thinking of her own experience.

"It was his choice to go out that night. He knew how bad things were getting, and he still went. There's nothing we can do for him now. We've watched the board for the last year and there's been nothing, not even a blip. You listed him as missing and if anyone knew anything about him, they'd have contacted you just like they do with all the others. Good or bad, we would have known."

"Which is why I can't stifle the fear he was taken to a lab. We have very few tips on those because they're so heavily guarded. He could have suffered as I did without being as lucky to have you swoop in and save him."

"If that was the case, then he's most likely dead. From the records we've recovered at the labs we've destroyed, they kept captives alive only a short time." As he gave her what comfort he could, he was thankful she stuck mostly to Shifters Underground and working with families. It sheltered her from what they learned about the labs and the knowledge of what happened when the shifter was no longer of any use.

He didn't want her to know the worst of it. If they hadn't rescued her, she'd have been incinerated alive.

Doctor Clarissa Greenwood stepped out of her new office at Hathaway

Medical and headed for the door. The air in the building seemed stifling all of a sudden, and the more she thought about her new position, the more it bothered her. As a scientist, she'd believed her promotion involved studying diseases to find the cures. She fumbled with the keychain locket in her pocket. It was the one thing she never left home without, a good luck charm of sorts that her brother had given her on her first day of college as she stood before the tall buildings, ready to run.

He had always believed in her, even when she didn't. Right now, she needed that support more than ever, considering what she'd just learned. Hathaway Medical expected her to experiment on live humans. *Shifters.* According to her bosses, and the government, shifters weren't humans. They were believed to be no better than the animals companies tested their products on.

Clarissa's heels clicked against the linoleum as she moved swiftly down the hall. All of a sudden it seemed as if the exit was too far away.

She wanted to *help* people, not torture them. And she was having trouble discerning the difference between a human and a shifter. All of it seemed wrong. She didn't understand why things were happening this way, or why the government thought they could just kill or imprison an entire species. She wanted no part in it. She needed to get as far away from it as she could.

"Doctor Greenwood, just the person I was looking for." Her boss headed straight for her, sending another wave of sickness through her. "We'll be conducting today's experiment on subject one-fifty-nine, so please join us in room twenty-two in an hour."

Her stomach rolled at the comment. *Subject one-fifty-nine* wasn't a subject. That was a person they were about to experiment on. A living, breathing, person with family and friends who were no doubt worried sick about them.

He paused and his gaze traveled over her. "You're looking pale, are you okay?"

"Actually, I'm not feeling very well. I thought some fresh air would do me good, but I think my migraine is only getting worse." She cringed as if the overhead light was bothering her, but in reality it was the man before her who made her ill.

"Why don't you just skip the session, then? There's normally a lot of noise and growls. You can watch it in your office, then go home for the day. Hopefully, by Monday, you'll be well enough to assist with the experiments."

I won't be here Monday, or ever.

"Thank you for understanding, Sir."

He patted her on the shoulder, then walked away. She hurried outside, into the sun. As she filled her lungs with fresh air, she put together a plan. She'd go back inside and gather what she could on her jump drive before the end of the business day.

Everyone was always ready to leave at five on Fridays. It was the one day overtime wasn't permitted. The company claimed they wanted their employees to enjoy relaxing weekends with their families in order to be ready to go on Mondays. To most, it seemed like a family-friendly place to work, especially with the in-house daycare, but to her it seemed suspicious.

What happened at Hathaway Medical on weekends that they didn't want anyone to know about? There were too many questions and not enough answers, but she was going to do her best to find out what she could. She shut her eyes, relishing the warmth of the sun on her face. Then she rolled her shoulders, stretched, and prepared to go back inside.

"Afternoon, Doctor Greenwood, is everything all right?"

She opened her eyes and found a security guard before her, his forehead creased with concern. "Andrew, I thought you were off today."

"They wanted additional security for an experiment, so here I am."

"That must have been the one I was supposed to be involved with, but with this migraine, Doctor Glass told me to watch it from my office."

After a quick glance around, he leaned in closer to her. "Record it."

She wasn't sure what to say to that, but before she could come up with a reply, he stepped around her and headed inside. She stood there a moment, trying to figure him out. Despite his relaxed demeanor, he'd always seemed to be watching for something as if he expected something to happen.

Had he seen too many experiments? Did he think the shifters they were torturing in the sublevels of Hathaway Medical would one day rise up against the staff? No, they were too drugged for that. Because of their fast metabolisms, the staff kept the prisoners extremely sedated.

She wandered back into the building as she continued to question his words. What was going to happen that made him think she should record it herself? She picked up her pace when an idea occurred to her, then pulled out her cell phone in search of the email her brother had sent her before he took a job in South America.

There was one thing that could give her continual access to what was happening—a small virus that would go undetected by even the best surveillance.

Chapter Two

Patrick's fingers flew over the keyboard in a blur as he typed out his ideas, the various alternatives to the concentration camps. A letter to President Ashworth might not have been the best idea he had, but he wasn't even sure he'd send it. Typing it out at least allowed him to get his thoughts in order, and Luke swore the email would be untraceable if he decided to send it, hidden by the same security that protected the origin of the Shifters Underground website.

He wrote about the possibility of the government giving shifters land to live on, their own towns where they could exist in peace. To him, that was still giving too much power to the government, as well as confining shifters. Still, the concept was better than the camps the shifters were already living in. They had to find a middle ground, and that's what the suggestion was. It would give them freedom and make them safe again.

A town with houses for each family, a few little shops, even a bar, and a restaurant. If they didn't think about the fact that it would be mandatory to stay within the bounds of the settlement—at least at certain times—they could begin to reclaim their lives. He hoped more freedoms would come over time as humans realized shifters were no threat.

Even the government had to see this was a better solution than an all-out war with shifters, who were faster, and stronger. Even so, winning the war didn't mean they'd win the battle. If there was a war, they'd be seen as an even bigger threat to humans.

Damn it, this is a lose-lose situation. He leaned back in his chair and let out a frustrated growl.

The house intercom mounted on his desk flickered to life, and Luke's voice filled the room. "Patrick, I think you need to come up here."

"What is it?" He kept his voice even, not wanting his brother to pick up on his frustration.

"Just get up here." The urgency in Luke's tone had Patrick pushing back his chair and heading upstairs. Luke wouldn't have pulled him away if it weren't important. Taking the east wing stairs two at a time, he dashed up the four flights without so much as missing a breath. The family had taken rooms on the fifth floor to give them an advantage, the reaction time needed if someone stumbled upon them. This left the first floor as their main living area, including the large castle kitchen.

While all the other siblings had made their offices or workshops on the first floor of the resort, Luke had occupied the suite next to his bedroom. This way, he was able to work at whatever hour he chose, and still be close to the bedrooms if something happened in the middle of the night.

Patrick was grateful the O'Reilly pride stuck so close together. They'd fight to the death for each other, and there was no one else he would rather have watching his back than his siblings.

He entered Luke's office. "What did you find?"

"I was researching these injections to see what I could come up with. To see who developed them and if I could find out where they were coming from. Maybe if we knew where, we'd be able to eliminate their supply chain before they became a problem for us. That's when I found this." Luke leaned back in his chair, giving Patrick access to the computer. He rubbed his chin, his fingers playing over his five o'clock shadow. "Hathaway Medical was behind the discovery of this injection and now they have a missing scientist, so I dug deeper. Doctor Clarissa Greenwood was employed there for less than two weeks, but a contact of a contact said she was appalled they were experimenting on shifters and took off."

"Wait…how long have you known they were experimenting on our kind?"

"Don't look at me like that. I just found out this morning. I wanted solid evidence before I brought it to you. A contact of a contact isn't enough, it could have been a trap. I've been working my ass off since I received the email," Luke added, seeming irritated.

"What do you know?" Patrick leaned against the edge of the desk, ignoring his brother's attitude.

"My contact sent me information on a shifter who might need our help. He wanted to know if we could extract him and get him somewhere safe. Andrew is a bear shifter, a retired Ranger. He was recruited for what he thought was a standard security job, only to find himself assigned to Hathaway Medical."

"Once he realized what they were doing, why'd he stay?"

Luke leaned forward and clicked a secondary tab on the screen, which brought up a picture of a young girl, her bleached hair streaked with pink and purple. "His niece."

Anger rolled through Patrick and his lion. The girl was just a child. She hadn't even hit puberty yet, and there was no chance she had completed the change. What did they want with her? The hairs on the back of his neck rose, reminding him he really didn't want to know. He'd witnessed what Jade had gone through and he could only imagine the torture they'd put this child through.

"Patrick, did you hear me?" Luke called to him, pulling him from his thoughts.

"What?"

"I said Andrew's sister was killed two months ago and the child is missing. He believes she's been taken to one of the labs."

"If she has, she's dead. You know as well as I do, they don't keep their captives long. You read the files on that hard drive I managed to salvage before we burned down that lab, so you know what they do." Speaking those words brought him back to that night. That horrible night when he'd seen the worst of what could happen to his kind.

Patrick, Austin, and Blake had crept up and watched as the guards at the lab did their rounds. If things went as planned, they wouldn't make another round until the next half hour, giving the O'Reillys the time they needed. They'd slip in, rescue the captive shifters, gather any information on other labs, and burn the place. At least, that was the plan.

But nothing that night had gone according to plan. He and Austin headed deep within the building conducting their search, their guns at the ready for anyone they might have encountered, while Blake set up the dynamite that would ignite on a timer once they were clear. Patrick would gather what he could, while Austin continued the search for prisoners.

He used the security card Luke had duplicated using the coding on the security system, and with an echoing click the door unlocked. He wrapped his hand around the handle and pulled it open. Inside, the laboratory appeared tame. He'd known it was anything but. He went to the first computer, hoping to discover more about the experiments, but it was password protected. With only fifteen minutes before the next round, he didn't have time to break it. Instead, he manually extracted the hard drive and tossed it into his bag.

Papers on the desk piqued his interest, so he shoved those in his bag as well. Later he'd go through them and see if they were of any use to them.

His ear bud sprung to life with Blake's voice. "Ten minutes."

"Almost done. Austin, status update."

"No prisoners. They're...dead. It looks like they were incinerated...alive."

"Fuck!" Patrick turned around and there in a cage, curled into a ball, something moved. No, not something, but someone. Her long blonde hair matted with blood. He dropped the bag on the desk and stepped forward. "Shit, Austin get down here."

"What's going on?" The urgency in Blake's voice forced Patrick to explain.

"I think...it's Jade." Not having time to find the key he grabbed the bolt cutters from his bag and unclipped the lock. "Jade." He reached out to push her hair away from her face, and even though her eyes were glazed over from whatever drugs they had her on, he recognized his sister, who'd gone missing a few weeks before while on a mission with Luke and Chase. One that was supposed to be easy and safe, but she got separated from the brothers and was gone. They had searched high and low for her over the last few weeks.

"Are you sure?" Austin's voice came through the transmitter as the door behind Patrick opened.

Without answering Patrick squatted down, his gun aimed at the door until he could make out Austin from the faint light of the computer screens and the light that streamed through from the hallway. "Damn it, I could have shot you."

"Is it her?"

"Yes." He set the gun on the desk, turned back to the cage, and pulled the electrodes and cords away from her, he reached for her. "Jade."

She only swatted at him, scurrying deeper into the cage. Her moans cut through the quiet and tore at his heart. His sweet sister didn't recognize him.

"What have they done to her?" Austin questioned coming to stand next to him.

"I don't know."

"But she's alive?" Blake asked.

"Yes." Patrick and Austin said nearly together.

"You've got six minutes, get the hell out of there," Blake ordered.

"Grab my bag." Patrick reached into the cage and took hold of her arm. "Come on Jade, we've got to go."

"No!" Tears ran down her face. "No, I...I can't...take anymore."

"I'm not going to hurt you, I'm your brother." He used his grip to force her from the cage. When he dragged her out, he could see the cuts, burns, and bruises that marred her body. Torture. His sister had been tortured.

"Oh shit!" Austin reached out to steady Jade as she tried to fight Patrick, but he seemed unsure where to put his hands. Everywhere they would normally touch was covered in some type of mark.

"Just grab the bag, I've got her." He lifted her over his shoulder and grabbed his gun from the desk. He couldn't worry that he was hurting her, not when they only had a few minutes to make it out of the building before the guards did their rounds again and Blake's explosion was set to go off. "We've got to go."

"Patrick, she's here with us," Luke's voice called through the memories and broke him from his thoughts.

"What?" It took him a moment to recall he was in the castle in Luke's office, not rescuing Jade again. He pinched the bridge of his nose, squeezing his eyes shut for a moment. Jade wasn't the only one reliving that nightmare. Those papers he had gathered, many of them discussed the experiments they'd conducted on her. She might not fully remember what happened there, only the agony that had come with it, but his mind was able to conjure up images of what she went through. If they hadn't gotten to her, she would have been dead the next day. He shook his head. *She's safe now.*

"You kept saying Jade's name over and over. You were thinking about the laboratory again, weren't you?"

"Shit." He pushed off the desk and paced the room. His lion needed a long run to get this out of his system, to reset his thoughts and get his mind back in the game. "What about this missing scientist?"

"Doctor Clarissa Greenwood." Luke leaned forward, his fingers clicking along the keyboard keys for a moment before looking back up at Patrick. "She has her doctorate in chemistry. According to Andrew, she was brought in to try to determine the correct dosage to keep the shifters sedated enough that they can't fight back but would still be able to suffer. They don't want to continue to sedate the shifters so much that they don't feel what's being done to them."

"Fuck. That will make the labs worse than they are now. The one plus side to what's happened with Jade is that she doesn't remember a lot of it. She sees the scars but everything that happened is somewhat blurred and unclear."

"She's starting to remember pieces of it. I can see it in her eyes, the nightmares are more frequent." Luke leaned back again. "Andrew doesn't believe Doctor Greenwood knew what she was hired to do. Otherwise, why would she take off when she had finally begun working on the project she was hired to do? He told her to record the last experiment she was there for. That was Friday. Now she's gone."

Patrick tried to figure how far she could have gotten in five days. "She'll have information on the layout of the building, where they're holding the shifters captive, and maybe she can help us determine the best way to get in."

"You're going to go after her, even though she might have known she'd be conducting experiments on us?"

He paused and turned to face Luke. "I don't see much of a choice. If they're torturing our kind there, we've got to do something. You know how hard it is to get any information on these labs. We need an insider if we're going to make a successful mission out of it. We want to get in, save as many as we can, and get out ourselves. We find her, and we take down Hathaway Medical."

"I'll get on it and see if I can find her." Luke scooted his office chair close to the desk, a clear sign for Patrick to get lost and let him get back to work. "I'll let you know when I find something."

With nothing else to do, he headed out to find Austin and bring him up to speed. They needed to come up with a plan and figure out who was going with him in search of Doctor Greenwood. Once that was settled, he'd squeeze in a quick run before it was time for their nightly family dinner.

Even though they had gone into hiding, they kept some of their normal routines. Family dinners gave them time to forget about the world, or that they were refugees in hiding. They tried not to think about what was happening outside of the abandoned ski resort they'd taken over, or that their father was still missing. They were a family, and they needed to stick together in order to make it through this. As a family, they were strong. He knew they could get through anything.

Five days on the run had begun to take its toll on Clarissa. She wanted nothing more than a shower, a hot meal, and a comfortable bed. Two days and four states ago, she had tried to reach out to her brother, Dean, but he didn't answer the phone. She couldn't jeopardize him by leaving a message.

She glanced around the corner, eyeing the pay phone at the edge of the park. She hadn't seen anyone suspicious, and she hated to take the risk, but it was the only way to contact Dean. If only he were in the states, instead of temporarily reassigned to Brazil. She needed his help to get out of this situation she was in.

With one last glance to ensure she was alone, she stepped out of the alley that had been her hiding place for the last hour and walked toward the pay phone. Not wanting to draw unwanted attention, she tried to keep her pace calm and act normal. If she ran, people would remember her. She knew she was being followed, and she couldn't give passersby an impression of her that would remain in their minds. A quick phone call, and then she had to get out of the area and find somewhere to hide away again. Knowing rain was about to pound the city, she was prepared to head toward the abandoned warehouses on the outskirts of town and find somewhere she could hunker down for the night.

She took the phone in her hand and deposited the needed coinage before dialing the number. As it rang, she hoped he would answer. Finding another pay phone would take some time and she couldn't risk coming back to the same place a second time. Pay phones had disappeared over the years so it wouldn't be easy to get to another one. The past couldn't survive with all the new technology, but she had ditched her cell phone before she started the journey. Carrying it would have given them a direct way to locate her.

"Hello." Her brother's sleepy voice echoed through the phone line.

"Don't say my name," she warned, taking a deep breath. "I'm in trouble. That place was just as awful as you heard." She pressed her back against the wall and kept her head down.

"Where are you?" The sleepiness was suddenly gone from his voice.

"You know I can't tell you that, but I'm not staying in one place long enough for them to find me. Just like Dad taught us. If they can't find me, they'll come for you. I'm sorry...so sorry." She tried to swallow the tears that were threatening to fall. This was no time to get emotional. If she was going to live through this, she needed to keep her head clear.

"There's nothing to be sorry for. We'll get through this. Can you get to *the place?*"

"Two days."

"Stay safe."

"You too." Knowing that Dean would find a way to get to her and to meet her at their place, she hung up the phone. For the first time since she'd left, she felt more confident she'd get through this. That she'd be able to fight whoever was after her. She didn't know why they were after her, or what they'd do to her once they caught her. If they caught her, she hoped they'd kill her quickly instead of tormenting her the way they did the shifters in their custody. She'd rather be dead than live through what she'd witnessed.

Watching over her shoulder, she headed toward the outskirts of town to the abandoned warehouses. She couldn't run forever. Eventually, they'd find her and then there'd be hell to pay.

Again, she wondered why they were after her. She doubted they'd found the virus she put on their computers, or they'd have blocked it. She was still getting information from their system. Which meant they either thought she knew something or they had some use for her. The idea they had a *use* for her churned her stomach. There were other scientists they could hire to replace her. What could she do for them that someone else couldn't?

Through the darkness behind her, she couldn't see anyone lurking. She found a broken part of the wall in the derelict warehouse, and shoved the board aside. As she slipped into the opening, she was careful to keep her bag from getting stuck on the jagged edges. The laptop she carried was her only proof of what was happening, and though the battery had died, she knew it was still recording what was happening at Hathaway Medical.

Tomorrow, once she was halfway to the spot where she'd meet Dean, she would look for a place where she could plug the laptop in for a while to charge. Maybe something on their system would explain why they were after her.

She found a corner in the warehouse that allowed her to see the whole space. The opening that had admitted her was the only spot that wasn't chained and padlocked. She had to be aware of her now limited escape options. She pulled the handgun from her bag, and set it down beside her. If someone found her, she refused to be taken. If she had to, she would take her own life.

With the gun close by, she tried to get comfortable. Exhaustion made her eyelids feel as if they had lead weights attached to them. Five days on the run meant she'd barely had any sleep, and the only food she'd gotten were from outside food vendors and vending machines. She couldn't risk being caught in a restaurant or a store with a camera. It would leave a trail she was working so hard not to leave. Even with all the precautions, they were still on her trail. She had barely escaped two nights ago when they'd caught up with her. How they managed to find her was something she hadn't figured out yet.

She leaned her head back against the hard metal and her eyelids sprung open as realization dawned on her. They weren't just finding her by luck, it was her scent that was leading them to her. They were using their shifter captives, forcing them to comply.

Unlike ditching her cell phone or never returning to the same place, she couldn't do anything about her scent. She didn't know much about shifters. Most of the world didn't, and the government used that fear to their advantage. What was she supposed to do to keep herself alive? And was being alive better than death? Maybe not, depending on what they had in mind for her.

Chapter Three

The O'Riellys' converted castle had not only became their operating center, it also became their home. The family gathered for dinner around the large custom table, with the uneven edges and lines in the wood telling the age of the tree it came from. Patrick sat at the head of the table. Austin found a seat to his right—the perfect place for Patrick's right-hand man—while Jade sat at the opposite end, and Luke, Blake, and Chase took seats around them.

Patrick shoved a bite of pot roast into his mouth and glanced at Jade, who was eyeing him curiously.

She crossed her arms over her chest. "I can feel your lion's impatience, and I saw you whispering to Luke. Why don't you just tell us what crazy mission you want us on now?"

"Not you, little sister," he said. A shudder of fear went through him at the very thought of sending her back out into the world again. He'd rather have her here, where they could keep a close eye on her. He wasn't willing to risk her again, and he knew she wasn't ready for field action.

Underneath her innocent look, there was a kick-ass warrior just like her brothers, but right now it was hidden behind the fear and anxiety caused by what had happened to her. It wasn't until recently that her outspoken, smart-ass attitude had begun to reappear. Though he wouldn't admit it to her, he was happy to have that side of her back. They didn't live in a world where they could afford to appear weak, and she knew it. Since he had rescued her from the lab, she'd gone back into her work for Shifters Underground and her training. She was learning to protect herself again, but even with how far she'd come, he wasn't ready to send her back into the field. Not yet.

"Patrick," she said. Austin adjusted in his seat, nudging his brother to let him know he had missed something.

"What?"

"I don't have to be involved, but at least tell us what's going on. I haven't seen anything urgent come through Shifters Underground." She leaned forward and tucked a strand of her blonde hair behind her ear. "What's so bad that you're hesitating?"

"I'm going after a woman, Doctor Clarissa Greenwood. I need someone to cover my back on this mission." He stabbed one of the potatoes on his plate and brought it to his lips. "Any volunteers?"

"That's all the information we get, a woman and her name?" Blake dished more roast onto his plate and didn't bother to look at Patrick. "Shifter?"

"She's human, but she might have some information that could help us." He side-stepped the full story while still doing his best to answer Blake's question.

"You've got to tell them," Luke said. When Patrick remained silent, Luke set down his fork. "We have to find her for information on how to get into a lab we've found. It's the best way."

The word *lab* stilled everyone at the table. Jade gasped. Her fork fell from her grasp and clinked off her plate. Each of the siblings looked at him for more information.

Seeing the fear spark in his sister's green eyes, he wished he could refute it, but it would do them no good. Ignoring the situation would mean leaving the shifters who were being held there in danger, not to mention countless others could be kidnapped and brought there against their will.

He had a duty to his kind, his family, and Jade to ensure that place was destroyed.

"A lab…" She paused, wrapping her arms around her body. "You found another one?"

He nodded and watched as she retreated within herself. The memories that had returned to her were obviously playing out in her thoughts. "Don't you worry, we're going to take this one down."

"What about this woman? How does she play into all of this?" Blake questioned before taking a sip of his coffee.

"She's a scientist Hathaway Medical brought on, but from what I understand, when she found out what she'd be working with, she took off. As of right now, she has a five day lead on us, but Luke is working to pinpoint her location. We've got to get to her before they do." He didn't need to tell them what the goons behind Hathaway Medical would do to her if they caught her. Her simple betrayal would be enough for them to want her dead. Tortured and dead if they thought she had betrayed them in other ways.

"Do we even know she's alive?"

He shook his head at Blake. "We can only suspect she is, from what Luke has found."

"I've picked up a phone call from a pay phone to her brother. I believe it was her, and they're meeting in two days in their spot. I'm not sure where that is, but I'll find it," Luke explained.

Chase pushed his chair away from the table and rose. "You can't honestly be suggesting that we bring a human here? One who might have experimented on us?"

"She won't be brought here if we even suspect she had anything to do with it." He took another bite. "We don't know what really happened there, or how much contact she had with the captives, but we do know this is our best chance to get into Hathaway Medical. If we don't do this, we're not going to be able to save the shifters who are being held there."

"Excuse me." A very pale Jade pushed back from the table. "I need…time."

Before anyone could say anything, she spun on her heels and hurried toward the staircase. Patrick knew she didn't like to think about the existence of the labs, that others were suffering the same things she had gone through. But it was a factor in their lives, one they'd have to deal with. At least until the day came that either the paranormal community stood up against it or the government put a stop to it.

"I'll go." Blake's statement brought Patrick back to their conversation.

"Me too." Austin nodded in agreement.

Patrick stirred his food around on his plate. "No, Austin, I need you here. I don't know how long we'll be gone, and I need you in charge until we get back."

"I still don't like this, but I'll go." Chase still stood behind the table, his hands on the back of the chair he had vacated.

"Blake and I are enough. There are other things to be done. Focus on Hathaway Medical while I'm gone, find out everything you can about them. When I get back, I want to work on a plan and go after them straight away." Patrick left his fork on his plate and stood from the table. He didn't feel much like finishing his dinner. "I'm going to check on Jade. Blake, I want you ready at a moment's notice. Once Luke has a location for Clarissa, we'll go after her."

"I'll be ready, and I'll make some devices in case we run into any trouble."

Patrick nodded. He'd leave the explosive devices to Blake. If there was one thing the middle brother enjoyed more than fixing things, it was blowing them up. There was no one else who could come up with various ways to blow things up like he could.

"Patrick, wait a moment." Austin cornered him at the bottom of the staircase before he could make his way up to his sister. "You should let me go on the mission, and you stay here. With the mention of a lab, it's bringing everything back for Jade and she needs you here with her. You're the only one she'll confide in. What am I supposed to do if she starts retreating into herself, closing us off again?"

"No, she'll be okay while I'm gone. I'm going to talk to her now. If things change, you'll call me and I'll come home. I need to go after Doctor Greenwood because if anyone has the ability to get through to her, it's going to be me. I might be able to use my knowledge to get her to see our side of things."

"What about the fact you're supposed to break down the chemicals in this new drug? We need a way to combat that, or we're all in trouble."

He had almost forgotten about the drug the government had developed. He combed his shoulder-length hair from his face with his fingers. "Did you get in touch with your contact?"

"He's going to get us some once it arrives on base. In exchange, he'll be staying here with us. They've already warned that military personnel will be tested, so he has to get out of there. He's made the arrangements so that he'll be one of the workers unloading the cargo. Testing is to begin the following day, so he'll get some samples and be gone before then. It's set to arrive next week."

"Very well. Just give me these two days to find her. If we haven't found her by then, I'll come back, and you can take over the hunt with Blake or Chase. I think I can convince her to help us. She obviously didn't want to test on shifters, or she'd have stayed instead of putting her life in danger."

Austin didn't look convinced that Patrick would be back in two days, but instead of saying anything, he just glared at him. Patrick was their Alpha; he didn't have to justify his actions to anyone. Instead of using that moment to show his dominance, he added, "You have my word. We need a counteractive measure, and I can't find one to help us if I'm out hunting a woman we're not even sure is alive."

"Fine." Austin crossed his arms over his wide chest. "See what you can do for Jade before you have to leave. No matter how much I try, she just won't talk to me."

"She finds comfort with Chase when he's in lion form. That's why I'm leaving him here. If she has a nightmare or a bad day, have him go to her and just lay beside her."

Austin glanced toward the table where Luke, Blake, and Chase were still eating. "What is it about you and Chase? She won't open up to the rest of us."

"She doesn't talk to Chase, either, just cuddles against his lion body. Each of them are running from something, maybe that's why she relates to him."

"What about you? Why you?" Austin turned his gaze back to him. "She was always close to both of us, but ever since you rescued her, she clings to you."

"It's only been a few weeks since we got her back." *Nine weeks and three days.* He had been unable to forget the date, and even now that she was safe, he couldn't stop keeping track. "She needs time."

"She might not have time. We need her at her best *now*." Austin tipped his head toward the steps, letting Patrick know he wanted to put more distance between them and the other brothers. "With each passing day, things are getting worse. Nolan, my military contact who's getting us samples of the new drug, mentioned there are plans to start doing sweeps door to door once the drug comes out, testing *everyone*. For the past few weeks, they've been rounding up anyone they suspect of being a shifter and imprisoning them. There's terror in the streets. While normally the military and police work to control the chaos, they're only adding to it. Terrorizing citizens, imprisoning anyone they want. There seems to be no law and order any longer."

"The world was going to Hell before the existence of shifters became known. Now it sounds like things have gotten worse." None of them had left the castle since they rescued Jade so this adventure would be the first one in over nine weeks. They'd find out how bad things had really gotten. They'd have to stick to the shadows to make sure they weren't caught up in any of the drama that was happening, and to be sure to stay away from anyone who might be in possession of the drug. "By the way, did Nolan mention a name for this drug?"

"I didn't even think to ask. Didn't the article Jade find mention it by name?"

"I was just double-checking the facts. I want to do some research online once I talk to her." Patrick stopped at the landing on the fourth floor. "I think you should go back downstairs, see if you can help Luke or Blake, and let me handle her."

"I hadn't planned to follow you there." Austin leaned against the wall, his hand on the banister. "Whenever one of us leaves the castle, we're risking everything and everyone still here."

He turned toward his brother and nodded. "There's not much choice. Can you really just sit here, safe and sound, while there are others out there who need help?" When Austin remained silent, he added, "I didn't think so. It's not in your nature, just like it's not in mine. We have to do something. I think it's only a matter of time before we have to stand against the government."

"We've been thinking that for months, but with this drug, and the way law enforcement is targeting people, everyone is scared."

"All the more reason we need to build our army and be ready for whatever comes our way. We're strong together, but we'll be stronger with more shifters around us. Nolan joining us will be the beginning of it, but he won't be the last."

"A fight's brewing and you're gearing us up to be on the front lines." Austin started down the steps, leaving him standing there for a long moment.

The fight was coming whether the siblings were ready or not, so it was better to be prepared. He'd rather see each of them dead than caught in a lab as Jade had been. The lion within him growled at the torture these so-called doctors and scientists were performing on shifters. What they were going through was pure Hell on Earth.

He climbed the last flight of stairs to the fifth floor and tried to put his thoughts together. He needed to go into Jade's room to put her at ease, not make her more terrified of what the future held. Sometimes, he wished he could pass the job of oldest sibling on to someone else. Instead, it was his job to take over the family's pride and the position of Alpha, leaving all the responsibility resting on his shoulders. Not that he'd be capable of being a follower. The beast within him was too controlling and dominating to be under anyone's rule.

Halfway down the hall, and just across from his suite, he found Jade's door open. When they'd moved into the resort, he had taken the center room because it had the best view and allowed him to watch over the grounds when he couldn't sleep. They had decided Jade should take the room across the hall from him, so she'd be surrounded by the brothers if anything happened. Austin and Blake each had their own rooms on one side of Patrick and Jade's rooms. Luke and Chase had rooms on the opposite side. All six of their suites were situated close together, allowing them to protect each other if the time came.

"May I come in?" Respecting her privacy, he stood in the hallway. She didn't bother to look up from where she sat in the small sitting area across from the bed. The bedroom was cozy and painted in welcoming colors. The accent wall behind the bed was a warm mauve, adding just enough color while the other walls were a snowy white. Since they had been there, she'd made it her own space, with the sparrow gray comforter and white and pink pillows accenting the bed.

"If you must," she said.

"Are you okay?" He strolled toward her and she glanced up, her eyebrow raised.

"I can't recall the last time I didn't feel this terror. It's become a constant companion and I don't even remember half of what happened to me." She ran her fingers her through her hair. "Maybe that's part of the problem…not knowing what happened."

"If you want to know I can help you with that." Not wanting her to stumble across them, he'd hidden the recovered documents and hard drive in the safe in his room. If she were ready, he'd give her what information he had. If that weren't enough, he could try some of the tricks he had learned in medical school to help her remember.

"Every time I close my eyes, I see enough of that place. Even through the haze that still hangs over it, I remember bits and pieces. When I look in the mirror…" Her voice cracked and he thought about the scars that marred her body. "I'm not sure I ever want to know the whole truth."

"There might come a day you do. When that time comes, let me know, and I'll do my best to help you. You might never know everything that happened there, and maybe that's a good thing."

"There are others who are suffering the same fate, and yet we sit here doing nothing."

He sank down on the sofa next to her and took her hand into his. "We can't run off half-crazed every time we get a lead. We need to put together a plan and go there with our best chances. Otherwise, we could end up captured or killed."

"You think this scientist will be willing to help?"

"I hope I'll be able to get to her. She'll help. We'll close down this lab, too." He squeezed her hand in reassurance. "Austin can be a little too threatening at first, but if you want me to stay here with you, I can send him to find her instead."

"Stay with me, why?" She tipped her head to look at him.

"The thought of another lab might make the nightmares harder."

"I can handle them." With a deep sigh, she leaned back against the sofa. "Okay, so I haven't been doing a very good job of it, but don't let that stop you. You need to go and find this woman. I hate to think of the captives suffering one more day there. We've got to stop it."

He turned enough to be able to see her and still keep his hand over hers. "We're going to, I promise."

"Then you have to go. Don't worry about me, I'll be fine."

"I always worry about you and the rest of the family, but as long as you stay here I know you'll be safe. I don't want you venturing too far from the castle while I'm away. Got that?"

She nodded, but it did little to quell the fear within him. Since he had become Alpha of their outlaw band, he had a deep connection to each of them that wasn't only family but was what a true Alpha would have. He could sense them, their emotions, and if they were in trouble.

When she was a prisoner in the lab, they'd kept her so drugged that it minimized their connection. He could have mistaken her for dead if there hadn't been a slight tug between them. He couldn't determine where she was, but every once in a while he'd feel the terror within her. When his guard was down he could feel the pain they inflicted on her, just as if they were doing it to him. It tore at him, making his lion testy, but he held it together for his pride. As any good Alpha would, he tried to send his strength to her, to let her know they were coming for her. Maybe that's what got her through it and kept her fighting.

Subject has more fight within her than previously studied subjects. Unable to determine the cause. Use extreme caution when handling the subject. Those statements were repeated over and over in the files he had found on her. While she'd always refused to take anyone's shit, she was naturally more outspoken than physically combative. According to the files, her attitude had become more pronounced when she was captured. Now it seemed as though it had all but dissipated. Even her outspokenness had gone. She was more reserved than she had ever been before.

Oh Jade, somehow we're going to help you find the person you were. I miss my baby sister—the woman she was.

Sometimes he felt as though he was still trying to rescue her. More than ever, he was determined to get her back.

Chapter Four

The sun was sinking into the horizon as Clarissa eased open the back door to the old cabin. Childhood memories came rushing back. This was the only place her family gathered, and had time together, without her father rushing off to deal with some emergency at work or her mother juggling her social schedule to the point that she forgot to be a parent. For the one week they'd spent there every summer, they were a real family again.

The cabin was completely isolated. Even if someone knew where they were going, it was easy to get lost. When Dean had given her the computer virus, they'd decided that if anything should ever happen, and they needed to meet secretly, they'd do it there. They wouldn't be able to stay long because eventually someone would find them, but it was the only place they'd both feel safe enough to go to alone.

She didn't bother to find a candle for light. The last rays of sun were enough to illuminate the small cabin, and Dean was nowhere in sight. *Where are you?*

Even though she knew she was safe there for the time being, she couldn't bring herself to risk looking out the window. Instead she hunkered down in the corner, hidden within the shadows while still being able to keep an eye on both the front and back doors. She'd sit there and wait as long as she had to. If her brother didn't show up, she didn't have any other plans.

She was counting on him to help get her out of this mess.

How was she supposed to hide from the powers behind Hathaway Medical if they were using shifters to follow her scent? She couldn't run forever and eventually they'd find her. She was betting they'd catch up to her soon, and it terrified her. She was going to do her best to avoid capture, even if that meant ending her own life. If they caught her off guard and captured her, then her worst fears would come to life. From everything she had learned about them, she knew they wouldn't kill her quickly. They'd take their time, drawing it out until she begged for them to end her life. She swore to herself that she wouldn't beg for her life, or for them to end it. She'd at least die with some dignity.

The headline from that morning's paper ran through her thoughts. *Woman torn limb from limb by shifters.* Three wolves had broken into a woman's house, terrorizing her until they ripped her apart while she fought for her life. Splashed there on the front page was a picture of the bloody crime scene, instilling fear in every citizen.

Would shifters actually do that? Or was this another stunt by the government to remind everyone they should fear the shifters? Either way, it had accomplished what they intended. She was terrified. The image kept running through her thoughts until she wondered if she could end up a victim of shifters. Would Hathaway Medical release the shifters who were seeking her out to kill her?

A twig cracked outside and the wind howled almost in warning. She pulled the gun from her bag and stood. Doing her best to stay in the shadows, and keep her back pressed against the wall, she aimed the gun at the door. *Please let it be Dean.*

The handle turned and the door slid open, casting another ray of sunshine across the floor. Even with the extra light, all she could see was an imposing figure. It was a man, but no other discerning features were clear.

As quickly as the door opened, it shut again. "Clarissa?" Dean whispered, his head turning as he glanced around the cabin.

"Oh, Dean!" Her hand shook badly as she lowered the gun. It nearly slipped out of her grip. "I thought you'd never make it."

"I came as quickly as I could. It took longer to get a plane back to the states than I expected." His backpack hit the floor with a thump and he moved toward her. "You okay?"

"Never better." She couldn't keep the sarcasm out of her voice as she closed the distance between them and wrapped her arms around him. "What have I gotten us into?"

"Nothing more than I have." He hugged her tight for a moment before stepping back. "Let's sit down."

"What's going on?" She sat down on the sofa and pulled her legs up under her.

"I got transferred overseas almost at the same time you were recruited by Hathaway Medical. I didn't find it suspicious until I got there, and once I found out what they wanted me for, I was worried about your safety. When you told me you were running, I was ready. I had already put in for leave to come back here and try to get you away from them."

"What happened? What did they want you for?" She leaned forward, trying to see him, but he tipped his head away from her and out of the light.

"I saw things you wouldn't believe. The torture…" He leaned back against the sofa. "One thing is for sure, we need somewhere safe to hide."

"I don't know if anywhere safe still exists. Hathaway Medical has shifters on my tail. It's the only way I can explain how they keep finding me. That or they have people spread out all over the country or the world." She wrapped her arms around her waist. "I've had too many narrow escapes to believe otherwise."

"I'll figure out something. In the meantime, I'm sure you're starving. I know I am. I've got some sandwiches in my bag." He moved and the glow from one of the windows cascaded off his cheek. Butterfly bandages covered a long fresh wound that ran from the middle of his ear, almost to his jaw. She reached out, and he leaned out of the light as if he had realized what she'd seen.

"What happened?"

"It's nothing." He got up and grabbed the bag and began digging out the sandwiches. "I don't want to talk about it."

"Dean." She wasn't going to let it go, not when it was clear he was trying to hide something. They needed to trust each other and that meant telling each other everything. "Tell me what happened. How bad where things over there?"

Before he could answer, they were startled when the front door was flung open and a man stood in the doorway, his ominous figure blocking most of it. Dean dropped the bag and pulled a gun from the waistband of his jeans. "You step one foot into this house, and I'll shoot. Don't think I won't."

"I have no issues with you. I'm looking for a Doctor Clarissa Greenwood and I know she's here." A deep voice sent chills up her spine.

"She's none of your business and if you want her you'll have to go through me."

She glanced toward where she had set her gun aside and cursed. There was no chance she'd get to it before things got out of hand. Wanting to calm the situation until she could grab her gun, she decided to approach it from another angel. "Did Hathaway Medical send you?"

"No."

Another figured moved just behind the man in the door, sending a wave of nausea washing over her. "Who's there with you?"

"My brother. Unless you want someone else to stumble on us, I suggest you put down the weapon and let us in."

"How do we know we can trust you?" Dean kept his gun aimed at the other man's head.

"You'll have to take my word for it, unless you want me to drag a body in front of you. We caught someone stalking just far enough behind Doctor Greenwood that he'd gone unnoticed by her." When they remained silent, he turned his head and said to the person behind him, "Fetch the body."

"No!" She shot to her feet. "Don't! That won't be necessary. I don't want to see that."

"Then may we come in?"

"No," Dean said. "You can leave, that's what you can do." He kept his gun pointed at the man in the door. "Whatever you want, we can't help you. We know nothing and just want to be left alone."

"We're here to help Doctor Greenwood. Who are you, anyway?"

She placed her hand on her brother's arm. "Dean, let them in. It's freezing, and leaving the door open will draw attention if anyone is still out there."

"We don't know who they are or what they want. We can't just let them in."

"As I said, we're here to help. If we wanted to kill either of you, we'd have done so already. Now we're coming in unless you want to deal with the others we spotted in town yourselves." He folded his arms over his chest. "What's it going to be?"

"Come in." She stepped around her brother, blocking his line of sight. It might have been a bad idea, but her sixth sense kicked in, sending her into action. He looked imposing and dangerous, but something told her to trust him. "Tell me who you are."

"I'm Patrick O'Reilly, and I'm also a doctor." Once inside, he was followed by another man who could have been his twin except he was a little smaller and seemed younger. "This is my brother, Blake."

The door clicked shut behind them as if to remind her of the decision she'd made. She wasn't only risking herself, but Dean as well. "Why have you come here? How do you know my name, or that I'd be here?"

"I know you worked at Hathaway Medical." With that, Dean grabbed her arm and tugged her back, training the gun on Patrick again. "There's no need for the weapon, at least not when it comes to me."

"I'm not so sure about that." Dean's grip tightened. "Get out of here," he told Clarissa. "I'll deal with them."

Patrick leaned against the wall, a smirk on his face. "If you'd just listen to me for a minute, you'd understand I'm here to help. Clarissa—if you don't mind me calling you by your first name—do you remember a security guard named Andrew?"

"Andrew…he warned me to watch that experiment." She thought back and tried to remember what he had actually said to her. Had he known what would happen when she realized what was going on? If he had suspected she'd run, then was she wrong about Patrick and his brother? Had they come to take her back to Hathaway Medical? She had risked Dean on a hunch, and now it looked like it was biting them both in the ass.

Dean's gaze left Patrick for the first time as he looked to her for answers. "What does he mean?"

Patrick cut in. "Andrew alerted us to your situation and sent us to help you."

"Then you're here representing Hathaway Medical."

He shook his head. "No, I'm here representing the shifters."

In a split second, Dean had pushed her down in front of the sofa, and a deafening gunshot exploded. Someone dove at her brother, knocking the gun from his hand and across the room. Without a second thought, she crawled toward it, keeping low and away from the scuffle. Her hand closed over the top of the gun, the smooth metal cool against her touch, when an arm wrapped around her waist.

"I wouldn't do that if I were you. I told you we bring you no harm."

"Then leave." She turned her head to look at him and found herself face to face with Patrick. His shoulder-length golden blond hair had a slight wave to it, but it was his eyes that drew her in. She could feel her body reacting to him. There was something about him that made her feel safe. Something told her that as long as she was with him, she'd always be protected. *That's insane. He's a shifter. Danger follows him everywhere.*

"You trusted me enough to invite us in, so trust me for a little bit longer," he implored her.

"Then stop playing games and tell me why you're here," she snapped. "How does Andrew play into this, and how did you know I'd be here? Andrew would have never known that." Something crashed in the background, reminding her that Dean and Blake were still in a physical altercation. "Before you do that, get your brother off Dean."

Patrick whistled loud, once again making her ears protest. "That's enough, both of you." Blake turned to look at them, and Dean used that moment to get another punch in, hitting his opponent squarely on the jaw. The other man was above him, straddling his chest as he tried to gain control.

"Damn it, Dean! Stop this." She stood, taking the gun with her as she rose. Patrick kept a surprisingly gentle hand on her arm. "We're going to sit down and hear them out. If you can't handle that, then step outside and cool off."

"I come all this way to help you and you'd rather trust these two? Fuck, Clarissa, their shifters. You've seen what can happen—"

"You're right, Dean. I've seen what can happen when they're tortured. When they're pressed into a corner, poked and prodded. But none of that's happening here."

"Do you think they care that you didn't perform any of the experiments? They only want to eliminate another one of the people involved."

"You don't know us, so don't pretend to know what we'd do." Blake just shook his head, refusing to budge.

"Blake, let him up. He's going to behave so we can sit down and talk." At Patrick's order, Blake rose and offered Dean a hand.

Despite what had happened, including Dean shooting at them and the physical altercation, Blake's actions exuded kind consideration. That surprised her more than anything else so far. "The gun went off," she said as if realizing it for the first time.

"Everyone is fine. Blake and I stepped out of the way, you can see where the bullet met the wall near the door. Now, how about we put the gun aside before someone gets injured?"

"Don't do it, Clarissa," Dean warned.

"I'm not asking you to give it to me, just put it aside." Patrick looked over at Blake. "Turning on a light will be like a beacon for anyone who might have followed, so see if you can find some candles."

"There's no electricity, anyway. Candles are in the first cabinet on the right in the kitchen." She sat the gun on the end table but she couldn't take her gaze off it. Was she doing the right thing or jeopardizing their safety?

"You're being stupid. Dad taught you better than this." Dean stood on the other side of the room shaking his head.

"We don't know they mean us any danger."

"I thought that once too, and then this happened." He turned toward her, allowing her to see the full impact of his injury. "I tried to save one of the captives when I knew they were going to kill him, and what did I get for my troubles? This! He attacked me. Maybe the government is right in some of the things they're doing. Not all of it, but maybe some. Shifters are dangerous."

"You got that because the shifter was drugged," Patrick said. "He didn't know what he was doing." He sank down onto a chair as Blake lit two small candles and placed one on each end table. With the curtains drawn, no one would see the tiny flickering lights from outside.

Dean spun to look at him, his body tight with anger. "How would you know that?"

"Because I know what goes on in those labs. I've seen the documentation of what torture these so-called doctors are putting my kind through. When they're done with us, we're incinerated alive. You're going to stand there and tell me the government is right in their actions? How would you like to be tortured and then burned alive?"

"How do you know?" Clarissa asked. "Those labs are locked and heavily guarded. Did Andrew tell you what happens there?" They would kill him for leaking the information. Even though she barely knew him, the thought of it made her ill, especially knowing they'd torture him first, because that's what they *always* did.

"No, I've seen these places firsthand." He and Blake shared a glance before he turned back to her. "My sister was held in one of those labs."

She sucked in a deep breath. After what she had seen, she hated to think his sister had suffered the same fate. "Was she…did they…burn…"

"No, we rescued her just in time and destroyed the lab." He leaned forward, placing his elbows on his thighs. "That's part of the reason I'm here. I have an offer for you."

"What sort of an offer?"

"Don't take it, Clarissa," Dean begged. "I'll figure a way out of this for both of us."

"I'll make sure you're safe in exchange for some information on Hathaway Medical," Patrick said, ignoring him. "We want to take the lab down and rescue any prisoners. You need our help, so this is a good solution for both of us."

"Why do you think I'll help you?" She pulled her legs under her, tucking herself against the sofa. "Even if I do, how can I be sure you won't cast me aside once you have the information you need?"

"I think you'll help me for the same reasons you didn't stay at Hathaway Medical. You couldn't stand to see what they were doing, and you wanted no part in it. If I'm wrong, then I've come a long way for nothing and risked our secret further."

"Even if she doesn't help us, they'll find her before they find us." Blake stood near the fireplace, his arms crossed over his chest. "It won't be long before they catch her scent again."

"They, as in shifters? Are the people behind Hathaway Medical actually using shifters to track me?"

"They're drugged, heavily guarded, and chained, but…yes."

"We masked your scent from town, but we don't have long before we need to get a move on if we don't want them to find you," Blake growled, deep and throaty. It scared her enough that she reached over to grab the gun, only to have her wrist caught by Patrick's hand.

"There's nothing to fear. He's not going to shift, just once again voicing his displeasure at me."

"For what?" She glanced between the brothers before finally settling her gaze on Patrick.

"Because we couldn't rescue the shifters they were using. It would have been too dangerous in town, with the residents around, and we had to get to you before you moved on." He removed his hand from hers and adjusted in the chair.

"Then we should have killed them," Blake said. "Death would be better than being on the end of a chain like some fucking search and rescue dog."

"I have to agree with him." She nodded toward Blake. "That's no life, and what's being done to them at Hathaway Medical is even worse."

"Sounds like you've made your decision." Dean shook his head. "I risk everything to come to you, and you're willing to trust someone else."

"We can help you too, Dean," Patrick said. "You're welcome to come with us, but you're going to have to make a decision soon."

"I want you to come with me," Clarissa said. "Please. Take Patrick's offer. I'm sure whoever's on our tail knows I have a brother, and they'll be looking for you."

"You're really going to do this?" Dean shook his head. "How do you know they won't turn on us?"

"Call it intuition. Plus, I want to bring down that lab, and I'll risk my own life to do it." She turned to Patrick. "If I help you, can you promise to close the place down, keep others from suffering?"

"You have my word."

"I'll blow the building sky high," Blake agreed.

Consequences be damned, she was going to dive in head first. "Then I'll help. If we can get to a place with electricity, I can charge up my laptop and that will give you all the information you need."

"We're going to need the layout of the building, the guard schedule, that sort of thing, as well as your files. That will help us determine the best course of action to get in and out. We'll need to go over all of that with Austin."

"Like I said, everything you need will be on my laptop. I put a virus on their system that will give us complete access. But who's Austin?"

"The next oldest of the O'Reilly family after me. He's former military, that's how he knows Andrew, and he's the best when it comes to strategy and planning." He leaned forward. "A computer virus? If it's not completely untraceable, you'd have risked yourself further."

"It's untraceable," Dean said. "I designed it. The South American government is beginning to think like ours, and they're planning to open laboratories like we have here. The company I was working for began to take on freelance jobs almost a year ago, and I was sent to Brazil in order to prepare their computer systems. I was given access to the systems here to be sure I understood what was needed. It would seem as though the two governments are going to work together. With that in hand, I was able to create a virus that would go undetected by their security measures and give me complete access. In case...well, in case a situation like this arose."

"A computer expert." Patrick smirked at Blake. "We'll have to see how Luke handles some competition."

"Luke's another brother and the geek of the family," Blake said. "He's the only one who ever took to the coding, and all that computer crap, which is why he runs a lot of our stuff. He's the reason we found you."

"What?" She raised an eyebrow in question. She'd been so careful. How had someone she didn't even know find her, and what did that mean for the people who'd been hot on her trail since she left?

"He tried to narrow it down based on where you were when you left, the two calls you placed to Dean, and anywhere that's familiar enough to you, locations only you'd know about. He found this cabin, and we left immediately to find you." Blake stepped closer. "If you're up for it, I suggest we leave soon. We don't have to make the complete journey tonight, but we need to get more space between us and them."

"I've been on the run for nearly a week, I'm exhausted and sore, but I won't stop now. Dean?" She looked over at her brother to see if he was willing to go tonight or if he wanted to rest.

Dean glanced at each of the brothers before shaking his head. "I can't fully trust them, not yet. They have to earn that."

"Dean—"

"It's okay," Patrick said. "It's understandable." He hit his hand against the armrest of the chair. "If we're going to leave, Clarissa, I need you in the bedroom. There's something we can do to block your scent and give us more time."

"Absolutely not." Dean's voice raised a few notches. "I won't let you have sex with my sister to mask her smell."

"What?" She looked at them with wide eyes. She couldn't have heard them correctly.

"Not sex." Patrick gave her brother an incredulous glance, seeming annoyed he'd jump to conclusions. "Blake, get the spare clothes. I borrowed a few of my sister's things. You're going to need to change into her clothes. The smell of her will throw them off of your scent. Once you're changed, I'm going to make sure there's nothing left of your scent."

"How?"

"You'll find out once you've changed and are laying on the bed." He smirked before adding, "There's little choice unless you want to risk them following us, and I won't put the rest of my family in jeopardy."

She nodded, grabbed one of the candles, and took the clothes that Blake held out to her. If they were willing to help her get her life back, and out of this crazy mess she'd found herself in, then she'd do whatever they asked.

Chapter Five

Through the glow of the candles, Patrick caught a glimpse of Dean staring at him with what appeared to be uncertainty and possibly hatred in his eyes. He wasn't sure what to make of Clarissa's brother. His technical skills could come in handy and would give Luke a break, but Dean would have to understand who was in charge.

"If you're coming with us, you're going to need to change as well." Blake dug into the bag and began to pull out a pair of jeans and a sweater.

"Why? They don't have my scent."

"You've had contact with Clarissa, so her aroma lingers on your clothes. It's a precaution. We don't want to take any unnecessary risks." Blake held out the clothes. "These should fit you."

"We've all had contact with Clarissa," Dean pointed out, remaining still. "Will the two of you change as well?"

"No." Needing to stretch his legs, Patrick rose from where he was sitting. "Our natural animal musk will overpower everything else. It will be all the shifter trackers will be able to smell without getting close to us."

"Animal musk." Dean shook his head and finally took the clothes from Blake's outstretched hand.

"You seem to have a problem with our species. Are you sure you wish to entrust your safety to us?" Patrick watched Dean closely, trying to decide exactly where he stood when it came to shifters. Would he become a threat?

"How can I not have some reservations about your kind after what was done to me?" There was a heat of anger in Dean's eyes as he stared at Patrick.

"Have you ever been drugged and tortured?" He didn't give him a chance to answer. "I doubt it, but it's a normal reaction to strike out at someone when you've been through what they have. They didn't know what you were doing, what your intention was, so they fought."

"How do you know so much about it?"

"Besides the fact I'm a medical doctor, it's just clear logic." Patrick pulled his long-sleeved shirt from the waistband of his jeans and tugged it up midway to reveal his scars. "The other reason is because something similar happened to me." He stepped closer, showing Dean the evidence.

"What happened?"

Patrick ran his hand over the scar closest to his heart. The smooth skin was puffed out a little more than the rest. It might have been the smallest of the scars, but it was the one that held the most meaning to him. "You can't possibly understand what the captive shifters go through, but I can. Jade, the youngest of my siblings, was captured and held in one of those labs. She was tortured as they conducted test after test on her. It was pure luck that we got to her in time. When we went to take down the lab, we had no idea she was one of the prisoners."

"I'm sorry, I didn't know."

"You wouldn't have." He let his shirt fall back down. "Jade fought me when I tried to pull her from the cage they kept her in. They had her so drugged that she didn't recognize me or our brothers. But things got worse as the drugs began to leave her system. My medical training didn't prepare me to see my sister so strung-out, belligerent, and fighting us at every move. She was convinced we were going to kill her. Two nights after we rescued her, she screamed out in her sleep and I went to her. That's when she stabbed me."

"She just missed his heart," Blake added as if he realized Patrick wouldn't admit how bad it had really been. "Even though shifters are harder to kill, if our heart is destroyed, we'll die."

"Your own sister tried to kill you?" The disbelief was clear in Dean's voice.

"She didn't intentionally try to kill me, she was only lashing out in fear. She grabbed what was closest to her and stabbed me." He shoved the bottom of his shirt into his jeans, closing the matter.

"I'm changed." Clarissa stood in the doorway separating the living room from one of the bedrooms.

"I'm coming." He turned to Blake. "I want to leave when we're done." Knowing his brother would see to Dean, he turned on his heels and strolled toward Clarissa. Seeing her in the candlelight, clad in low-slung jeans and a yellow sweater, made her look so young and innocent. It made his inner beast stand up and want to protect her.

Thoughts of her had his lion purring, and he remembered something from before that hadn't registered at the time. Physical heat had poured through him when he wrapped his arm around her waist to keep her from pointing the gun at Blake. His beast had been so preoccupied with trying to ensure her safety, that he hadn't even pushed for more contact. The heat in their touch could only mean one thing. *Clarissa's my mate.*

"Why are you standing there looking at me like that?"

He blinked, bringing her back into focus. "Come on."

"What are we doing now?"

"You're going to lie back on the bed and I'll do all the work." He smirked.

She slipped past him and into the bedroom. "That sounded sexual, and you said this wasn't about sex."

"You're right, it isn't, but it *is* very intimate." He stalked forward, letting his inner lion out enough to get another taste of his mate.

"Intimate? I don't know you…maybe this isn't such a good idea."

"It's the only way we can get you away from here and somewhere safe." With each step he took toward her, she retreated just a little farther into the room until the back of her thighs were pressed against the side of the bed. "I promise it won't hurt a bit."

"I hadn't thought of pain."

"Lie back." He brushed the front of his body against hers.

"Wait…maybe…maybe I should know what's going to happen first."

"You're going to lie back and I'm going to press my body against yours—"

"Oh, no you don't. That sounds like some cheap trick."

He placed a hand on her arm, just below the shoulder, and instantly the heat he remembered feeling earlier sparked back to life. The first signs of mating would only get stronger the longer they were together. "You don't trust me, and I understand. I'd have asked Dean to come in to make you more comfortable, but from the way he's reacted to me so far, I suspect he'd pull me off of you before I could finish."

"Why?" She bit her lip and gazed up at him with big, honey brown eyes.

"Because he wouldn't want me touching you. His fear that I'd hurt you would get the best of him. Or because of the intimacy of it. Take your pick." He nodded to the bed. "Now, please, we don't have much time."

She hesitated for another moment before she finally sank back onto the mattress. Their eyes met as she reclined. She pulled one of the pillows beneath her head. "Now what?"

"I need to replace your scent with my own. It will only mask it for a short time, but it will be long enough for us to get far enough away without them catching a whiff of it and following."

"How are you going to do that? Isn't my scent a part of me?"

"It is, but my beast can mask it temporarily." *It would mix with yours if we mated, throwing them off your scent permanently.* But that wasn't an option. Not yet, anyway.

"Beast?" She rose up to rest on her elbows. "You're going to shift?"

There was a mixture of terror and excitement in her eyes that made him want to tease her, but he resisted the urge. "No. My beast is always within me, even when I'm in human form. There's no need to shift."

"What a relief. I'm not sure I'm ready to see your animal yet." She paused, averting her eyes. "Mind if I ask what your second nature is?"

"Second nature. So proper." He smirked. "I'm a lion." He spoke with ease because unlike the rest of the world, he didn't see the animal side of him as a curse or an experiment gone wrong. To him, it was a blessing, something he was proud of. Though times were tough right now, things would get better. He'd see to it.

"I wasn't sure how to word this…this…ability." Seeming nervous, she bit her bottom lip. "I'm not even sure *ability* is the right word."

"Shifting is a magical thing, and even though the world thinks I should be ashamed of it, I'm not. My lion is as much a part of me as my internal organs. The human society that we live in just doesn't accept those who are different, but we're here just like everyone else, and we want to live in peace."

"That almost sounded like a public relations statement."

"I just want you to understand who my siblings and I are. We're no danger to you or any other human. We're always in control of our animal, no matter what form we may take. That's what Hathaway Medical and the rest of the government organizations don't understand. We shouldn't be experimented on, nor should any other human." He hated that he sounded like he was lecturing her, but if he was going to take her back to Forever Creek, she need to understand his kind. He didn't want any surprises later that would send her running. Once she knew their location, if she got spooked and ran off, she'd be a liability.

"But the government doesn't classify you as human." With that statement, she wasn't able to meet his gaze.

"What about you? Do you think I'm human?" Silence thickened the air until he wasn't sure she'd answer.

"You look human enough to me." She reached out and laid her hand on his chest. "You feel human, too. That's all that matters to me."

He placed his hand over hers. "This is just one side of me, kind of like a coin. Will you still feel the same way when you see my lion?"

"If I felt any different, then I wouldn't have left my position at Hathaway Medical. What the government is doing is wrong. I'd like to do something to fight it, but what can I do? I'm just one woman against the government. There's nothing I can do, but I don't condone their actions."

"My family and I are fighting against it, and you can help. We'll take everyone who's willing to help, and stand against the government. We're creating an army to fight for our right to live our lives without fear."

She pulled her hand from under his and leaned back on the bed. "I can't. What chance do I have to fight them? What can I do to aid you or your family? The answer is nothing."

"You're a scientist. We can use your skills." Even if they couldn't utilize her, he'd have found some reason to keep her out of danger. She couldn't just return to society. After all, she was a wanted woman now. The government would keep it under wraps for now, but once they lost her scent, they'd go to the media with her picture and do whatever else they had to in order to keep their secrets safe. As long as she was alive, she was a threat to them.

"You said before that you're a doctor, so you don't need me."

"I have a medical degree. Before my family went into hiding, I had a family practice. While I might be able to handle some of it, especially how drugs hit our systems, I can't do it all. I could use your knowledge."

"Should I feel cheap that you just want to use me? I've been wanted for my brain before, but normally it's by an employer."

"Cheap, no...but valued, yes." He reached down and took her hand into his. "I'm sure you've heard about the drug they're pushing out to the military and first responders. It will be in the hands of the general public before long."

"Lycan Ultra Neuro Acid, right?"

He gave her a quick nod. "Yes, LUNA. I've got a sample coming and I need to determine what's in it so we can counteract it. Help me do that."

"If I say no, what then? Do you take away your promise of protection?"

"No." He gave her hand a gentle squeeze. "You're as much of a threat to them as I am. They won't give up until you're dead. As long as you don't put my family in jeopardy by doing something stupid, like running off and telling the world where we are, we'll protect you. If you're stupid enough to do something like that, you'd get what's coming to you, but it wouldn't be by our hands. You would be at the mercy of the government and their hired hands. If they thought you had information about us, they would make sure your death was a slow one." A shiver of fear vibrated through her body, but he held tight to her hand.

"Are you trying to scare me?"

"Not on purpose, but it's time you had a dose of reality. The world is screwed up right now. People are scared, and instead of thinking logically, they're lashing out with that fear. You need to understand what will happen if you don't follow every order I give you." He squeezed her hand and let the heat of their touch caress over him. "I'm going to get you through this and make sure you're safe."

"*Every* order?" Her lips curled up into a smirk that didn't quite reach her eyes. "Hmm, I've never been very good a following orders. Dean says I have this unnatural need to push the limits on everything. He also says I've never met a boundary that I didn't try to push or break. So, you might have your work cut out for you."

"I'll make you a deal. You don't push the boundaries until I get you somewhere safe, and then I'll cut you a little slack. I understand this is new to you and you're scared, but right now the most important thing is to get us all out of here before they have a chance to find us." He nudged her knee until her legs were on either side of his. "Now, are you ready?"

"Just one more question. You mentioned you saw them in town, so why haven't they made their way here yet?"

"Blake shared a tip, sending them in the opposite direction. It should buy us some time, but not a lot before the shifters realize there's no scent leading that way. Then, our scent will throw them off."

"Then we better get this done." She took a deep breath and let it out slowly. "Don't make me regret this."

"Deep breaths. The last thing we need is for you to pass out." When she did as he directed, he nodded. "Very good, now just keep doing that. As I mentioned before, this is going to be very intimate. I'm going to press my body against you and run my hands along your body. With every place I touch, and the longer we do it, the stronger my scent will become. If you feel uncomfortable and want to stop, just say so, but if we don't get it strong enough, we might have to do this again at some point, and I don't think Dean will be cooperative."

"He would kill us both."

"I would never let that happen."

She rose her eyebrow in suspicion at him, before leaning back on the bed. "Let's do this before Dean barges in."

"Remember, you can stop this at any time." He knelt between her legs.

"I think it's best to do as much as possible now. You don't understand what my brother is like."

"I think I do." He wrapped his hands around each of her ankles, the warmth burning a little hotter and began to slowly slide upward. He took his time, not only to enjoy the moment, but to also make sure he touched every inch of her. "There are six of us. I'm the oldest, and Jade is the youngest. She's our only sister. We're very protective of her, especially after all that's happened."

"You say that like it's more than just the threat to your kind. There's something lingering in the way you said it." When he didn't say anything, she leaned up on her elbows and looked down at him. "Patrick?"

"Let's just say Jade's been through a lot. All of us have, but it's only going to get worse before it gets better."

"The president has pushed for these changes, for the shifter camps, and even though it's not been publicly addressed someone in his office is behind the push for the labs. If it's not him, then it's someone he's put in charge of the shifter crisis. There's a statement on my laptop that orders Hathaway Medical to have at least six more labs operational within three months or they'll find someone else to take over the contract."

He stopped moving just as he'd begun to slide along the curve of her thigh. *Six more in the next three months.* Anger had his lion trotting within him, demanding something be done to stop it.

"Patrick." She placed her hand on his shoulder, pulling his attention back to her. "I'm sorry…I shouldn't have…"

"What? You shouldn't have said anything?" He shook his head. "I need to know everything you can tell me about this lab, their operation, and about Hathaway Medical, in general because my brothers and I are going to take them down."

"It will get you killed or worse."

"We're not going to live in fear any longer. We have to stand up and fight or the government and the rest of the population are going to wipe out my kind. I can't stand by and let that happen." He rolled his shoulder, trying to release the tension. "Don't worry, angel. The government is going to be suffering from their own consequences soon enough."

"What do you mean?"

"LUNA's going to be their own downfall. They don't realize it yet, but there are plenty of shifters working within the government, military, police departments, or as firefighters. When they start the testing, those shifters will have no choice but to leave and go into hiding. There will be more job openings than ever before, making it harder to control crime or fight against us as the shifters begin to unite for their freedom." He continued his journey and slid his hands along her thighs. "All hell is about to break out."

"Why is it that the more you tell me about this, the more I think that if there's an all-out war between humans and shifters, humans will lose?"

"I hope it will never come to anything like that." He rose up on his knees to hover over her, while he slipped his hands beneath her, grabbed hold of her butt, and lifted her to meet him. Her pelvis and the tops of her thighs pressed along the front of him. "I promise, whatever happens, you'll be safe."

"But what happens if something happens to you? Then where will I be?"

"My family will protect you."

She raised an eyebrow at him. "You know what I mean. From what you've told me about your family, it doesn't sound like you're going to be sitting on the sidelines while the rest of your kind is out there fighting a war. You're going to be on the frontlines, aren't you? Then what about me? If you lose, the rest of the human population will classify me as lower than a shifter. I'd be a traitor."

He cupped the curve of her ass as he fought the urge to pull her into his arms. "Now, listen to me, you have nothing to worry about. Things are going to be just fine. We're going to find some common ground with the government. Once they realize how much LUNA is going to affect them, they'll have no choice."

"Unless that backfires and they realize how strong the shifter population is." She closed her eyes as if she didn't want to think about what she said next. "They could seek to eliminate you because of it."

"My angel, did anyone ever tell you that you worry too much?"

"Dean says that, but that hasn't changed anything. I'm still a worrier." She nodded toward her hips. "Is this part of the treatment or are you trying to see how long I can hold myself like this before my muscles protest?"

"I could hold you here all night, I would, but we have other things we must attend to. But don't think you'll get out of it that easy next time."

"Who said there'd be a next time?" She sneered.

"Oh, there *will* be a next time." He leaned closer to her, his chest pressed against hers, and his hands slid past her hips, toward her midriff. As much as he was enjoying the feeling of her body under his touch, the first time he was able to explore the curves of her body should have been more romantic.

Not with the threat of danger lurking just around the corner. He promised his lion the time would come soon enough. *Focus on getting her out of here and back to Forever Creek safely.*

"Patrick." Her voice was barely above a whisper, but it was enough to bring him back to the present.

He looked at her in question, only to see her gaze cast down toward his hands. He silently scolded himself when his attention lingered on the way the sweater was pressed against her breast, curving the material.

"Patrick." She called to him again.

Damn it, he was getting distracted too easily. This mating was affecting him already and he hadn't even claimed her as his. It would only get worse as time went on, but before it did, he had to get her somewhere safe.

He realized why she had called his name when he saw his hands below her breasts. His thumb gently brushed against the underside, but he hadn't moved past them, leaving a tension in the air. His animal urged him to lean forward and close the distance between them. For his mouth to claim her, to lay at least a partial claim on her until they were able to get somewhere safer and he could complete the mating.

"Are you planning to stay there all night? If so, at least you could make it more entertaining for me." She glanced back up at him and wiggled her eyebrows. "Come on, big boy, show me what you've got." Her voice held a teasing tone, but his lion trotted forward in anticipation.

"There's no time now. I can hear Dean getting impatient, and I'm not sure how much longer Blake can keep him out of here. But don't forget you asked for it because I'll show you just what I'm made of later on, and you'll never look at another man the same."

"A girl can hope."

It might have been innocent flirting, but his lion wanted to prove it to her. Instead, he forced himself to move his hands and to continue what he had started. He was nearly done, and then he could put a little distance between them. At least until they were back at Forever Creek.

Chapter Six

Clarissa had allowed her fear to be replaced by desire. It was a relief to feel something other than total dread, but she was worried she was leading him on. Even if she wanted to, she wasn't sure they were compatible. Didn't he need to be with someone of his own kind? Could she have a relationship with someone who was so different that he had the ability to shapeshift?

"You look as though you just thought of something." He slid his hands down her arms, and she could feel the heat of his touch through the sweater.

"How often can shifters change? Is it based on the moon cycle?"

"We can shift at will. Even young shifters have the ability, but sometimes their emotions get in the way and they can shift without meaning to, or it can take longer for them to return to their human form. Why? Are you worried you'll have a lion pawing at you any second?"

She tried to laugh it off, but the image of a lion above her sped her heartbeat and iced her blood. "I…I didn't…"

"Angel, I was joking. You have nothing to worry about. I'm in complete control of my animal." His hands returned to her shoulders. "Now things are about to get a little more intimate."

"How?"

"You might enjoy it more if you just lie back and relax." Without hesitation, he leaned into her and nuzzled her neck.

"Wow." She was torn between pressing herself closer to him, or pulling away.

"Shh, angel, we don't need Dean coming in." He kept his voice low as he tangled his hands in her long, blonde hair. "Do you remember the lover bites from high school?"

"You mean hickeys? Don't you even think about giving me one of those."

"Not completely." He lifted his head to look at her. "I need to bite your neck. Not enough to draw blood."

"Don't even think about it."

"All I need to do is leave a mark from my teeth. It will fade in a few hours, but it will be the final step to mask your scent completely. All the tracking shifters will be able to smell is me. If we don't do this, and they have some training, they'll find us quickly."

"Training?" She adjusted enough so that she could look at him without getting a cramp in her neck.

"My brother, Austin, was military and still has contacts within the service. We've seen the paperwork that suggests they have trained some of the shifters as trackers." He closed his eyes and let out a low growl. "I can't believe I just said trained and shifters in the same sentence. We're not dogs or circus animals that can be used to perform."

Wanting to give him comfort, she reached up and cupped his cheek. "I'm sorry."

"Sweet angel, you have nothing to be sorry for. It's those bastards who will pay for doing this to my kind." He pressed a gentle kiss on her palm before finally meeting her gaze. "Now, I need your decision."

"I hate pain, but do it. I don't want to be the reason they find us. I still can't believe you and Blake are risking yourselves to help me. Dean, too, but from what he's said he'd have been in the same position." She let her hand fall away from his face and glanced up at the ceiling. "How did the world get so screwed up?"

"That, my angel, I don't know. A few bad decisions by idiots and the world turned upside down." He brushed her hair away from her neck. "I need you to relax. This isn't going to hurt much."

"Much." With a cringe, she let out a deep breath. "I'll do my best."

"You'll feel tension, but I promise the actual pain will be minimal. I wouldn't do anything to hurt you."

She looked up at him and found sadness in his eyes that she hadn't seen before. Had she done something to cause it? Or was there something else she was missing? She wanted to reach up, to tuck his shoulder length golden blond hair behind his ear. "I'm sorry."

"For what, angel?"

"My fear of pain. But if you think this is bad, you should see me when I have to get a shot. I hate needles."

A fist slammed against the bedroom door, causing a loud bang. "What's going on in there?"

Dean's voice echoed throughout the room and she jumped, her nails digging into his arm. He didn't even flinch. "Holy shit, Dean, keep your voice down," she called out.

"I want you out here, right now. You've been in there so long, I was worried he'd killed you."

She closed her eyes and tried to regain her patience. At the moment, she'd had enough of his protective attitude. Days ago, all she wanted was her brother, and now she wondered what the hell she had been thinking. It was so unlike her, but she wanted to return to the intimate moment she was sharing with Patrick. As much as she loved her brother, he was giving her a headache. Maybe Dean was right not to trust Patrick and Blake, but she couldn't get the thought out of her mind that if they didn't trust them, they wouldn't make it out of there alive.

"We're almost finished," Patrick called to Dean when she remained silent.

"Clarissa?"

"I'm fine, Dean. Just give us a few more minutes, and keep your voice down." She waited a moment until she heard him moving away from the door. "I'm sorry about him."

"He's seen things that have made me cautious of my kind. I can't blame him for wanting to protect you. It's what anyone would want to do."

"Don't let that fool you. He's always been like this. I guess that's why I called him home. I wanted someone to watch my back. We've always been close, but lately we've gotten closer. He's been calling me nearly every day for the last few weeks as if he knew something was going to happen." She stared up at the ceiling. "Did he know what Hathaway Medical was doing all this time?"

"That's something you'll have to ask him." He gently massaged her shoulder. "Just wait until we get out of here. I don't want you two fighting, at least not until we're somewhere safe."

"What if he says he knew? That he's participated in the experiments on…on your kind? Will you leave him behind?"

"As long as he doesn't betray my family, he's welcome to come with us. He said before he knew what was being done, but didn't mention taking part in the experiments. If you really think it was otherwise, then it needs to be confronted before we get back to my family. I won't risk them or our location. If he's going to deceive us, I need to know because I won't give him any more of a chance than he already has."

She wanted to say that her brother would never do anything like that, but a few days ago she couldn't have pictured anyone doing what she had seen done in the labs at Hathaway Medical. Humanity was something she wasn't sure she understood any longer, and it made her doubt everyone's actions. It wasn't just the world that was going to Hell, it was humankind. They were scared and letting their fears control them. With everything she'd seen, she couldn't help but wonder what would be next. Had her brother's anger stemmed from his own guilt?

He pulled back a little farther from her, his eyebrow raised as he stared down at her. "You're really doubting him."

"Not so much him as humanity. When did we change so much that it was okay to experiment on people? To torture someone because they were different? If that's what it means to be human, I'd rather be dead. I didn't become a scientist to participate in this. I did it to help…" She let out a deep sign. "I wanted to find cures for the illnesses that plague civilization. Instead, look what I got wrapped into."

"Did they tell you why they wanted to hire you? If your specialty was diseases and not animals, there had to be a reason." Before she could answer, she saw the realization dawn in his eyes. "Fuck!"

"That's one sentiment. They're using some as test subjects. Injecting them with diseases and looking for a cure. They wanted me to come up with the perfect match of chemicals to keep them drugged, but so they could still feel it. They're using shifters to try to eliminate diseases."

"But we're immune to diseases, the flu, even the common cold. We don't get sick. If they injected a disease into a shifter, the shifter's body would reject it without showing any symptoms."

"That's the reason Hathaway Medical has started to test on shifters. They're the first, but won't be the last. They're sure the cure for every disease can be found within your blood."

"More than ever, we need to make sure these labs are shut down. I won't stand by while my kind is being testing on. Especially not when the tests are pointless."

She reached up and cupped his cheek with the palm of her hand. "I'll do whatever I can to help. Any information I have on my laptop is yours. Anything I can do, any questions you have I'll try to answer."

"Let's get you somewhere safe, and we'll go over what you have. We need to find a way into Hathaway Medical to try to rescue anyone they're holding there. Then we'll destroy the place."

"What good will that do? They'll only find another place to do it."

"True, but it will destroy what they've done so far and they'll have to take time to set up again. It's all we can do right now, but it won't be for long. We'll fight the government if we have to because we deserve to be able to live in peace just like everyone else." He ran his hands down her arms. "Enough about this for now. Are you ready?"

She tipped her head to the side. "Let's do this."

"This will take a few days for my animal musk to wear off. Until it does, it will mark you as mine. If we run into any shifters before we get back to Forever Creek, you'll need to go with the flow. If I put my arm around you, don't shy away from it. Any hints that this mark isn't true could bring trouble."

"If we run into anyone, we're already in trouble. My face has been all over the television and newspapers. They'll report me."

"No, most shifters will stand united. They won't turn you in, and not for fear of the government, but because of a bond we all have. It doesn't matter what animal we shift into, there's a connection between us. However, if they suspect we're trying to deceive them, things could get tricky."

"How long will it take us to get back to your place?"

"Depends on what we run into and how long you and Dean can keep up the pace. You've been on the run for days and you're exhausted. Dean's not as bad off because he must have slept on the plane and he's worried about you, but it will catch up with him. Ideally, I'd like to make it back to Forever Creek tonight. If not, then tomorrow."

She stifled a yawn. "I'd love a nice warm bed, steaming hot shower, and a hot meal. I'm not sure in what order."

"Then we should get on our way." He leaned back down until he hovered over her and tipped his head into the curve of her neck, his warm breath sending goose bumps down her shoulder. "Just relax."

His voice was low as it caressed over her, and in a strange way it relaxed her. She took a deep breath and let her eyelids fall shut. Whatever was about to happen, she didn't want to see the build-up to it. She wouldn't let her nerves get the better of her before the pain came from his bite.

"Shh, angel." He placed soft kisses over the curve of her neck. "Deep breath."

"Just do it already. The build-up is—" Before she could finish the sentence, his mouth closed around the skin just behind her ear, so the mark would be hidden from view. His teeth sank into her flesh, and a dual pain shot through her, but it was nothing like what she'd expected. He held the bite for a moment before pulling back and running his tongue over the fresh mark.

"I told you it wouldn't be painful." He kissed along her neck, soothing away the pain that had been there moments before.

"That's all?"

"Yes, angel. That's enough to mask your scent and keep the trackers off our trail." He pulled back to look down at her. "If you give me a chance next time I'll make sure it's full of pleasure."

"You seem so confident there will be a next time." She stared up at him as questions ran through her mind. A sparkle in his eyes made her wonder if he was serious.

"Oh yes, angel, there will be a next time." He popped off her, stood up, and offered her a hand.

"Yo, Patrick, time," Blake called through the door.

"Time?" she questioned, as he pulled her to her feet.

"Two minutes," he told Blake before turning back to her. "We figured how long we had to get you out of here, and Blake is just reminding me that time is ticking away. We need to move. Once they realize they've been led in the wrong direction, they'll find the scent you left in town. It'll lead them straight here."

"Just great." She felt the fear creeping back into her shoulders and her stomach churned. The time they'd been alone in the bedroom had made her forget about everything that was happening. She had focused on Patrick, and getting through each minute. Now she was about to be on the run again, but this time she wasn't sure where she'd end up.

"It's going to be okay."

"What?" She forced herself to look up at him and stifle the panic rushing through her.

"The terror gushing off you is piquing my lion's interest." He ran his hands up her arms. "You're going to be fine. I'm going to get you through this."

She gave into her desire and leaned forward. She pressed her head against his hard chest as he wrapped his arms around her. There was a comfort in his embrace she couldn't deny. She'd just met him, but it was as if her body was telling her they'd known each other for years. There was a connection between them she wanted to both embrace and run from. She wasn't sure which side of her was winning, but she had to be insane to think she could get involved with a shifter. At least more involved than she already was.

Without thinking twice, Patrick stepped out of the bedroom, his arm loosely around Clarissa's waist. Dean's reaction was much like Patrick should have expected if he'd given it any thought before they entered the living room. Rage heated his eyes as the two men stared at each other from across the room. A smirk tugged up the sides of Blake's lips as he watched the two men in a silent dispute.

As if Dean realized he wouldn't get a response from Patrick, he turned his attention to his sister. "What the fuck do you think you're doing, Clarissa? You have no idea what he's capable of, and yet you stand there allowing him to have his arm around you."

"I'm a grown woman and my decisions are my own. Patrick and Blake have been kind enough to help us. The least you can do is be grateful and stop acting like an ass." She stepped away from Patrick and went to her brother. She grabbed his arm and pulled him toward the kitchen, putting some space between her and the O'Reilly siblings.

"Get off me." Dean pulled his arm from her grasp. "Little sister, you're in a lot of trouble, and you need to be careful who you trust. How do you know they don't work for Hathaway Medical? Maybe they're here to gain your trust and then lure us both back there."

"That's not true. Don't ask me how I know, I just do. I'll trust them, not just because we need help, but because it feels right. My instincts have never been wrong. I knew something was wrong with Hathaway Medical, but I let the job prospects talk me into ignoring my intuition." She reached out to him, but he pulled back. "Dean, I love you and want you to come with us, but if you can't, I understand. In order to go with them, we're going to need to trust them."

"Trust should be earned."

"As far as I'm concerned, they've earned it by coming here. They didn't need to follow Andrew's lead and find me. They didn't have to risk themselves to come help us."

Dean glanced at them before looking back at her, and shaking his head. "They want something from you."

"I'd freely give any help I can to stop what's happening at Hathaway Medical. I've seen what's being done to them. I can't stand by and do nothing. Anything I can do, I'll do." She let her gaze move to his laceration and tried not to cry. Seeing him injured tore at her heart. "With what's happened to you, it's understandable you'd be on edge. But they explained why the shifter attacked. You can't hold that against the person who did that to you, and certainly not against the O'Reillys."

"Every morning I see the wound, and eventually it will heal, but there will always be a scar and a constant reminder of what they can do if provoked."

"What about us, Dean? Humans…are we so innocent?" She didn't give him a chance to respond. "We're the ones locking them in cages so small they can't even turn around. Torturing them. Sometimes in the name of medicine or for the good of humankind. Other times just so we can see how far we can push them. If anyone is to be blamed, I think it's time we start looking at ourselves. At the government for what they've allowed to happen, for LUNA, for those labs, and the damn concentration camps. Damn it, they're people too. Think of all of those organizations trying to get labs to stop testing make-up, shampoo, and other products on animals, when what's happening to shifters is a million times worse."

"When did you become an activist for animals? You use lab rats in your studies, how is this any different?"

"They're people." She raised her voice a notch before she regained control. "Maybe I've always had a double standard. I've never believed in testing on dogs and I've boycotted companies that do. Yet, all the while, I've used rats in my studies because that's what scientists do. We can't get clearance to try a drug on a person until we've gone through certain testing. So, I've done what I've done to try to cure diseases."

"Isn't Hathaway Medical trying to do just that? At least part of their organization is. That's why you were brought on, to use shifters to find cures," he argued.

"You're right, I was, but I didn't know I'd be working on people. No matter what might come of it, I can't support it. I didn't become a scientist to do the experiments they're doing. They have more than just medical experiments going on in those labs. If I can be of use to Patrick and his siblings, I'll do it because I want to see those labs closed as much as they do."

"They are animals." He stepped toward her, anger heating his words.

"Your attitude has changed. You used to believe they were people too, not just animals. What happened?"

"*This* happened!" He screamed at her, pointing at the wound across his face. "You can't trust someone who is capable of doing this to a person. I was lucky but a few inches lower and he could have gotten my throat. I'd have died."

"Dean, I'm sorry, but this isn't their fault. That shifter was drugged, he was fighting for his life. You'd have done the same thing in his situation."

"You're going to choose them over your own family."

She stood her ground, not backing up as he crowded her space. Out of the corner of her eye, she noticed Patrick had stepped closer, Blake only a pace behind him as if they were ready to get between them. She kept her attention on her brother. The last thing she wanted was for his anger to be directed at them. "I had hoped it wouldn't come to that. But if need be, then I guess so."

"Fine, go with them, but I won't." He stepped back and grabbed his coat from where he had tossed it before tugging it on.

"Dean, you've come all this way to help me. You knew what was happening was wrong. That's why you sent me the computer virus. Why are you changing your mind now?" Tears filled her eyes as she tried to blink them away.

"What the government is doing is wrong." He glanced at Patrick and Blake as if worried they'd attack. "I'm just not sure these…animals should be allowed to mix with humankind. I still believe they're dangerous when provoked, and the world is at risk if we let them run free. Maybe they have the right idea with these shifter camps."

"Oh, Dean." Her heart broke, knowing she was being forced to make a decision between her brother and doing what was right.

"Come with me."

She shook her head, and he turned to grab something out of his bag. Patrick seemed even more tense if that were possible.

She forced the tears away and tried to calm the situation. "If you leave, you'll be in danger. Please, Dean, don't do this."

"We've each got to make our decisions, and I hope the one you've chosen doesn't get you killed." He pulled out a folder that was about two inches think, along with an external hard drive. "Here's everything I've

gathered. Maybe it will help you on your mission. Good luck, little sister."
He slipped the bag over his shoulder and strolled toward the door.

Blake stepped into his path and held out what appeared to be a business card. "Here. If you change your mind or need backup, call us."

"After everything I just said, you'd still help me?"

Blake nodded, and Dean took the card, shoving it into his jacket pocket.

"See, Dean, you've got them wrong." The tears rolled freely down her face as he turned the door handle.

"For your sake, I hope so." With that, he was gone, leaving a hole in her heart.

Patrick came to her and wrapped his arm around her. When she'd called Dean, she had never expected all of this, and she certainly didn't anticipate her brother walking away from her when she needed him most. Patrick and Blake might be there to help her, but she still wanted her brother. Family was supposed to stick together, and instead hers had just walked out the door. Sometimes blood wasn't thicker than water.

Chapter Seven

Skirting around the town instead of through it was their best chance to get Clarissa safely back to Forever Creek without being recognized. Patrick had helped her hide her hair under one of Jade's hats, giving anyone who looked their way an impression her hair was shorter. Even with the hat covering part of her face and the thick winter jacket, he couldn't take his eyes off her. He wanted her.

"It's freezing," she bitched, shoving her hands into the pockets of the jacket.

"Just a bit longer and we can stop to warm up. Let's get away from these houses and out of sight." Blake paused and scanned the area before he waved them forward.

"Come here." Patrick wrapped his arm around her shoulders and pulled her close. Even with her heavy winter jacket, he was sure his body heat would help her until they could stop and he could warm her up properly.

"I'm okay." She still let him wrap his arm around her and hold her close as they made their way across the road to the shelter of the trees. "I just don't remember it being so cold earlier."

"It's only going to get worse as the night goes on. The darkness is cloaking us so we can move around without being noticed, but it makes it colder. You'll have to let us know when you get too cold because it doesn't affect us like it does you. Our body temperature is warmer than a human's, and we're able to keep ourselves warm or cool as the situation would call for it."

"What's your temperature?" She was careful to duck her head as they returned to the cover of the trees to avoid bumping into one of the branches.

"Between one hundred and one, and one hundred and two. A nice temperature to keep you warm," he teased.

Blake stepped around them and stopped so quickly that she walked into the back of him. "What's wrong?"

"Shh," Patrick whispered, tightening his arm around her as every muscle in his body went rigid. He cursed himself for being so preoccupied with his attraction to her that he hadn't been paying enough attention to their surroundings. He was grateful Blake was on his game, sniffing the air for any traces of danger. At least he knew his brother could take care of himself and others if the situation called for it.

"Ten o'clock." Blake pulled a gun from under his jacket. "Two males."

"Wolves." Patrick bit out the word with disgust. Wolves always seemed to cause problems, especially when he didn't have time for them.

"We're downwind from them and could still find another way around."

"It will take too much time." He shook his head and rubbed her shoulder. "Remember what I told you earlier. Can you still do it?"

She nodded. "Wolves? As in regular wolves, or..."

"Shifters," he finished for her.

"Look what we have here, Richard." A man stepped out from between the trees and instantly Blake raised his gun.

"We don't want any trouble, we're just passing through."

A second man with short dark hair stepped up, the stench of alcohol clinging to him. "Hmm. Who's the pretty human? Don't see many of them around our kind. What ya do, kidnap her?"

His words slurred together, and Patrick wondered just how much the wolf had to drink. It took a lot for alcohol to affect their kind, so for him to be slurring he had to have gone through a number of bottles.

"She's mine." He made it clear by rubbing the side of his face along the top of her head, marking her with his scent again. As long as his scent was strong enough, no shifter would suspect he hadn't completed his claim on her, and no shifter in their right mind was willing to mess with another's mate.

"Come on, man, we just wanted to have some fun." The first wolf stepped closer, and Blake kept the gun aimed right between the man's eyes.

"I wouldn't take another step if I were you. I'll shoot to kill."

A third man stepped out from Patrick's left. "Richard, Carl, get back to the house. Now!" Authority echoed in each word. "I apologize for them. They're just trying to let off some steam."

"No harm done." Patrick watched as the two hightailed it through the woods, back to wherever they were supposed to be. The newest arrival was clearly an Alpha, and the respect they had for him was obvious even in their drunken state.

"I'm Cotton. Are you passing through the area to somewhere in particular, or trying to find a place to hide away from the government? If you need somewhere safe, some of us have taken over an old abandoned house just on the other side of the woods. You're more than welcome to join us."

"Thank you, but we're just passing through," Patrick said. "We're on our way to meet with the rest of our family."

With the threat gone, Blake holstered his gun. "If you don't mind me saying so, those two you just sent off seemed to have respect for you. But you're not their Alpha, are you?"

"No." Cotton leaned against the tree and hooked his thumbs through the belt loops of his jeans. "Richard and Carl belong to another clan, and their Alpha is back at the house. Funny thing is, until the world went to Hell, we were rivals. They respect me because I've proven to them I'll take no shit from them or anyone, not even their Alpha. If I wanted to, I could fight him and win control over their pack, but I don't want to do that."

"What do you want?" Patrick ran his hand down her arm to chase away the shiver he'd felt seconds before.

"To stop what's going on." Cotton shook his head. "Sounds stupid, I know. After all, what can a single person do against the government?"

"Not a lot, but there's a group of us preparing. You could join us."

"Sounds like a death wish," Cotton replied, pushing off the tree.

"Death is always a possibility, but I'd rather go down fighting than be a victim of one of their labs."

"I'd sign my own death warrant to avoid that fate," Blake added.

"A wolf mixing with a bunch of lions, who would ever think that was possible?" Cotton smirked. "I have something I must attend to, but I'd like to give it some thought."

Blake held out another one of the business cards he had given Dean earlier. "You can contact us through the information on here and we'll arrange something if you want to join us."

"Very well." Cotton pocketed the card and nodded toward Clarissa. "Now, I suggest you get her out of here."

"You know me?" Another shiver shot through her, but this time Patrick suspected it was more from fear than cold.

"I was in town earlier gathering supplies when someone held up a picture of you, asking if I'd seen you in the area. I can't smell them, but I'm sure they're still around here somewhere. I don't know why and I don't want to know, but they're determined to find you, so if I were you I'd get out of here."

"We're going," he reassured her. "I've got an SUV not far from here. We'll be out within the hour."

"Do yourself a favor and complete the mating. Otherwise, she's fair game and others might see her as a prize to get back at the government." With that, Cotton disappeared into the trees.

She tipped her head back enough to look up at him. "Complete the mating? What's that supposed to mean?"

"Not now," Blake interrupted. "Let's get moving, and Patrick will explain everything to you once we get out of the woods." He started ahead, keeping a lookout for anyone who might double back.

"He's right. We don't know if the first two will circle around to cause more trouble, or if they recognized you and are heading into town to let someone know they saw you." She sidestepped out of his embrace, leaving him with an empty sinking feeling. He'd barely known her a few hours, and already his lion was becoming attached. How much worse would it be once their mating was finalized?

"Patrick, what does he mean by mating?" She balked when he tried to take a step forward without answering her. "Was Dean right? Are you just using me?"

"No, angel." He pulled her around to the front of him so he could look her in the eyes. "He smelled my scent on you, and he jumped to the conclusion we had started something we haven't."

"Are you saying I'm not your…mate…or whatever?"

He might have bent the truth a little before, but he couldn't lie to her when she asked directly, no matter how much the timing might call for it.

"Clarissa, please, we need to carry on."

"Answer me."

"You call to my lion and to me as a man, just the way a mate would." When she took a step back from him, he reached out and took hold of her arm. "There's nothing to be frightened of. It's not like when we get somewhere safe I'm going to throw you over my shoulder, carry you to the bedroom, and have my way with you."

"You're not?"

"Well, angel, if you want me to, that can always be arranged." He wiggled his eyebrows at her, suggesting he'd be more than willing. "Though it wouldn't be with force. It would be because you wanted me."

"Don't you have to stay with your own species? I mean, isn't that like inbreeding?"

"We're not that different. Except for the fact I can shift into a lion, there's nothing else that separates us." He cupped the side of her cheek, using his thumb to push away a stray hair that had fallen from under the cap. "We can mate with anyone, it doesn't matter if they are human, or another breed. It's just like a human relationship. It might grow from instant attraction, but for it to work both parties have to want it to. There has to be love between them, not just sexual attraction."

"Patrick, we've got to go," Blake called.

"He's right. Come on, angel."

"Maybe this is a mistake. I want to help, but I'm not sure that I should get romantically involved."

"One step at a time. Let's get you out of these woods, to the SUV, and then back to Forever Creek. As for the mating, nothing will happen unless you want it to. I would never force myself or my second nature lifestyle on you."

With a nod, she turned toward Blake and started forward. Patrick wrapped his arm around her shoulder and they caught up with his brother in silence. This was all new to her, so he'd have to be patient and give her time to adjust. She had been tossed into the world of shifters, on the run, and now had a cold bucket of water tossed over her with this mating idea. He didn't doubt she'd come around because no matter the differences between them, she could feel the draw to him. The mating was working its magic between them, and for her it would feel like an instant attraction. She would find herself drawn to him, thinking about him, and eventually seeking his touch, but she wouldn't completely understand why until the mating ritual was complete.

She had been through enough, and he'd have to take it slow with her to avoid pushing her away. Eventually, he'd have his mate. *Mate.* He still couldn't get used to the idea. It was a dangerous time to be mating, and it was even worse that his mate would be human. If he were ever caught and placed in one of those labs, she'd feel what was happening to him. He might be able to shield her somewhat, but ultimately they'd break through all his defenses and she'd experience some of the pain through their connection. He couldn't let that happen. Now, more than ever, he had to make sure he was never captured. He'd die before he'd let them imprison him.

They arrived back at the SUV, and Patrick took the wheel, with Blake in the passenger side. Clarissa sat in the back, low enough no one would see her through the dark tinted windows. They had a several hour drive ahead of them, and every minute of it would be torture for him. To have his mate so close but be unable to touch or claim her, would be agony.

He wasn't sure how long he drove with the silence hanging in the air.

But it had been long enough that he began to think she might have fallen asleep. Not that he'd blame her after the days she'd had lately. Exhaustion must be taking its toll. Even with the adrenaline and his shifter abilities, he was worn out from the last two days, ready to crawl into a nice warm bed.

Even though the hour was late, he took the back roads, avoiding anywhere the population was too dense. They'd take no risks, at least not until they got the information they needed. Then the risks would be on him and his brothers. They'd go to Hathaway Medical, rescue those they could, gather anything that might be useful, and then destroy the lab so that at least one more was out of operation. *One down, countless others to go.*

"Would anyone like to tell me where we're going?" At her question, Patrick glanced in the rearview mirror, but without any streetlights or even the light of the moon he couldn't make out much more than her figure.

"Forever Creek," Blake answered.

"We've taken over an old ski resort. The main building is a castle with five stories, so there's plenty of room for my family and anyone else who needs a safe place," Patrick explained, keeping his eyes on the road. "It's roughly three hours outside of Denver, Colorado. Now that the resort is no longer functioning, the town has closed down. All the residents have had to move, but that was a long time ago. It's safe, I promise."

"The town was Forever, and the resort before it was shut down was Forever Creek Ski Resort. It's set just outside of the White River National Forest and the nearest town is Parachute, Colorado, which has less than a thousand residents, so it's a good place for us," Blake added.

"That's the old resort that looks like a castle, isn't it? I think I've seen it."

He nodded. "You're going to be safe there. No one could stumble upon us. In all the time we've been there, we've never seen anyone else nearby. I know you're scared, but you're going to be fine. I'll protect you." *With my dying breath, I'll protect you, my mate.*

"You mentioned a sister, Jade. How many other siblings are there? Is there anyone else at the castle?"

"Besides Blake and me, there's Austin, Luke, Chase, and Jade. Jade's the only woman, so she'll be excited to have another female around. As for anyone other than us O'Reilly siblings, not at the moment. You'll be the first, but I suspect two more will be joining us shortly."

"Two more? How do you know you can trust them? What if the government sends a spy?" Trepidation was creeping into her voice again.

"We're like human lie detectors." Blake stifled a yawn. "No one could deceive us long enough to learn anything or even convince us to bring them here if we didn't believe they were completely truthful and trustworthy."

"Get some sleep, Blake." As his brother put his head back against the headrest, Patrick glanced back into the rearview mirror at her. "If you're thinking about Dean, he's angry, scared, and unwilling to trust, but he'd never do anything to harm me or my family. Otherwise, we'd have never invited him to Forever Creek. His anger is of the result of fear and what happened to him. He doesn't want anything to happen to you."

"I don't know what happened to him…what he saw…but I swear he's a good man. He'd want to help if he could." She sighed. "But I guess he just won't. Damn it. Something is off with him, and I left him. He could get himself killed because of this."

"What he does or doesn't do isn't your fault. You're his sister, not his mother. If he didn't want to come with us, you couldn't have made him." He wanted to pull the car over, slip into the backseat, and wrap his arm around her. "What we can do is be there when he's ready. Blake gave him a way to reach us, now we just have to wait."

"What if he never calls? Then what do I do? Just assume he's dead or keep holding out hope that he'll come back?"

"Keep hoping until you have undeniable proof."

"How am I supposed to do that when I know the chances of him getting killed? Especially with him out there all alone."

"Take it one day at a time." Now that the road was no longer curvy, he was able to put his foot down on the gas pedal and hopefully make up some of the time that had been lost while they had been detained with the wolves. "I know it's not easy, and I wish I could tell you that it will get easier, but it doesn't. I know because the night before we went into hiding, my father went out for a stroll and never returned. We don't know if he's alive or dead."

Blake had been silent, his eyes closed as if he were asleep. Now, he spoke. "If he was captured for one of the labs, then he's dead. Even so, we all hope. It's against the odds that he's alive, but we still hope. Maybe he's in one of the shifter camps."

"I'm sorry."

"My brother Luke set up a forum for shifters. It allows us to share information, follow up on leads, get help, pretty much anything we might need." Patrick paused for a moment as another car pulled out of a driveway, but when it turned in the opposite direction, he let out a sigh of relief. "It was Jade's idea to do a missing persons section, and she does what she can to help reunite families who have lost loved ones or at the very least give them closures. I think she wanted to start it to find anything she could about our father, and even with the time that has passed, she searches relentlessly for any trace of what might have happened to him."

"I'm sure it's hard not knowing what happened. Has she found anything?"

"Nothing. We might never know."

"Maybe not knowing is for the best." Blake readjusted in his seat. "I'm not sure Jade could handle knowing he was tortured in one of the labs until he died. She would take that harder than all of us, considering what she's been through."

"Dad knew how bad things were getting when he decided to go out for that stroll. He should have stayed in, and then he'd still be with us." *He'd be running the pride instead of me.* Patrick had been thrust into the role of Alpha over their pride long before he should have been.

The loss of their father had made the family look to him on what to do. He remembered the following day, when they woke up to find Dad gone. They had waited as long as they could to see if he'd return, but as hours passed and the uproar in their town grew worse, he had no choice but to order them to leave.

If they had waited even an hour longer, they might not have made it. One of Austin's contacts later told them a team of law enforcement officers had come through town, going door to door, checking out each of the residents. They had tried to determine who were shifters and who weren't. In the end, a number of families and residents had been taken into custody for additional questioning.

Did he regret his decision to force his family to stick with the plan? For the most part, no. There was too much danger there for them to linger. A small part of him wondered if his father had ever made it back to their old house. If he had, what did he think when he arrived and they were gone? Would he have come to Forever Creek looking for them? It was crazy to think like that. After all, they would have found him by now if that were the case. It was more likely he was dead, and Patrick hoped he hadn't suffered.

Blake's right, maybe it's best we never know.

Chapter Eight

Clarissa tossed her coat and shoulder bag at the foot of the king size bed. She stood in the middle of the beautiful room, trying to take it all in. The warm brown walls brought out the gold comforter on the bed. On either side of the bed, the wrought iron lamps with their black shades and gold swirls cast a glow, lighting the room. On the other side of the bed was a small sitting area, with two chairs and a small coffee table.

Even though Patrick had mention the castle had been closed down for years, everything was very luxurious. All of the furniture remained in place as if the resort had never closed. The castle was stunning, and each room she saw lived up to anything she could have expected. The O'Reilly siblings had put a lot of work into the place to bring it back up to standard, and she wondered how much time they'd spent cleaning it when they moved in. Blake had installed solar power as their main source of electricity and heating. Otherwise, since they couldn't have the electricity through the electric company turned on, they'd have had to lug gallons of gasoline for the backup generator, and that would have been too suspicious, making it easier for someone to find them.

The siblings had worked together in order to build what they had here. Even though they all tried to make her feel welcome, the sensation of being the odd one out prevailed. She was human, and her new companions were each hiding the form of a lion beneath the surface. Chase, however, did not conceal his lion. When they'd made it to the castle, and Patrick had ushered her inside, and out of the brewing snowstorm, they found Chase stretched out on one of the sofas in the main living area in his lion form.

Even though she knew they had that ability, she hadn't expected to find him lounging in animal form, purring as he licked his paw. It was too primal for her to truly understand. One thing was for sure, she didn't want to think about how their bodies went from standing on two feet to four. There had to be unimaginable pain involved in the transformation, and the very thought of it made her stomach churn.

Now that she was here and had met the family, giving them all the information she had, she wondered what would happen next. It was clear Patrick and the others were planning on taking down Hathaway Medical, and as much as she wanted that, she wondered what it meant for her. Once they had their information, and questions answered, they'd have no use for her. Patrick had suggested she help him find something they could use to counteract LUNA, but she suspected he'd be able to do that himself, and that he really didn't need her help. Could she stay there if she weren't able to contribute to the fight?

A knock on the door to her room pulled her from her thoughts. "Come in."

Patrick opened the door and stepped in. "I know you're tired, but I wanted to check with you before you got into bed to make sure there was nothing you needed."

"I'm fine." She wasn't sure that was completely true, but there was nothing he could bring her to make things better. She just wanted to wake up from this nightmare and have the world back to how it was a year ago, when humanity didn't know about the existence of shifters.

"I've got Luke going through the Hathaway Medical computer system. While he's doing that, Austin and I are going to discuss possible plans for an attack on the facility."

"Aren't you tired?"

"I'll sleep soon enough. Right now, I want to talk to Austin about a few things, and get it out of the way." He shoved his hands into the front pockets of his jeans. "Everything's going to be okay."

"I'd really like to believe that." She sank down to sit on the edge of the bed. "Everything is just so upside down. I'm not sure things will ever smooth out again."

"Things will look brighter after a good night's sleep. If you need anything, I'm just two doors down on the right. Room five hundred and fifteen. Luke is also right across the hall in his office, which is attached to his bedroom. He's normally always in there, day or night, working away."

"Does everyone have bedrooms on this floor?"

He nodded. "We're all right here in the center of the building. Jade's across the hall from me, with Austin and Blake on the other side."

"What about Chase? Should I expect to see his lion form strolling the halls?" She didn't want to open her door to see a lion wandering by.

"His room is between us, but I've asked him to be cautious of where he is when he's in his lion form. At least until you've grown more comfortable around us."

She ran her hands down her thighs. "I know you said that even when you shift, you still function as a human but seeing a big lion still springs fear through me. Irrational, maybe, but it's still hard to adjust to."

He crossed the distance and squatted before her. "I understand, and we will do everything we can to help you adjust to this. We want you to feel comfortable here. This is now your home, for as long as you need or want it to be."

"Need." She shook her head. "I've been giving this some thought and I realized I'll never be able to have a real life again. I should have just let them kill me. Everything I worked for is gone, just like that. Not to mention the mess with Dean."

"Hey now, angel." He cupped the side of her face, rubbing his thumb over her cheekbone. "Things are going to get better, I promise. Eventually, Dean's going to come around."

"Maybe, but I deserted my position, turned information over to you. I'd never get a position as a scientist again. I gave up so much, thinking I would have a better position at Hathaway Medical, that I'd be able to do more, to change more. In the end—"

"Have you considered that in the end it might have brought you just where you're supposed to be?"

"Why?" She looked up at him, gaining eye contact. "Because you think I'm your mate? Or because you want to use the information I have to take down another lab?"

"My angel has claws of her own." He smirked. "But what I meant was, you're doing the right thing instead of falling in line with what the government wants. You're standing up for those who can't do it themselves. You saw what happened during one of the experiments, and you decided you weren't going to stand by and let this happen."

"Then I should have rushed down there and stopped it. Instead, I cowered in my office."

"You'd have only ended up getting yourself killed if you had done that. Instead, you gathered all the information that you could and saved yourself. There's nothing wrong with that." He took hold of her hand. "There's nothing wrong with living to fight another day."

"What if the person they were experimenting on is dead now because I did nothing? His blood is on my hands."

"No, angel." He brought her hand to his lips and kissed her knuckles. "That is not your fault. His blood is on *their* hands. Even if he's dead, you wouldn't have been able to stop it. Instead, there would have been two dead. Being here now, you can help, and because of you, we'll have the information we need to take them down."

"Sometimes it seems like whatever I do isn't the right thing. I was so appalled at what happened, what I had gotten myself into. How did I not know what was happening there? I had been there numerous times for interviews, and two tours before I finally accepted the position. I should have seen there was something going on behind closed doors."

"They'd have kept it hidden until they had you on board. Even now, I'm sure there are people who have worked for the company for years who don't know. They started out as a legit business, and even if there are some questionable practices behind the doors, the employees might not want to see it. You can't make someone see something they want to be blind to."

She nodded and thought back to the beginning of her time there. "There were things I should have questioned. Like how they have a strict rule with employees leaving at five o'clock on Fridays. No overtime, especially on the weekends. I now know it's because they spend the weekend focusing on their experiments. They still do them during the week, but on weekends they can do it without having to worry they'll be interrupted or someone would hear the shifters howling. The howls and growls laced with pain and fear...I'll never be able to forget it."

"I know, angel, I know." He rose off the floor and sat next to her on the bed. He wrapped his arm around her shoulder, keeping hold of her other hand. "I wish I could tell you that one day you'll forget, but I'm afraid it will always be with you. There will come a day when you don't hear them every time you close your eyes, but then you'll see or hear something and everything will come flooding back like it just happened."

She rested her head against his shoulder and just sat there. She wasn't sure for how long, but the comfort she could feel in his embrace made her believe she'd get through this. That, one day, what she witnessed wouldn't haunt her thoughts and dreams any longer. There was a small ray of hope that was burning deep within the darkness. If only she could get to it, help it grow bigger and brighter, then maybe she'd get through this.

"Some of them overlook things because of the benefits they offer," she said. Horror rushed through her as she tipped her head back to look at him. "The on-site daycare for their employees…"

"Angel, I don't understand. What about it? Some hospitals offer that, so it's not shocking that they would."

"No, you don't understand. There's a file on the system. They're using the children to control their staff."

"What do you mean?"

"I didn't read the whole file, and honestly, it didn't sink in completely until now. I read so much of the stuff on their system, trying to take it all just in case they found the computer virus. I think I remembered them threatening to inject the children with something that would turn them into shifters. I know they threatened to experiment on their employees, too. After all, they'd need human test subjects, too." Her body trembled at the thought of them hurting the children.

"Listen to me, Clarissa, we're going to stop them. I'll have Luke find that file because we're going to need it. Maybe it will help the government see what they're doing."

"Those poor children. If they're turned, Hathaway Medical will keep them in a cage just like the other shifters. There's no way they'd let the parents take them home."

"A person cannot be turned into a shifter. We're born."

Her eyebrows knitted together as she glanced back at him. "What about bitten? Whatever happens, then surely they could reproduce to infect these children."

"Sweet angel, you've either read too many paranormal books or you've listened to too many of the government's lies." He rubbed his hand down her arm. "We can't do that. I bit your neck earlier and you weren't concerned about it. Why think of it now?"

"You didn't break the skin." She rested her head against him. "Oh, hell. I didn't think about it then, and if that had been true, you could have changed me before I knew what happened."

"Even if I could, I wouldn't have done it without your permission. Forcing someone to do something against their will isn't the way to start a mating. The trust would be completely gone before we even began."

"I can't even begin to think about this mating situation." She still couldn't get past her surprise over the whole thing, but until he walked into her bedroom, she had been able to push it from her thoughts. She hadn't wanted to face it, but she couldn't put it off forever. She wasn't sure she wanted to get tangled deep into the shifter world by mating with him, especially since he seemed determined to begin the war between humans and shifters.

She lifted her head, but couldn't bring herself to pull completely out of his embrace. It seemed like her body wanted things her mind was warning her against, yet her mind was losing the battle. *It's just like all those books I read in college. The shifter enters and the woman is to be his. There's no stopping the mating bond.*

She tried to push those thoughts away and focus on the present, instead of some fictional world, but she couldn't help but wonder how her life had become a paranormal novel. Instead of a romance, it was a thriller with bad men chasing after her.

"Every time I begin to adjust, it seems like there's something else I don't know about all of this. Are there any other hidden secrets about your species you'd like to tell me? Anything else like this mating that's going to jump out at me when I'm not expecting it?"

"Chase would have something smart to say like our children are born in animal form—"

She pulled from his embrace so quickly she almost slipped off the edge of the bed. Her body trembled with the idea of giving birth to a lion cub. She wasn't an animal, and her body couldn't deal with the strain of it. "What? You can't be serious."

"No, angel. I only meant that my brother would have something like that to say to try to lighten the mood." He squeezed her hand. "It doesn't matter if our mates are human or shifters, when they give birth all babies are born in their human form. Normally, around their first birthday, they began to embrace the ability to shift. Even then, it's difficult for them to control it. Most shifter families with young children have to live in rural areas, so no one spots one of them shifting. It's the reason most are homeschooled. Though in some clans they have their own schools, depending on the size."

"How long does it take for you to control your changes?"

"Over the years we grow better at it, but until we make it through puberty it's touch and go. It's harder for some but basically it depends on controlling our emotions. High ranking shifters have an easier time of it. Low ranking shifters within a pride can have more trouble controlling their emotions, and therefore their ability to shift, causing them to change forms at inopportune times."

"The world has so much to learn about you." She stifled a yawn as exhaustion tugged at her. "I've so much to learn."

"I'm not that different than you, but tomorrow I'll answer any of your questions. Now you should rest." He placed a gentle kiss on her cheek and rose. "Remember, if you need anything just come find me."

"I'll be all right. As you said, I need some sleep. I'm sure once my head hits the pillow I'll be out."

When he turned and strolled out of the bedroom, she reached up and placed her hand over where he had kissed her. She could still almost feel his lips there. She wasn't sure what to make of shifters, but she couldn't deny her attraction to Patrick. There was a heat between them that she had never felt before. She wasn't sure if she should give in, like her body so desperately wanted to, or if she should fight her attraction to him.

Weighing all she had learned about shifters, she stood and wandered over to the large bay window. Through the darkness, she could just barely make out the mountains surrounding the area. During the day, or even at night with the light of the moon, she was sure it must be beautiful. She'd have to wait to take in the magnificence because there was just a faint glow from the moon behind some clouds. Most of what she could see was the heavy snow falling.

The mountains would be different than her childhood home in Florida, but at least she felt a measure of safety here. Her thoughts left Patrick and returned to her brother. Where was he? Was he regretting his decision? She had no way of knowing, and that made it harder to bear.

"Oh, Dean. I hope you're safe…wherever you are."

As he climbed the stairs to the fifth floor, fatigue wrapped around Patrick like a second skin. He felt as if he was climbing the mountain outside the hotel. Even his lion within was barely stirring. The planning session with Austin could have waited until morning, especially since they couldn't bring down Hathaway Medical until Luke had finished going through their system. He had to back up the information they needed, otherwise it would all be destroyed. To make the most out of the mission, they needed to be completely informed.

Luke would work around the clock, only stopping when he simply couldn't go on without sleep, and get it done as quickly as possible. Then, Patrick would lead the team to take down the lab, despite Austin thinking it was a bad idea. The family felt they had a duty to protect Patrick. After all, he was the Alpha. Austin reasoned that he shouldn't be risking himself on the frontlines.

Even with Austin's fierce argument, Patrick was determined to see this through. He'd be on the team to destroy Hathaway Medical. It was the least he could do for his mate, after all, the terror they'd instilled in her, and the manhunt they'd sent after her. With every lab, he took down, it was another retribution for Jade. They might have destroyed the lab she was kept in weeks ago, but this one would be yet another lab that could never harm shifters again.

As he came down the hall, he could see Luke's office door slightly ajar, letting the rest of the family know he was still up working if they needed anything. Yawning, he pushed the door open and entered. "Got a minute? Or is this a bad time?"

"Naw, come on in." Luke took a long drink from the coffee mug he held in his hand before setting it back on the cluttered desk. "What's up? I figured you'd be in bed by now."

"I just finished going over possible plans of attack with Austin. Find anything?"

"A ton of shit that I'll never be able to erase from my mind." He pinched the bridge of his nose and let out a deep sigh. "When you rescued Jade and brought back the stuff you found there, it was nothing compared to this."

"Do you mean they've advanced their experiments?"

"Not really advanced, just decided to record them more. Photography and video. Some of these have been viewed so many times I wonder if there isn't someone getting off on them. How anyone can stand to watch someone being tortured like this is beyond me."

As he settled into the chair across from Luke's desk, he nodded in agreement. What he had read was bad enough but to actually watch it or see the aftermath captured in photos would bring it to another level. His mind had already done enough to reconstruct what had happened to Jade, and the others who had been held captive in various labs.

"What brought you in here? If you came to put more pressure on me to get this stuff onto my own system, I'm working as fast as I can. A lot of the files are encrypted and need to be unsealed first. It's going to take a little time."

"I know you're working as quickly as you can. No, I'm here because Clarissa thought of something else. Something that might be more terrifying than what's going on in the labs."

"After what I've seen I'm not sure there is anything worse."

He ran his fingers through his hair and tried to swallow the lump in his throat. "She remembered that Hathaway Medical has an on-site daycare for their workers. They're using the children to control the parents, possibly more. They threatened their employees, claiming anyone who doesn't follow the rules and do their work would risk having their child turned into a shifter."

"That's not possible." Luke appeared incredulous. For the first time, Patrick noticed how red-rimmed his eyes were, and wondered when he'd slept last.

"I've been thinking about this. Though we can't bite someone and turn them, there might be another way. Our blood is so mixed with that of our beast that it could be possible to give someone traits of ours if they were nearly drained of their blood and had ours used in replacement. It might not give them the aptitude to shift, but it would give them some of our abilities such as to purr or growl." Even as he said it, he hoped he was wrong. He stared past Luke, watching the royal blue curtains wave as the floor heating vent kicked on, sending warm air throughout the room. It was surprising that with the dark wood desk, and the blue curtains that nearly spread the whole length of the wall, that Luke still looked at home there instead of his pale skin and blond hair clashing with the decor. This was his space, and rarely anyone intruded, the only exception being Patrick or Austin.

"Could you really do that? Drain someone of their blood and replace it with ours? That seems ridiculous." Even though he appeared disbelieving, Luke had paled as he clenched the arms of his chair.

"If you have medical knowledge and equipment, then yes."

"Fuck."

"My sentiments exactly." He stood and rolled his shoulders. "See if you can find anything that might lead you to believe they carried through on their threat."

"I'll put some keywords into a search and get it going. If I find anything—"

"I don't care what time it is, find me. I want to know immediately. We might not be able to reverse it, but we can be damn sure they don't experiment on these children any more than they already have."

He left Luke to get back to work, and headed for his own bedroom. Exhaustion tugged at him, but his brain was working overtime trying to digest everything he had learned. What made these people think that what they were doing was right? He understood medical testing because he was a doctor—but not like this. Not with shifters being forced into it, and especially not with torture involved. If the government wanted to do testing, it should have been conducted like any other drug test with volunteer subjects. And there was no way it should be done on children.

Something had nagged him since Clarissa recalled that horrendous memory, making his lion restless. It was almost as if his beast was warning him that it wasn't just a threat. Could they have possibly carried out their warning? He sure hoped not.

Chapter Nine

Screams pulled Patrick from a restless sleep. He climbed out of bed without thinking. The stress of finding this new lab must have been preying on Jade's mind. Austin had mentioned she had a nightmare while Patrick was gone, but it had been mild considering those she'd had in the past. Now, it seemed to have changed.

Once he was in the wide hallway, he heard her desperate cries. "No, no. Damn it, stop!" Heart-wrenching sobs and shrieks pierced the walls of the castle. "You can't do this, they're innocent!"

"Patrick," Austin called to him as he stepped into the hallway.

"Not now, I've got to check on Jade."

"That's just it. It's not Jade, it's Clarissa."

With Austin's statement, Patrick paused and listened. Sure enough, the cries were coming from the other side of Chase's room, not from across the hall. "Oh, hell." He rubbed his hand over his face, trying to wake himself up. "Go back to bed, I'll check on her."

"If it wasn't bad enough with Jade having these nightmares, now it's Clarissa, too. But maybe they can find some comfort with each other. Or maybe with you...her mate." Austin leaned against the wall, a smirk tugging up the corner of his lips. "When were you going to tell me?"

"It's not official." Patrick reached for the handle on Clarissa's bedroom door.

"Maybe not yet, but it will be. I smell you all over her and don't give me that bullshit that it was for her protection on the journey here."

"We can discuss this later." He slipped inside and shut the door behind him. The soft glow from the attached bathroom gave him enough light to see. She was stretched out in the middle of the bed, the sheets tangled around her legs as she lashed out with her arms, fighting someone he couldn't see—a nightmarish phantasm.

He crossed the room in two quick strides and came to stand near the bed. His lion rushed forward, demanding to touch her, but he knew she could strike out at him. She wouldn't mean to, but in the midst of a nightmare she wouldn't be thinking clearly. "Hush, angel. You're okay, you're safe."

"Oh, please. No, stop, they're just children!"

"Shit," he whispered before lowering himself onto the edge of the bed. Clarissa wasn't like Jade, who was a shifter and could hurt someone if she let her beast out unintentionally. She was human, and there was very little she could do to hurt him.

Careful to avoid her swings, he placed his hand on her shoulder. "Clarissa, wake up. Come on, angel. I need you to wake up." He ducked out of the way of her next swing but caught hold of her wrist. "I need you to wake up."

She moaned and her eyes fluttered opened. "What…" She tried to pull her wrist from his grasp, but he didn't budge.

"You were having a nightmare."

"Why are you holding my wrists?"

His embrace loosened, but he didn't let go. "To avoid being hit. You were thrashing about."

"Nightmare." Her voice was light as if she didn't want to remember it. "An awful nightmare."

"I know, angel. Do you want to talk about it?"

She shook her head and slipped her hands from his embrace. Leaning against the headboard, she slid her legs up until she could pull them tight against her chest and sat there with her arms wrapped around them. "Awful, just awful."

Without invitation, he scooted onto her bed beside her and wrapped his arm around her shoulders. "Come here, angel."

Without hesitation, she slid into his embrace, her hand on his bare chest. When he'd rushed from his bedroom, he'd thought it was Jade crying out, and hadn't even bothered to grab a shirt. The plaid pajama pants were fine then, but now he wondered if she'd think about this a moment later, when the fear wasn't icing her veins, and question his intentions since he was half-dressed.

Mating for a human was like being tossed out to sea with the waves knocking them in one direction and then the opposite, over and over. Her delicate human body was going through changes to adjust to what was happening, to expand her lifespan to match her shifter mate. Her emotions would have been erratic just from the mating, but everything else was only making it worse for her.

All he could do was sit there and hold her until she was ready to talk. There was nothing he could do about the dream, nothing he could do about what was happening inside her when it came to their mating. He'd be there for her every step of the way, to hold her, a shoulder to cry on, someone to talk to when she was angry and frustrated. He was determined to give her anything else she needed. Together, they'd get through this.

He pulled the blanket up around her and ran his hand down her arm.

"It's going to be okay."

"I'm not sure my world will ever be okay again. So much as changed recently, and I just don't know how to adjust to it. I almost feel like I've been kidnapped and transported to another planet."

His hand paused on her shoulder. "Because you know shifters exist?"

"That was a shock in itself, but that's not the reason I feel like I'm in a different universe." She ran her hand up his chest, her fingers teasing along the contours of his muscles. "What happened to civilization? We're not wild creatures that need to go around attacking those who are slightly different. There's enough room in this world for all of us. I just don't understand why they're doing this."

"They're scared."

"That's not a good enough excuse to torturing people. Maybe it's valid for locking them up in those camps, but not to experiment on them." She tipped her head back to look at him. The sadness and tears glistened in her eyes. "I'm ashamed to be a part of this world. To know my species would do something so disgusting."

"We're going to stop this."

"A band of shifters and one lonely human up against the whole of civilization?" She shook her head. "I hate to be a pessimist, but I don't think we stand much of a chance."

"It's not just me and my siblings. There are other shifters out there ready and willing to fight. None of us want to live in fear any longer."

She pulled back from him enough to get a good look at him. "Have you considered what might happen to you or your family if you try to stand against the government? They'll kill you."

"Oh, angel, they'll do much worse than that. We all know because we've seen what happened when Jade was captured. She suffered the actual torment, but as the Alpha of the pride, I felt it, too. The others saw the files I brought back. Each of us knows what we're risking."

"If you know, then why do it? Why risk being a lab experiment when you're safe here?"

The fear rolled off her, permeating the air with its odor and piquing his lion's attention. "I wish I could tell you the end justifies the means, but since I don't know what the future holds, I can't. For that, my angel, I'm sorry. But I do know someone has to stand up and try to make this better."

"Why you?"

"Before things got so bad, my family had a beautiful home. Even though we were all older, Jade had just turned twenty-one and we still lived at home. None of us really had the desire to move out."

"Isn't that unusual?"

"For humans, maybe, but not for shifters. Even though some of the animals we shift into are solitary creatures, we're still human. We seek at least part of the time, the company of those like us. You'll find many shifters living in groups or clans. Sometimes they're families, others are groups of the same species, and more recently there are some groups that have gotten together just to stay alive. No matter our living arrangements, each of us still need time alone."

She leaned back into his embrace and tugged the blanket up around her. "Sorry, I interrupted you. Tell me about your life before all of this."

"It will be a good story to get you back to sleep," he teased, leaning his head against the pillows, settling in. "Our house wasn't fancy by any means, but it was large enough to give each of us our own space. That's no easy task with six siblings and my father. Seven bedrooms upstairs, with the large living, kitchen, and dining rooms downstairs. My father also kept a small office off the dining room for his trading business. He was a financial genius."

"You say *was* but you don't know that he's—"

"Dead," he supplied. "You're right. We don't know, but I know my father. If he were alive, he'd have found us. Plus, if he's not dead, that means he's in one of the labs. That would be worse than death."

"What about one of the camps? He could be there."

"It's possible, but knowing Dad, he'd have found a way to let us know he was alive. Shifters Underground hasn't offered any hints to his whereabouts, and Jade's been searching every day since he went missing, not counting the time she was held captive. If he were alive, we'd have found something."

"What's Shifters Underground? That name almost reminds me of the Underground Railroad." She tugged the comforter high enough to cover her arm, as well as his torso, as she continued to tease along the contours of his chest.

"It's kind of like that, at least in part. We help shifters who need to get somewhere safe. But it's so much more than that. There are boards for people to share information, like towns to stay away from, and places that are safe. Jade started a section for people to find lost loved ones and she handles most of that. She scrolls through the website, our boards, the information we collect, trying to find anything she can. I can't begin to count how many families she's reunited or brought closure to."

He leaned his head against the top of hers. "But we're straying from the subject. You wanted to know about life before all of this."

"It's all fascinating."

"It was an average life. Dad was an investment banker, helping people invest their savings. He had some high powered clients, a few shifters, but mostly humans who didn't know about his second nature. He provided a stable income that put most of us through college."

"Go on. I want to hear it all." Sleep coated her voice as she snuggled a little closer to him.

"We lived in a small town. It wasn't too far away from the city but far enough that I was able to set up a medical practice. People came to me instead of venturing into the city. A small family practice was what I always wanted, and for a short period, I had it." He missed the simple days of his medical practice, even when he'd get a call in the middle of the night when someone was sick or in labor. Unlike doctors in big cities, he offered house calls. He had set up his practice just like so many other doctors had done in the past, with house calls and bartering. Times were tough, and medical care was sometimes put on the back burner.

Thinking she had dozed off, he adjusted slightly, moving down into the bed so that once she had fallen completely asleep he wouldn't have to wake her. This way he could hold her all night if he needed to, and keep the nightmares away.

When she looked up at him, he could tell she was struggling to stay awake. "What about the others?" she asked, sounding groggy.

"Austin joined the Army when he was eighteen and put in ten hellish years. He was alone and had to keep his beast a secret. Once he returned home, he went to work for the police department part time and weapons training through the department. We were all glad to have him home, not just because he'd be safe, but because having him missing from our pride was like having a chunk taken away."

"Sounds like you two are close."

"We're all close, but Austin and I work together a lot. Luke went to college for his computer science degree. Blake has always been the handy brother, so he did construction and worked on cars. Pretty much anything to keep him busy. Jade had been in her final year of college when the world changed. She wanted to be a kindergarten teacher, and she'd have been good at it. So patient and caring, just like our mother." Thinking about the good old days, when things were easier, he let his eyelids fall shut. Poor Jade might never get her teaching degree, and they might never be able to live among civilization again, but at least they were alive. That's what mattered.

"You didn't mention Chase. What was he doing before everything?"

"Running." He let out a long sigh. "He was born running, and hasn't stopped. Nothing keeps his interest longer than five minutes. It's gotten worse with the uprising, and he's become antsy. With the shit he's seen since all this started, it doesn't help matters."

"Why?"

"Chase's lion picks up on the unease and just won't settle. He stays in lion form because it's easier for him to control his anxiety. If you put him on a task, he'll get it done, but to self-start something he finds his attention drifting and his lion pacing." He rubbed his hand along her back as if he was trying to soothe tension from her. But it wasn't tension from her that he was feeling, it was within him. "A week before we came up here, Chase was out when he saw something that still to this day he won't talk about. Whatever he witnessed changed him."

"You said before he wasn't dangerous."

"He's not, my sweet angel." He pressed his lips to her forehead, leaving a gentle kiss below her hairline. "Chase is still himself whether he's in lion form or human. Either way, he'd never hurt you or anyone else. He's just running from being an adult, from facing the realities of what happened to him that night, and what's happening in the world."

"He's young…I mean, isn't he? I just assumed he was younger than you."

"He's the youngest of the boys, twenty-five. Mom and Dad thought he'd be the last because of a complicated pregnancy, but three years later Jade was born. Mom's health never recovered after that, and a few months later she passed away. Dad had to raise all six of us. Being the oldest, I stepped up to help and we all protected Jade."

"Isn't she twenty-one? That would be four years later that she was born, wouldn't it?"

"They are three years and ten months apart, so not quite four years. She had just celebrated her twenty-first birthday before we went into hiding, but that was nearly a year ago. A lot has happened since then. Next month, for her birthday, we're going to make it special. It's the first one without Dad, but we also didn't know we'd have her back. When she was captured, we all thought the worst."

"You were lucky." She squeezed herself tighter against him. "Not everyone is so lucky."

"That, my angel, I know. We've learned to never take a day for granted because it might be our last." He slipped a stray lock of her long hair behind her ear. "Now, you should get some rest. You've had a rough few days."

"Stay with me? Just hold me."

"I'll be here as long as you want me to be. I'll keep you safe."

She pulled the blanket up along his chest and he didn't even bother to tell her he didn't need it. Instead, he just reflected on the thoughtfulness of it. Never before had someone offered him such a simple gesture. He had done it for others, but no one had ever done it for him.

"I told you about my past," he added. "Tomorrow you can tell me about yours."

"It's not that exciting."

He didn't care if she thought her life had been boring. He just wanted to know everything about her. The normal life she had before getting all wrapped up in this had such appeal. It was the only thing he'd ever wanted—a normal life—but something told him he'd never get it. At least not completely.

Even though he'd told her to get some sleep, he couldn't shut off his brain. Memories rushed through his mind as he longed for the past. The family had been close before, but coming to Forever Creek had made them closer. They were one unit, standing together, fighting for each other. If this ever ended, he hoped they'd keep this new bond they'd formed. But most of all, he hoped they'd get through this alive. His worst fear was that he'd lose one of his siblings. The thought of someone else suffering the tortures Jade had gone through terrified him. If they managed that, then they'd truly be blessed.

Clarissa pulled a bright red sweater over her head and tugged her hair out from under it. She glanced at the mirror above the double sink vanity to see how it fit. The sweater clung to her curves a little more than she liked, but in an attractive way without making the sweater seem too tight. This was another one of Jade's outfits. Thankfully, they were nearly the same size. When Clarissa left, she hadn't had time to gather clothes. She just took off, wanting to put distance between her and Hathaway Medical, as if she could run from what she had seen. She'd have to do something about her clothing situation, instead of borrowing Jade's things every day.

Stalling, she ran her fingers through her hair and pulled it back into a messy ponytail. When she could delay no longer, she took a deep breath. *Time to face the O'Reillys. By now, they all must know Patrick spent the night in my room. What must they think?*

She strolled from the adjoining bathroom into her suite and paused for another moment before she finally opened the door and stepped into the hallway. Quiet. Only Luke's door was open, and she could hear light taps on a keyboard, letting her know he was in there working. Everyone else must have made their way downstairs to work on their plans for infiltrating Hathaway Medical, or whatever it was they normally did here.

There was an elevator, but she walked past it and headed for the stairs. She needed time to get herself together, to try to ease the tension knotting in her stomach. She hated the sensation of not belonging. It wasn't just that she was human. The siblings had a bond she couldn't compete with. She didn't want to come between any of them.

As she descended the stairs, she reminded herself that she had no right to think she could be included in what they had. She was an outsider, one who'd worked for the enemy. There was no way they'd ever accept her. What she needed was to figure out a way to get her life back, and then she could leave the O'Reillys to do what they had to. She might never be able to work as a scientist again, but as long as someone wasn't hunting her down to silence her, that didn't matter. She could find other work.

When she arrived at the bottom of the steps, she saw Chase on one of the sofas, stretched out in lion form. Apprehensive, she quickly scanned the area trying to locate someone else. Instead, she was alone with a lion. She could call out and she knew Patrick or one of the others would come, but it would only make things worse. Patrick's words played through her thoughts, and she kept telling herself he wasn't dangerous. Chase's big brown eyes stared up at her, and it was almost as if he was telling her he wouldn't move, that he didn't want to frighten her.

"Come on, you can do this." She forced herself to let go of the banister and step away from the staircase. "Sorry, Chase. This is just so new to me."

He let out a soft purr, almost as if he understood.

"What am I doing?" she wondered aloud. "Do you even know what I'm saying?"

"We understand everything that goes on in our lion form." Jade stood in the doorway to the kitchen, a mug of something steaming in her hands.

"I feel the need to apologize again…"

Jade shook her head. "There's no need."

"I've been thinking about this, and I think part of the reason all this is happening is because humans don't understand. They don't realize shifters aren't going to harm them. They assume if they see one in animal form, they'll be instantly attacked."

"Have you listened to yourself?"

Clarissa forced herself not to bite her lip. "Umm…did I say something wrong?"

"No, that's not what I mean." Jade moved away from the doorway and went to sit on one of the other sofas. "You said humans don't understand, not *we* don't understand. They don't realize, not *we* don't. When Patrick first found you, you lumped yourself in with humans, but now…"

"I *am* human." Her words were halfhearted. If she were honest with herself, she'd admit she was ashamed to be lumped into the same group as the ones who were doing this. Humans were better than this, so much better.

"I'm not denying that," Jade said. "I'm just saying you're not classifying yourself with them any longer. You're like your own species now. Maybe species isn't the right word…class, maybe? Let's put it this way. You stand apart from them because you *do* understand. Or at least, you're beginning to."

Clarissa didn't notice she had made her way to the sofa until she sat down next to Jade, forcing herself to overcome her apprehension with

Chase. "What they're doing is wrong, so maybe you're right. I don't want to be lumped in with them. I just want a normal life. Shifters should be allowed to live in peace just like humans."

"That's why you're here, to stand against what's happening to us."

"I'm not so sure about that." The moment she saw the disappointment appear in Jade's eyes, she wanted to take it back. "I told Patrick I'd help as much as I could, but I'm no one special. What chance do I have to do anything when it comes to this fight? After all, they'll just smear my name more because I worked for them before I switched sides. That's not going to help you guys."

"It doesn't matter what you did in the past, what any of us did before we came here. What matters is what the future holds. Each of us have the duty and responsibility to make this a better world for our children. You can't just turn the other cheek and hide. You have to pick a side and fight for your rights. Is this a world you'd want your children to grow up in?"

"I get where you're coming from, I really do, but this isn't my fight. Being here, all I'm doing is bringing more danger to you and the others. As for children, I'll never have any. They'll see to it that I don't live long enough for that."

"So, you're just going to give in. To let them win, and eventually kill you." She rose from the sofa and looked at Clarissa one last time, an expression of disdain on her face. "Maybe you're more of a coward than I thought. Patrick deserves a better mate than that. He needs someone who will stand beside him and fight." Without another word, she turned and walked away, appearing disgusted.

Tears moistened Clarissa's eyes as an ache rose in her chest, and she wrapped her arms around her slim form. *Is she right? Am I a coward?*

She dug deep, wondering if she was afraid to stand up for what was right. It made her sick to think Jade's words were true. Instead of doing the right thing, she was willing to stand aside and do nothing.

That is bullshit. Forcing away the tears, she searched for courage. She knew she had to do something.

Chapter Ten

Patrick sat in his office, unable to focus. His thoughts kept returning to Clarissa as he wondered what she was doing—or what she *wasn't* doing. When the sun had just begun to cast the first rays of sunlight over the land, he had left her in bed and headed for his office. He'd work on some of the files for Luke until the samples of LUNA arrived, bringing along a new member to their outlaw gang—Nolan.

He had met Nolan years ago when Austin was still in the military. Nolan would have devoted his life to the Army, but now he had no choice but to leave the service. There was no time to officially be discharged or retire. He had gone AWOL with the drug samples and was heading their way. They were lucky to have him on their side.

Even with the excitement of finally being able to get his hands on LUNA, and see what he could do to counteract it, he was still having trouble focusing. Clarissa had taken over his thoughts, making him want to go find her, hold her in his arms again. For the first time in weeks, his lion was uneasy, pacing within him like a caged beast. One thing was for certain, he didn't like having his mate out of his sight.

Debating on going to find her, he pushed back his chair and started to stand when Austin stepped into his office. "What's up?"

"Nolan called. He made better time than he thought he would, and he'll be here tonight. I know you're helping Luke go through some of the files. Need me to take over anything?"

"I'll finish what I have here, but you might want to see what else he can give you. I'd like to go this weekend while Hathaway Medical is closed. We need to get through the files before then, or at least have the stuff backed up on a separate system." He pushed in his high-back leather chair and cracked his knuckles. "Have you seen Clarissa?"

"She was sitting in the living area talking with Jade. What happened last night with her? Is she okay?"

He nodded. "She'll be fine. She needs time to adjust." *Adjust to shifters and this mating.*

"You need to claim her before the mission," Austin stated matter-of-factly, as he sank into the chair in front of Patrick's desk.

He raised his eyebrow at his brother. With any other Alpha, Austin would have been watching his step. With Patrick, he was on semi-safe ground. At least he wouldn't reach over the desk and rip out Austin's throat for his bold comment. Though it reminded him that with new shifters coming into their ranks, he needed to embrace his inner Alpha more. Pushing that aside, he leaned over the desk, pressing his fists on the ink blotter. "What are you talking about? I'm fine. She needs time."

"Time neither of you have. If you're going on this mission, you need to make your claim now. It's the only way you or your lion will be able to focus on the tasks at hand. You know I'm right."

Right or not was beside the point. It only added more pressure to the situation. Things had gone smoothly with her after her nightmare. They had cuddled and talked, but he had a feeling she wasn't ready for the mating yet. She had barely begun to wrap her mind around all of this, and come to terms with the fact that people wanted her dead. Time might not be something they had much of, but he had to give her what he could.

"Earth to Patrick, are you even listening to me?"

"I heard you, but it's not like I can just go upstairs, toss her on the bed, and claim her as my mate. You know she has to accept this mating before it can be final. Pushing her won't help move things along."

"Neither will sitting in your office working. Go spend time with her, convince her you're an okay guy and let the rest of us handle this stuff."

"Just *okay*?" Patrick tipped his head to the side in question. "Here I thought I had everything under control and was running this family like a well-oiled machine."

"You were tossed into your role as Alpha unexpectedly, but you've handled it well. You've managed to keep this family together, and bring us here. Look at all we've done in the last year, including rescuing Jade. None of that is anything to smirk at." Austin stretched his long legs out and stood. "You might not want to hear it, but with Nolan and most likely Andrew joining our pride, you need to embrace your Alpha side. Rule this family instead of just being a leader."

"Funny you should say that. I was just thinking something similar."

"This is our family, and now our home. If you can't be a true Alpha, you might need to consider not allowing others to join us here. None of us would be happy to have someone else rule over us, and it won't be easy to find somewhere like Forever Creek again. We're safe here. The advantages of the area and the remoteness are unbeatable."

Austin left before Patrick could reply, not that he was sure what he would have said. After all, he was right. If Patrick weren't willing to fight to remain Alpha and to rule their pride with an iron fist, he'd lose his position and most likely his life. If another Alpha stepped into power, it would mean they would eliminate him, and probably see his siblings as a threat. The only one who might be safe would be Jade because as a female they'd see value in her. She could find a mate and produce offspring for the pride.

He turned to the window and glanced out at the winter wonderland. Fresh snow was falling in large flakes, quickly adding to the drifts that had already accumulated. He would have loved to have been transported back in time, to simpler days. When the six of them didn't have a care in the world. No one was hunting them, and they could have enjoyed a snowfall just like this by building snowmen, maybe even finding a nice quiet spot to shift and enjoy the snow in their animal forms. Instead, he was stuck inside with his mind on the lab they were going to take down, LUNA and most of all Clarissa.

Having her as his mate would put her into a whole different kind of danger. She'd have to accept shifters, show no weakness, and most of all be strong and supportive through everything. If any of them were going to get through this, she'd have to stand up and fight by his side. Not actual hand to hand combat, but in other ways. He'd have to have her by his side, in order for them to be a strong leading pair. Was she ready for that?

A light knock on the door behind him echoed through the space. "Not now."

"Sorry, Patrick, but it's important."

He turned to find Chase standing in the doorway, in a pair of black jeans and a light gray, long sleeved shirt. He was taken aback for a moment to see his brother in human form at this time of day, but quickly composed himself. "Everything okay?"

"It's Clarissa. There were some words said over what's happening in the world, how she needs to stand up and be the mate you need. Jade left the room and a few minutes later Clarissa stormed off. I'm not sure what's going on in her mind, but she seems upset."

"Where did she go?" He turned to glance back outside, and hoped that she hadn't decided to head out into the storm.

"Toward the library. Other than that, I don't know. She's only been on her own a few minutes."

"Damn it. What the hell did Jade say to her?" Not expecting an answer, he slipped past Chase and jogged toward the library.

"Don't blame Jade," Chase said as he followed closely behind. "She was only forcing Clarissa to see the facts as they are. You need a mate to stand by your side, not one who's terrified of us. How do you expect to claim her if she can't even handle my lion form?"

"She's getting better," he snapped.

"She came into the family room where I was, just a bit ago. Jade distracted her, but before that she was clenching the banister with a death grip. How's she going to handle it when you shift? Her mate, the man she sleeps with, the man she'll have children with. Do you think she's going to handle that well?"

Without bothering to reply, Patrick turned the corner and picked up his pace. Chase might be right on some aspects, but there were other areas he didn't want to think about at the moment. What he needed to do was convince her that he was just like anyone else, he only had a slight quirk that allowed him to shift into a lion. It wasn't something he should hide, or be embarrassed by, or that she should be afraid of. There were many benefits to his second nature, and not just for him, but for both of them. They needed to focus on the positives and the things they had in common instead of his differences.

The French doors to the library stood open, giving him a clear view of her sitting behind one of the antique cherry wood desks, books scattered around her. The castle had a library was stocked with the best books money could buy. It stood two floors tall, with shelves that spanned every available wall space, going straight up to the ceiling. It held almost any book a person might desire. From what he had gathered on the history of Forever Creek Ski Resort, this had been the owner's sanctuary. He had wanted to learn everything he could on nearly every subject, and had created a library to do just that.

Patrick paused at the doorway and watched her. She had twisted her long blonde hair up into a bun at the crown of her head, but a few strands had escaped and dangled over the nape of her neck. She was mumbling to herself as she wrote something down on a notepad.

"Am I interrupting?"

She set the pen down and glanced up. "I hope it's okay that I came here."

"I want you to treat this place as your home. That means using the library, going for a swim in the pool, hitting the gym, or getting in the sauna. I heard about the disagreement with Jade, and I wanted to make sure you're okay."

She leaned back in one of the plush high back chairs that were situated with each of the antique desks. "It's fine. She was just bringing to my attention something I should have realized before."

"And that is?" He ventured further into the library.

"I can't be hesitant when it comes to this. I need to be completely involved or I should get out now. While I'm not sure I'm ready for this whole mating thing, I need to come to terms with where I stand on everything that's happening. I need to be here for all of you...whether I'm your mate or not."

He ignored her comment about whether she was his mate or not, because in time she would come to terms with their destiny. "Where exactly do you stand on things?" He leaned against the desk in front of her and watched her closely.

"I'm here to help, and that's what I'm doing." She patted the book in front of her. "I remembered the coordinates for one of the shifter camps and something about how they space them. I've been looking at maps of the states, trying to remember the pattern."

"Pattern?"

"Yeah. I can see patterns other people don't. I've always been able to. Everything from behavioral patterns to the way people speak, the things they say, and what I read." She shook her head as if she was realizing she had fallen off track. "Anyway, I saw a map with some of the shifter camps on it. If I could only think, I should be able to remember the whole pattern, giving us locations for all of them. Maybe we can do something about it."

"There's no *maybe* about it. You remember, and we'll deal with them." He tipped his head back. "Come here."

"Why?" Even as she asked, she pushed back the chair, seeming nervous.

"Because I want to hold you."

She took her time coming around the desk, but when she got close, he reached out and wrapped his arms around her, drawing her near.

"The seven of us can only do so much at one time, and right now we need to deal with Hathaway Medical. If you can remember the locations of any of the camps, we'll dismantle them next. The shifters there are safer than the ones in the labs, so the labs have to be our first priority."

"They're still being held prisoner."

"Yes, angel, but they're not being experimented on like those in the labs. They're not being incinerated alive when the tests and tortures have been completed."

She pulled back to look at him, her eyes wide with fury. "What?"

"I thought you knew." He rubbed his hand along her back and wished he had kept his mouth shut.

"Are you sure? I mean, incinerated…why not something more humane?"

"I found the proof when we took down the last lab. Jade was going to be incinerated the following day. Thankfully, we saved her before that happened." They were almost too late, and the thought of it still made him sick to his stomach.

"Oh, Patrick." She reached up and cupped the side of his face, caressing his cheekbone.

"It's okay. We saved her." He fought the urge to kiss the palm of her hand.

"But what about all the others who weren't saved? What if they're doing that to a shifter at Hathaway Medical? We should be there stopping this."

"We will, angel, we will. I'll go this weekend, once all the employees are gone. That will limit the collateral damage."

"You?" Her tone hitched up a notch.

"Yes." He held her a little tighter to stop her from pulling away. "I'll take Blake and Chase with me. I'll take the lab down and bring you some closure on that. We'll save anyone we can, and since we had your laptop with the virus, we won't need to spend valuable time trying to go through the paperwork or computers. Luke has already sent out an email containing an additional computer virus. Hopefully it will infect the administrative personnel's computers, and they'll continue their work somewhere else and bring us along with them."

"Couldn't Blake and Chase do this alone?"

"I need to do this for us. I promise you I'll be back as quick as I can."

"What if they capture you? Patrick…I couldn't lose you, too. Not with

Dean out there, and who knows where he is. I haven't known you that long, and...I'd like to get to know you. I'd rather not lose that chance."

"I know, angel." He pressed his forehead to hers. "Nothing will happen. I've done this before, and I'll be back before you know it. We'll do it at night when only the security guards are on duty. I'll be back by the time you wake up the next morning."

"Take me with you."

"Absolutely not. Your face is all over the news. You will stay here where you're safe. Austin and Luke will be here to make sure nothing happens to you and Jade.

"Three going, and four staying here. That hardly seems fair. Maybe Austin should go with you. He can put his military skills to use."

"You worry too much. Austin and I have already gone over the plan of attack. I know what we're going to do. I've got to lead my family through this. Now more than ever."

She closed her eyes and let out a soft breath. "This is about you being Alpha, isn't it? Jade mentioned that you needed a mate who would stand by you, not cower behind you. She doesn't think I'm good enough for you."

"Now, you listen here." He guided her chin up with his index finger. "You're an amazing woman, full of courage others only dream of having. I don't know what Jade said, but if she thinks you're not the woman for me, she doesn't know you at all."

"You should have a shifter as a mate, not me."

"You're the woman I want." He smirked. "Do you realize you're talking like you've already made up your mind?"

"Have I?" She shook her head. "I mean, it's not like I have a choice or anything, do I? In college, I used to read paranormal romance. The human doesn't get a say. You claim us anyway, and then we're chained to you for eternity." Hints of disgust laced her words, saddening him.

"I hate to disappoint you, but that's not how it works."

"Don't lie to me." She pulled out of his embrace and stepped away from him. "I might not have a choice in this matter, but I refuse to stand here while you lie to me."

"Clarissa, I'm not lying—"

"Bull crap. I can feel the draw between us. It's like something magical. But I guess in the end, that's what you are. You're a magical being, not some scientific experiment gone wrong."

"Will you let me explain?" He paused, waiting to see if she would interrupt him again. "You feel the connection like a live wire between us. Sizzling through you, connecting you to me, and when we touch it sparks to full life, filling you. It's a warm energy without causing you any pain, but it's always there, keeping you on edge. You feel it, don't you?" When she nodded, he continued. "That's the mating link. It will always be there as long as you choose this."

"Choose?"

"Yes, you have to decide if you'll accept me as your mate. Until you make that decision, it will stay as it is. If you decide you can't handle me as your mate, then you'll no longer feel it."

"But you will?" She moved to the middle of the library where a sofa and two chairs sat before a large stone fireplace. She lowered herself onto the soft cushions.

"Once you make the decision not to accept me, the connection will fizzle out until there's nothing left. For me, it will leave a hole, an emptiness, but you'll be able to move on with your life. Find another man who meets your needs."

"What about you? Will you be given that same opportunity?"

He couldn't keep the frown off his face. "This happens so rarely that no one is really sure. Some say that eventually we will find the right person, one who can accept us, and we'll mate. But others say we would have missed our chance, and that we didn't try hard enough to convince our first mate."

"How awful."

"For me, yes. But for you, either way, you will eventually have a man you can spend the rest of your life with."

"Which brings me to a whole different question."

He nodded. "Go ahead. I'll start a fire." He went to the fireplace and knelt, collecting wood from the basket they kept and began to build a fire for them.

"The rest of my life…" She shook her head and started again. "What I'm trying to say is, from what I read, your species lives a long time. Longer than any human. Why would you or any shifter ever want to be saddled with a human who'd die before you?"

"I'm assuming you read about our life span in one of Hathaway Medical's files?" He lit the kindling and waited for it to catch, stoking it to create a nice big fire and warm the cavernous library. "They don't have all the facts about us."

"So, you don't have an extended lifespan?"

He tossed one final log onto the fire that was now fully engulfed, and stood. "No, we do. We can live for hundreds of years."

"Then why…"

"Why mate with a human if they'll die long before us?" He lowered himself to sit next to her on the sofa and wrapped his arm around her shoulders. "Once the mating has been completed, our lifelines sync, so we're able to have many long years with our mates. Before you ask, it doesn't mean that when one is killed the other will die. It allows humans to age more slowly, to age with us instead of before us."

"What's the point of living hundreds of years if you're old and feeble? I wouldn't want to become a burden on someone, especially not my children or my family."

"Unlike humans, we don't have that problem. Our bodies stay active even as we age, and we go on doing the things we've always done. It's very important to us that we can continue to do things for ourselves, especially Alphas. Once we stop leading our pride, we're of no use to anyone."

"Can you ever just step down as Alpha, or is that something you are appointed to for life?"

"To step down is most likely going to get an Alpha killed. Normally, anyone who wishes to take over the pride has to challenge an Alpha and only if the challenger defeats the Alpha will they gain control of the pride."

"By defeat, you mean…to the death, don't you?" The uncertainty was clear in her tone, and she seemed to be waiting for him to deny it.

"Yes. No Alpha wants the former leader around. There'd be too much loyalty left over for the previous leader to allow the new one a fair chance."

She pulled back as if his touch were suddenly poisonous. "You killed someone to gain your position. How could you?" Tears glistened in her eyes. "I didn't think you were like that."

"Hold on, Clarissa." He reached out and took her hand. "That is *not* what I said, I only told you how it normally works. My case is different, and I didn't kill anyone to become Alpha. Hell, I'm not even sure I wanted this position, I only know I can't let anyone else lead my family."

"If it's so different, then what happened?" she snapped.

"I told you about my family, our house, and lives. There was no one else, and we formed our own pride. We didn't need anyone else. Our father was Alpha. Mom had been his right hand until her death." He paused, allowing the memory of those first few days to flow through him. Grief and uncertainty had filled him during that time, like never before. "When she died, I was pushed into her role and my father relied on me more than the others. It prepared me for the position I'm in now."

"Why don't you want to be Alpha?"

"I didn't say I don't want to be, I'm just not sure I'm ready. Dad was the leader of this family. Now I've been pushed into the position, and since then I haven't been able to help Chase get over whatever he saw. He lives in his lion form, and Jade was captured and tortured. I just don't think I've made that good of an Alpha so far."

She placed her hand on his and squeezed. "I disagree. You got Jade back and everyone is together again. You saved me and tried to help Dean. You've done countless other things, but what's important is everyone is alive and well."

"I'm not sure about well. Jade still has nightmares, and there are the issues with Chase."

"You're dwelling on the negatives." She turned away from him to look out the window. "I remember Forever Creek Ski Resort. There's something I didn't tell you. My father brought Dean and I here the year before it closed. When you mentioned the name, I tried to shut out those memories. He used to come here with his family and was trying to reconnect with us after our mother died. So many years ago, and all this time it's been empty. You must have had to work hard to make this place livable again."

"Most of it was cleaning, fixing broken windows, adding new locks, those types of things. Blake was able to install solar power units. Otherwise, we'd have been back in the stone ages without the electric company." He nodded toward the fireplace. "The solar power works for heating as well, but since there are fireplaces in nearly every room, we tend to use those more."

"What about the smoke? Can't people see it?"

"Maybe if they flew over, but we own the place. Well, Dad and I did. Like your father, he used to come here in its glory days. It went on the market some years ago, and Dad didn't want to see it go to someone who'd only demolish it. We bought it together and planned to remodel it as a family, make it a vacation hideaway. It was several hours away from home, but it would give us all the privacy we wanted to shift and run."

"You own this place? Wouldn't it be easy to trace it back to you if they find out you're a shifter?"

"Luke helped make it harder to trace, putting the property in a company's name so it appears less suspicious." He leaned forward and wrapped his arm around her again. "There's nothing to worry about now. Lean back and enjoy the fire."

"There's work to do. I've got to remember where those camps are. We can save them."

"We deserve a little time to ourselves before Nolan gets here. Now, come here. I want my arms around you." This time, he didn't give her a chance. He pulled her back against his body.

"Who's Nolan?"

"A Ranger who served with Austin. He's the one bringing us samples of LUNA, and he'll be here tonight. Jade's planning a special dinner to welcome him, and after that we'll get to work on breaking down the compound."

"There's so much work and so little time to do it in." She relaxed into his embrace. "But…when I'm in your arms, the worries of the rest of the world seem to slip away. Still, it seems too soon to be saying that."

"That's the mating bond. A mate's touch can ease physical and emotional pain." He ran his hands through her hair, pushing it away from her face, and placed a gentle kiss on her forehead. Having her in his arms eased his beast's demands, but it wouldn't be long before he would feel it gnawing at him again to claim her.

All in sweet time.

Chapter Eleven

With her robe tied loosely shut and her wet hair wrapped in a towel, Clarissa stood in the middle of the bedroom suite feeling lost. It was late, and she should be tired, but the books she'd brought from the library called to her. She was hoping they might help spark her memory. Even more than her pull toward the books, she could feel herself being drawn to Patrick. It was like a magical string being tugged, growing taut until she thought it would snap with tension. Her body sang for her to go to him.

They had spent hours in his makeshift lab working on LUNA, but their tests were just beginning, and they still had no answers. She wasn't surprised, but she couldn't help wishing they'd have some answers on it before Patrick and the others left. It would give her some peace of mind if they had something to counteract LUNA, in case they ran into any trouble.

She sank down on the mattress and pulled the towel off her head. Her hair spilled over her shoulders, sending a chill down her neck as the wet strands touched her skin. "I'm in too deep. I barely know him, and yet he's all I think about."

"Talking to yourself?" Jade stood in the doorway. Her hair was pulled back into a ponytail with only a few strands escaping around her face. The jeans and sweater she'd been wearing earlier had been replaced with black yoga pants and a long sleeve t-shirt to match. Still, she sent a ripple of jealousy through Clarissa.

Was it wrong to be envious of the fact that Jade always appeared ready to tackle the next problem, no matter the time of day or the issue at hand? She seemed quite unlike Clarissa, who felt overcome by her exhaustion. Jade looked refreshed like she was ready to begin the day anew. She had put in just as many long hours as the rest of them. When she wasn't cooking, she was busy with Shifters Underground.

If shifters were able to keep their energy going throughout the day and not let fatigue show, then humans were certainly at a disadvantage. Humans gave in and gave up when they became tired. Even now, Patrick was down in the lab, still working.

"Are you okay?" Jade asked when she didn't answer the first time.

"I'm sorry. I was just thinking."

"Aloud, until I popped in."

"I'm known for that." Her grip on the moistened towel tightened. After the last conversation with Jade she felt uneasy, but there was no one else who could answer her question. Instead of letting her discomfort bother her, or the fact the two hadn't seen eye to eye, she took a deep breath. "Do you ever worry about your brothers when they leave?"

"I always worry about my family."

Clarissa shook her head. "I guess I should have asked, how do you handle it when they leave?"

Jade strolled into the bedroom and came to stand near Clarissa. "It's normal to be worried about Patrick. I'd be concerned if you weren't, but he's going to be fine. They'll go, do what they have to, and they'll be back. The longest part for them will be traveling. They'll have to limit their time in Hathaway Medical to maybe twenty or thirty minutes, so the security guards don't catch them."

"What will happen to any of the shifters they find?"

"That will depend on their conditions. In the past, most of them have wanted to go out on their own to see about finding their families. We give them the Shifters Underground card in case they ever need our help." Jade leaned against the dresser. "What we don't do is bring them back here. It's too dangerous when they first get out. We don't know what happened to them, or what they're capable of. We have to protect our home."

"So, you just toss them out into the cold to be captured again?"

"No, we have safe places for them all around the country where they can stay until they decide what to do. This is command central for Shifters Underground, so it's important to keep it safe. For all of our sakes but also for all the ones we can save."

"After Patrick and I have deconstructed LUNA and find a counteragent, what can I do to help with Shifters Underground?" Even as she said it, she couldn't help but think of those who'd helped rescue slaves on the Underground Railroad. It was exciting to think she could help in some way but she also wanted to use it as a tactic to cross the wall between her and Jade. If she were going to mate with Patrick, Jade would be a big part of her life. Being that they were the only two women in the house, it would help if they bonded in friendship, if not as sisters.

"There's always something to do, but you're so much more skilled than I am. Reuniting families is a pale comparison to what you and Patrick have been doing in the lab. Though, if you have some free time, I'd love some help searching the database for missing people, to try to reconnect them with their families, or at least give them closure."

"What you do it just as important. You're bringing peace to those who are suffering. Never doubt what you're doing." She paused and looked at Jade. The two of them had already started moving in a different direction, but maybe that had more to do with the fact she had accepted that Jade was right. She couldn't fault the woman for stating what she needed to hear. "I'd love to help with what you're doing. Just give me a couple days for Patrick and I to find something to stand against LUNA."

"Did I hear my name?" Patrick stepped through the doorway.

"Seems like my bedroom is becoming a central spot." She smirked at him and tried to hide the fact she was glad he'd come to her.

"That's what happens when you leave your door open. It's an open invitation in this house. Which is why most of the time everyone's doors are partly open."

"I thought you were going to work longer in the lab?"

"I was, but I wanted to be with you."

"That's my cue." Jade straightened, and stepped away from where she'd been leaning on the dresser. "Sleep well, and…Clarissa…" She glanced at her brother before turning back to her. "This chat proved I was wrong this morning. I think you'll be perfect." With that, she slipped from the room leaving them alone.

"What was that all about?"

"I think your sister just gave us an approval, rescinding her original comment that I wasn't good enough for you." Towel still in hand, she rose from the bed. "Wanted to be with me, huh? Isn't that a little presumptuous?"

"I thought you'd be thinking of me as well, and from the look in your eyes when I entered the room, I don't think I was wrong. Though, if you want me to, I'll leave."

He turned on his heels, and she was tempted to let him walk away. It would teach him a lesson that he shouldn't jump to conclusions with her. Next time, she promised herself. "Get back in here."

"I thought…" With a smirk stretched across his face, he raised an eyebrow at her in question.

"We may not know each other that well yet, and this attraction feels too sudden to me…but I'm not into self-denial, at least not when it comes to things I really want."

"My angel, should I take that to mean I'm something you really want?"

"Don't get cocky." She dragged her fingers through her damp hair and went to the dresser where she knew she'd find some of Jade's clothes. It took all her concentration to keep her attention on finding a nightshirt instead of going to him. She wanted to feel his arms around her, holding her like he had the night before. "Give me a minute to change."

"I like what you're wearing. It lets my mind wander to how enchanting you must look underneath that robe."

She tried to ignore how his words made her heart flutter with anticipation. There was no way she could deny she wanted him, obviously as much as he wanted her, but now didn't seem like the time. Plus, sex would only complicate things. Sex would complete the mating, making her his. She wasn't sure she was ready for that. Not yet—but her body screamed soon.

Instead, she pushed herself to a safer topic. "Did Austin get Nolan settled in? Will he be staying here permanently?"

"For now, he will be. He took a room on the third floor."

"Two floors down?"

He nodded and stepped closer. "While Austin knows and trusts Nolan, I don't. He's not family. I've been giving this a lot of thought…" His words died off, and he slid his hands up her waist.

"What?" she pressed.

"Whenever I'm around you, I can't seem to keep myself from touching you."

"You were saying that you gave something a lot of thought." She placed her hand on his chest, not to push him away but because she wanted to touch him, too.

"Thought…oh, right." He nodded as if he remembered what he had been about to say. "I've decided we're keeping this floor for family. Tomorrow, Blake is installing a passcode lock on the doors to this floor. No one without the code or one of us accompanying them will be given access. With Luke's office up here, the confidential information and our safety, this is imperative."

"Then I'll gather my things."

He stopped her as she started to turn away. "You're my mate, and you're not going anywhere."

"Actually, I'm not your mate yet."

"You're my mate. I just haven't made the claim official yet. I'm waiting for you to be ready." His wrapped his fingers around the tie of her robe. "Though, we can change that if you'd like."

"Let's stay on topic for now, and maybe I'll reward you later," she teased. She took his hand in hers as if to stop him from untying her robe.

"You're staying here, close to me. Preferably in my bed, but one step at a time."

"Is a passcode lock on the doors really necessary?"

"Yes. It's for our protection. Not everyone we bring here will be someone who knows one of us, like Austin knows Nolan, and we need to protect ourselves. Nolan is going out tomorrow to deal with something for another Ranger, and he'll be gone most of the day. Meanwhile, I'm going to get everyone on board to transport the lab equipment from downstairs to its new location in one of the rooms at the end of the hall. We're going to set up a conference area we can use if we're meeting with others. I'll keep an office downstairs so I'll be accessible to anyone who's here, but I'm going to have a second one off the lab so I can work on more confidential stuff if I need to."

"It sounds like all of a sudden you've lost faith in our safety here." She pulled her robe tighter around her body. "Why did Nolan's arrival change you this much?"

"It's not that." His brow furrowed for a moment as he considered her words. "In the future, we're going to have others here. That's a certainty. And when I return from Hathaway Medical, Andrew will be coming with me."

"Andrew the security guard? Why?" She thought of the last time she'd seen him. Standing outside, he had warned her, told her to record the experiments. Had he known she'd be appalled by what she saw?

"He's been on edge there for a while, but now that LUNA is being used, he can't risk trying to find another job. He's switched shifts with one of the other guards so that he'll be on duty late Friday night when we arrive, and he can help us get in."

"He's worried about LUNA? He can't be…"

"A shifter?" he finished, before nodding. "Bear."

"What? Why was he working for Hathaway Medical, then? I saw him holding down the shifter once, when they were experimenting. How can you let someone like that come here?" She eyed the man before her, mentally questioning his actions. She couldn't understand how he could bring someone who had played a part in the experiments into their home and lives. That only increased the dangers for all of them. A part of her wondered if Andrew was only helping the O'Reillys so he could get to Clarissa.

"Andrew's motives were unusual. Two months ago, his sister was killed, and the evidence points to it being someone who worked for one of the labs and had tried to take her. She struck out at the kidnapper, trying to protect her daughter. Andrew believes his niece might be in one of the labs. He's been spending all this time searching for her, but he hasn't found her."

"How old is she?"

"Eight. That might keep her alive."

"Why?" She couldn't think of one reason it would be good for her to live, to suffer through horrendous tortures. Life wasn't worth such agony, especially not when the little girl wouldn't understand what was happening to her.

"At that age, we shift unexpectedly, especially when our emotions get the best of us. They'll want to find out why she's able to do it so often." Even as he said it, she could see a glimpse of doubt in his eyes.

"But that will mean…" She couldn't bring herself to say *torture*.

"Pain, experiments," he said. "Andrew is hoping they will monitor her instead of experimenting on her."

"What about you? Do you think they won't experiment on her, that she's even alive?"

"Eventually, monitoring her won't be enough. They won't be satisfied with it, and they'll experiment on her. Maybe they will keep her sedated so she won't feel the pain." He closed his eyes for a moment, and something about it made her think he didn't believe what he was saying. "I don't know if she's alive. As awful as it sounds, and even worse how it feels to say it, I'd rather she'd have been killed with her mother, or after she was at the lab. As long as she wasn't incinerated alive."

"There's no win to this situation, is there? Either she's in a lab being tortured with endless experiments or she's dead. How's anyone supposed to deal with that?"

He pulled her tight against his chest and held her. "You deal with it by knowing there are others you can save. You fight to do the right thing."

"What about Andrew's niece?"

"We'll see if we can find her, even if it's too late to save her. He needs answers and closure. I've got Jade searching through Shifters Underground, and hopefully she'll come up with a lead. Andrew won't stick around long if he figures out another way to search for her, but while he's here we'll do what we can to make sure he's prepared for what he's up against."

"The world we live in…" She paused as she realized she had accepted this. All of it. She accepted that she was neck deep in the rising tension between shifters and humans, and a fight that might end up killing her. Most importantly, she had accepted that she was destined to be Patrick's mate.

The only light in the room was the faint glow from the moon. Clarissa cuddled against Patrick's naked chest, comforted by his soft purrs of sleep which echoed throughout the space. She wasn't sure what time it was, only that it was still dark outside. The bedside clock was on the nightstand behind her, but if she rolled over she might disturb him. She was enjoying snuggling beside him, watching him sleep. Instead of checking the time, she opted to close her eyes, and tried to let his soft purrs lull her back to sleep.

Something had woken her, but she wasn't sure what it was. With her eyes closed, her thoughts had a chance to wander, maybe a little more than she would have liked. She wanted to stay in the moment and let nothing distract her, but fate had other desires. Her eyelids sprung open and her body shook, waking him.

"What?" His voice was groggy. "What is it? Nightmare?"

"No. I know where the first camp is. I need to get a map." She rolled from his embrace and toward the edge of the bed.

"Write it down and come back to bed. There's nothing we can do about it right now."

"I need to see it. Maybe the others will come back to me, too." The nightshirt she had on wouldn't keep the chill away. She grabbed the robe she'd tossed at the edge of the bed and slipped it on. "Maybe someone can go with me and we can go scout the place while you're away."

"Absolutely not." Wearing only his boxers, he got out of bed. "I told you before, you're too recognizable. You need to stay here until things calm down. Even if that weren't the case, I wouldn't trust anyone but me to keep you safe on a mission like that. You smell like us now, and if they have shifter trackers it could put you in additional danger."

"How? What happened back at the cabin had to have worn off by now, and Jade said they'd only be able to smell me as a shifter once the mating was complete."

"True, but the mating has started and you've been in my embrace enough that my animal musk clings to you like a second skin. Shifters can mask their smell if they need to, and that of their mates, but without me you'd be a target." He came to stand behind her as she glanced over the maps and placed his hand on her shoulder. "When I get back, Austin and Blake, or Nolan, can scout out the camp."

"We need to do something about these."

"Camps are harder for us to take down. There are more guards, more shifters that we need to be concerned with. I love your motivation for this, but the labs need to be our first priority. Those are the places that are hurting and killing shifters. Camps are controlled places to keep shifters—"

"A prison." She turned to look at him, unable to believe he was willing to stand by and do nothing when it came to these camps.

"You could call them that, but those shifters are also in a semi-safe place. It's not the same as living completely free, but it is better than having to be on the run from the government. Right now, there are very few choices for shifters and freedom isn't one of them."

"Don't you think they're giving the labs free access whenever they need a new subject? Just drive over to one of the camps and pick them up. It's almost like a drive-through at a fast food place. But instead of a quick meal, they're picking up someone to torture." She lowered herself onto the chair by the desk and tried to keep her stomach from heaving. "How long until criminals start joining the ranks of the labs or these camps as security personnel, to get free access to someone they can help torture? Or criminals kidnapping shifters to torture on their own? After all, the government doesn't see your species as equals but as lesser beings who have no rights. A sadist could capture and torture a shifter, and there'd be no consequences."

"I've already thought of that, but we can only handle one problem at a time. We can't worry about something that could have always been a threat looming in the background. We need to focus on the labs. They have to be our biggest priority."

She nodded in agreement, but it didn't quiet her thoughts. She wanted the world they had before. Where everyone was safe, and no shifters were being tortured and killed. America didn't have concentration camps housing shifters. She wanted a safe world for the next generation to grow up in.

"What's wrong, my angel? You look like you've been splashed with cold water." He smoothed his hand along her back.

"I can't help but think this is a terrible world to bring children into. Heck, to even think about the future."

"We've got to live each day to the fullest. We'll make it through this and in the end we'll be stronger for it."

"We as a whole or we as in shifters?" She shook her head, not sure she wanted the answer. "Do you think we'll ever be able to live in a civilization as we did before, where shifters and humans can coexist together?"

"That is our goal, but we need the government to accept us as people. To see that while there are some among us who do evil things, we're not like that as a whole. Just as there are criminals among humans, there are criminals among shifters as well. While you can't throw a shifter into a human prison, there should be an alternative for them. But only for actual criminals, not for the whole species. As it stands, we're *all* being treated like criminals." He took her hand and brought her to stand before him. "Though you should know before this mating goes any further that it's unlikely we'll ever leave Forever Creek. Not permanently, at least."

"Why? If we can make the world safe again, why not?"

"Each of us has our own reasons, I'm sure, but as the Alpha I need to think about what's best for my pride. I believe staying here is best. Because of what happened, I don't think Jade will ever be able to trust people like she should. I'm not sure she could ever go back to living amongst others. I can feel the anxiety within her when we talk about others coming to the castle. She wants to trust, but she's just not there yet. She needs somewhere safe where she can be herself. That place is right here."

"What about the rest of you? That's not fair on the pride for you to stay here because of one."

"Like I said, I believe we each have our own reasons. Austin retired from the Army, and even though he looks well-adjusted he doesn't like large crowds or loud noises. Then there's Chase…I'm not really sure what's wrong with him, but eventually he'll be ready to tell me."

She met his gaze and stared into his sea glass green eyes. "Where do I fit into all of this?"

"Hopefully right by my side." He laced his fingers between hers. "I want you with me as I lead the pride, as we fight to get the government to accept us, but more importantly I want you in my bed for now and always."

She loved the sound of that, even though it hadn't been very long. To be with the man she was quickly falling for was like a wish come true, especially when she realized he wanted her as much as she wanted him. They'd get through the questionable times because they had each other. She rose up on her tiptoes and pressed her lips to his.

Chapter Twelve

Patrick hooked up the last computer monitor and glanced around the new lab. In just over two hours, they had moved everything up to the fifth floor and completely set up. With that off his checklist, he needed to head back downstairs to gather what needed to come up from his office. He didn't want the office on the first floor to look too sparse and unused, but anything he was working on needed to be kept upstairs.

His beast growled within him, angry they'd been pushed to the level of not trusting his fellow shifters. It broke something within him that he had to move anything that might spark someone's anger to his other office. All the confidential items they had gathered from the labs and their searches had to be tucked away. With others coming here, he needed to make sure none of it fell into the wrong hands.

He was stuffing files into a box when Chase stepped into the office. "Got a minute?"

"Sure." He sat down on the leather office chair. "What's up?"

"Blake and I can handle Hathaway Medical and—"

"I have no doubt that's true, but I'm going. I've already had this conversation with Austin, and I don't appreciate any of you questioning my judgment."

"It's not your judgment that's in question." Chase bit the corner of his lip, clearly uneasy. "You're leaving the day after tomorrow, and you haven't even claimed her yet. Each of us can feel the tension building within you. Your lion is on edge. Going on a mission now isn't the best decision."

"Unless you wish to challenge me for my position, I've given you my answer. I'm going to deal with the lab myself. If you can't accept that, then you can challenge me, stay here, or keep your mouth shut," Patrick snapped. His lion growled within him, begging to be released. His beast wanted to remind everyone that he was Alpha here, and it was time they respected that.

"Patrick." Austin stepped in, leaning against the doorjamb with his large arms crossed over his chest. "The way you're acting right now…it's unlike you. Don't you see why we're concerned?"

"I'm fine. I'm in control," he reasoned, even as he tried to repress his beast. Maybe it wasn't the complete truth, but he was their Alpha and he'd handle this the best he could in order to keep everyone safe.

"You're fine now because Clarissa is just down the hall. But when you leave…" Austin paused for a moment and came farther into the office. "If you don't claim her before you leave, your lion is going to spaz out. You need the connection alive between you two in order to focus on the mission at hand. If you don't, someone could get hurt…or worse."

Even if they were right, Patrick hated the pressure his brothers were inflicting on him. His beast wouldn't take the separation very well without knowing his mate was safe. "She needs to be ready. I won't force her into a mating she isn't ready for."

"Neither of us said to force her." Chase glanced back at Austin.

"A little pressure never hurt anything," Austin added. "Clarissa probably feels the tension and need as well."

"I heard my name. Are you talking about me?" She stopped in the hallway, a filled cardboard box in her hands, the tops of files sticking out.

"Come in." Austin went to her and took the box from her. "We were just telling Patrick that he needs to claim y—"

"That's enough, Austin!" Patrick shot up from the chair, anger coursing through him. "Leave her out of this."

"She's as much a part of this as you, and she has a right to know."

"Know what?" She moved past Austin, toward Patrick. "What aren't you telling me?"

"For this mission to be successful…" Chase paused as Patrick's growls echoed throughout the office. With a deep breath, he continued, "He needs to complete the mating."

"Chase, I warned you. Both of you." He glanced toward Austin.

"Is this true?" When Patrick didn't answer, she turned back to Austin.

"He doesn't want to rush you, but if the mating hasn't happened his lion will be on edge. He'll be more focused on you, or what's happening back here. It will put the whole thing and their lives in danger."

"Get out. Now!" Patrick hollered, his beast's growl lacing his words. If anyone else had disobeyed an order from an Alpha, there'd have been hell to pay. However, these men were his brothers, so he kept his lion's natural impulses in check. At least, for now. "*Out.*"

"You're not getting rid of me that easy." She straightened her back and met his gaze.

"Clarissa," Chase began, his voice low. "I think you should come with us."

"I'm not leaving," she told Chase as she eyed Patrick. "I have a few things to stay to him."

"I think you've met your match, and she's not backing down." Austin smirked as he headed out the door, Chase following only a few steps behind.

"You should listen to them." He didn't want her to be afraid of him, but at that moment his lion was more on edge than ever before. He needed to shift and give his beast an outlet for the anger that was burning within him.

She stalked forward. Annoyance had her glaring at him, as she crossed her arms over her chest. "How dare you not tell me this? If not completing this mating is going to put you and the others at risk, I had a right to know. How do you think I'd feel if one of you came back injured, and then I found out I was partially to blame? Or worse, what if one of you didn't come back at all? Do you think we could ever move past that, or would there always be some resentment between us?" The questions rolled off her tongue, each one faster than the last, leaving no time for him to answer them.

"I'd have handled things and we'd be fine." It came out as more of a growl than anything else.

"Handle things?" She shouted, throwing her arms in the air and then running her fingers through her hair. "I'm a *thing* now? Not a person but a thing." Her eyes widened before she slammed her hands down on the back of the light brown chair that sat across from his desk. "Who the hell do you think you are?"

"Damn it, Clarissa, that's not what I meant and you know it."

"Do I?"

"I won't force you into something you're not ready for. No matter what the consequences are. You asked me about resentment, but have you considered the resentment you would have if I forced this mating onto you? How would that work, because once we're mated there's no going back. There's no divorce or separation. Once the mating happens, the only way out is through death." He watched as the anger left her eyes. "I care more about you than to let that happen."

"And I care more about you than to let you rush off on this mission without your head in the game." She stepped around the chair and took a seat. "You could get killed."

"That possibility is always there, and you know it, but we take every precaution to make sure we come home after each mission." He wanted to walk around his desk, go to her, and wrap his arms around her, but he denied himself that privilege. The last thing he needed was to make her more confused. Time. She needed time.

"Sometimes no matter how many safeguards you put in place, it's not enough." She wrapped her arms around her. "Knowing that I care for you, how could you go off and risk yourself and your brothers?"

"Caring about someone and being ready for what would be a lifetime commitment are two different things. I was trying to protect you. That's what I do." He tried to apply reason to his actions, but part of him knew he should have told her. He had chosen to hold off the mating until he returned, putting himself and the others in danger. It would also force her to feel the longing that came with his absence, but when he returned he'd hoped it would bring them to the place they needed to be.

"You didn't give me a choice. You just guessed I wasn't ready. Who are you to decide what's best for me?"

"I'm an Alpha, that's what I do. I make the decisions that are best for my pride. I protect them no matter the cost. Sometimes people get hurt in the process, but I don't take decisions lightly. I suffer with the decisions I'm forced to take every day, but in the end I do what's right for my pride, no matter the personal cost."

"That's where you're wrong. I'm not one of your pride members, and I sure as heck don't need you to protect me." She shot up from the chair and stormed out of the room.

He watched her as she ran from him, while nagging doubt rose within him as he wondered if she'd ever be ready for the life he lived. This was his mate, and if he let his role as Alpha interfere with claiming her, he'd regret it for the rest of his life. He needed to find a way to show her the positives of being the Alpha's mate. He needed for her to truly understand what it would be like to be a part of a pride.

After dashing from Patrick's office, Clarissa wandered around the castle, trying to find somewhere she could be alone. She had to get her thoughts in order before she could face any of the O'Reillys, but everywhere she thought she'd find sanctuary someone was already there. She could have been alone in her bedroom, but that would only remind her of the time she'd spent cuddled in his arms. That was the last thing she needed at the moment.

"How can I possibly consider spending the rest of my life with someone who can't even respect me enough to tell me the whole truth?" She pulled open the door to the indoor swimming pool. "Maybe we're too different after all."

She paused by one of the chairs, slipped out of her boots, and rolled up her pants. She might not be able to go for a swim, but she could at least put her feet in, and enjoy a quiet moment to get her thoughts together. Turning toward the pool, she caught a glimpse of herself in the wall of windows that looked out onto what used to be the ski slopes. "Look at me, standing here talking to myself. Maybe I'm nuttier than I thought."

The pool was Olympic size, nine feet deep at one end. She chose to sit near the steps. Dipping her toes into the crystalline liquid, she nearly pulled back from the frigid temperature of the water, before taking a deep breath and letting her feet sink in. She swung her legs back and forth, her thoughts jumbled, and watched the wind pick up the snow and toss it forcibly into growing drifts beyond the windows. There was something so peaceful about it, yet so unnerving.

She was miles from anyone, alone with a houseful of shifters. Until now, she hadn't considered it, but as she remembered the way Patrick's growls mixed with his words, she couldn't help but wonder just how close his animal lurked beneath the surface. What would have happened if she'd pushed him further? Would he attack her, and would she ever be at risk around these people?

She remained uncertain how far a shifter would go to if he was pressed, and whether his beast would emerge if provoked. She was concerned, but her heart tried to remind her there was nothing to worry about. He would never hurt her.

"What am I going to do?" she wondered aloud. "He obviously doesn't trust me." She reached down and dragged her fingers through the water, sending little ripples across the surface.

"You okay?" Startled, she straightened where she sat and glanced toward the door. Jade was standing there, the door open just enough that she could peek her head in. "I can get you a suit if you want to go for a swim."

"Thanks, but I'm okay. I just came here to…" She started to say *to be alone*, but suddenly she didn't want that any longer. She wanted company. Maybe Jade wasn't the best person to talk to because Clarissa couldn't openly discuss her fears with her, but she was the only person around. "Are you busy? Maybe you'd join me for a few minutes."

Jade nodded and stepped into the open area, letting the door click shut behind her. "I saw you wander past the kitchen, and I almost didn't follow. I thought maybe you wanted to be alone, but something about the look on your face and the sadness in your eyes made me think twice. So, what's up?"

She kicked off her flip-flops and sat down beside her.

"Why didn't anyone tell me?"

Jade's nose scrunched up as she considered the question. "Maybe we should backtrack. Tell you what, exactly?" She sunk her feet into the water and cringed visibly at the cool temperature.

"No one told me…" She felt her face heat. "That…that Patrick needed to complete this mating *before* his mission."

"Ah, that." Jade leaned back, splashing the water a bit with her toes. "Which one of my brothers let it slip, and more importantly, are they still alive?" she joked.

"Austin started to, but Patrick interrupted him. Chase was the one who let the bomb drop. Yes, they're still both alive…well, last I saw of them. They took off while I stayed behind to have a few words with your brother." All of a sudden, she wasn't certain it was a joke. She turned to Jade and tried to swallow the fear that chilled her veins. "You don't honestly think he'd kill them, do you?"

"Not Patrick, but another Alpha would. They disobeyed a direct order. Patrick specifically told us to stay out of this mating, that the two of you would work through it in your own time. He wanted to give you as much time and as little pressure as he could."

"So, because he's your Alpha you have to do everything he says? What kind of life is that?" she asked, incredulously.

"That's how shifters survive. We need that command structure. Otherwise, things would get out of hand, especially in larger prides," Jade explained. "Patrick is still new to his role as Alpha. He hasn't been willing to embrace it as much as he should because we're a very tight-knit family. Now that he's allowing outsiders here, he's going to have no choice. Either accept his role as Alpha or risk being overtaken…and none of us want that."

"What would happen then?"

"For another Alpha to take over an established pride, he would have to challenge and defeat the ruling Alpha. If Patrick lost, it would put all of us at risk."

Clarissa sat there for a moment, trying to digest what she had just learned. "Then why allow anyone else to come here? He already has Nolan here, then Andrew will come here, and he offered a safe place to Cotton, the wolf shifter we met when he found me."

"He's giving them a safe place in exchange for their help. Anyone who comes to Forever Creek will play a role in our future. We all have to fight together in order to regain our freedom."

"You really do believe shifters can live amongst the rest of civilization again, don't you?"

"I have to." Jade's eyes darkened, and Clarissa could have sworn she saw tears threatening to fall. "Otherwise, all that we've lost so far has been for nothing. All that we stand to lose in this battle has to be for something. We deserve to live without fear, just as everyone else does. If you didn't believe it, too, you wouldn't be here."

"Believing and wanting are two different things." She stopped swinging her legs and turned toward Jade. "I want to believe it could happen, but I'm not sure the government will ever allow it."

"If all of us banded together, they'd have no choice. Shifters could stand united and strong, and our numbers would far outweigh those opposing us."

Clarissa thought about that for a moment, conjuring images of Patrick standing at the frontlines, demanding their freedom. One new question popped into her mind. What would happen to a human mate of a shifter if the shifter were captured? Would the government put her into a camp like they were doing to the shifters who weren't in labs? Or could she be killed?

She knew the powers that be weren't above stepping on someone's liberties if they thought it was in the best interest of the country. Now she wondered how many other humans with shifter mates would be at risk. How many had already been captured or killed? Were any of them in the labs, where scientists might study how the mating affected a human body?

"Clarissa," Jade called out. "You traveled miles away. What are you thinking about?"

"Mates." She shook her head and pushed the thoughts aside. Jade was dealing with enough, trying to relocate shifters in danger, reconnect lost family members. The last thing Clarissa wanted to do was get her started thinking about their human mates and what happened to them. Instead, she forced herself to change the subject, to focus on what they had been talking about initially. "Why wouldn't he tell me that this unfinished mating would jeopardize the mission?"

"Because my brother is hardheaded. He thinks he can control everything, and that it's his job to protect us all from the dangers in the world. He was always like this, but now that he's our Alpha he's become a little more protective." Jade ran her hand over her midsection. "Especially with me."

"He wants to keep you safe." Clarissa caught the sudden change in Jade's voice and the way her hand went to her abdomen. Could there be scars hidden under the sweater from the time she'd spent as a captive?

"He wants to do the same with you." Jade smirked. "Patrick has a big heart, and he'll go to the end of the universe for someone he loves."

"I don't want to be protected." She tucked a stray hair behind her ear. "I guess that's not completely true, or I wouldn't be here. Still, I deserve to know the truth. How could this mating possibly work otherwise? If he's going to keep important things like this from me, how can I have a strong relationship with him? Trust is the most important thing in a relationship."

"Just trust? What about chemistry between the sheets? Love and romance?"

"Those things are important, too. Especially in the bedroom," Clarissa admitted with a wink.

"I know you said you don't want to be protected, but with the danger we live in, a protector isn't a bad thing."

"I guess you're right. It's just such a change for me. When he excludes me from something like this, it is hurtful. I felt like he doesn't trust me."

Jade nodded. "Patrick can be like that, but he's doing it so you don't worry as much. Go talk to him, let him know how you feel. Until the mating has been complete, both of you are on shaky ground. Once you've committed to each other, he'll no longer be able to hide things like this from you. The two of you will be in tune with each other and there will no longer be secrets between you. Give things time. Everything will work out."

She tipped her head to look at Jade. "I know you weren't happy that he was destined to mate with me, and you didn't believe I was good enough for him."

"But you're proving me wrong."

"Maybe…but that's because you opened my eyes to what I should have seen." She pulled her legs out of the water, and turned toward Jade. "He needs a mate that is willing to stand by his side and fight for the good of the shifters. I wasn't sure I was willing to do that but I am. How much help I can be is still to be determined, but I'm on your side. We'll fight together."

"Welcome to the family." Jade leaned forward and hugged her.

That one word sent joy spreading through her. *Family…*

Chapter Thirteen

It was beginning to snow as Patrick headed back to the resort. Ice crunched under his lion paws, and with each step his pace slowed. His beast enjoyed being set free, and didn't want it to end. Giving himself just a few more minutes to feel the fresh air tease through his fur, he lowered himself to lay in the snow, on the last incline before reaching the castle.

For months now, this had been home, but he'd never felt completely comfortable. Now that he'd found Clarissa, it was beginning to seem more like a place he could enjoy living in. He caught a glimpse of movement in the pool room. Staying low, he scooted forward, ignoring how the snow cooled his stomach as he slid into a better position. Focusing, he could make out Clarissa and Jade sitting at the edge of the pool, their legs dangling in the water as they talked.

A twinge of jealousy coursed through him. He wanted that same natural ease with Clarissa, but now he was concerned he might have pushed her further away. However, he knew the relationship she was developing with Jade was important. She needed another woman to talk to, and so did his sister.

He could feel the connection come alive as Jade caught a glimpse of him on the hill, watching them. *Let go of your ego and get down here. Show your mate you're only trying to keep her safe.* Jade's voice echoed through their mental connection. *She needs your reassurance.*

She's pissed I'm trying to protect her. He didn't move.

You're our Alpha. Being controlling and protective is in your nature. But she's not a shifter and doesn't understand. So, get down here and explain it to her.

He rose to stand on his paws and slowly wandered down the hill toward his mate. If she had been a shifter, she would have understood his role. She would have realized why he was protecting his pride. But a human would see it as being smothered. For the rest of their lives, he'd have a thin balancing act to follow when it came to keeping her safe and keeping his mate happy. In the end, her safety would outweigh her happiness. She could be mad at him and alive, but if she got killed because he hadn't protected her, there was no going back from that.

As he strolled up next to the wall of windows he saw the way Clarissa watched him. There wasn't fear in her eyes, only concern and curiosity. He loved the way her gaze followed him as he made his way toward the door.

"It's Patrick." Jade slipped her feet out of the water, stood, and made her way to the door to meet him. She scooped up her flip-flops along the way. "You two need to talk."

"Talk? How is that going to happen if he's like that?" Clarissa watched as Patrick strolled into the pool area and disappeared behind a wall where the showers were.

"Give him a moment and he'll change. Meanwhile, I'm going to leave you two alone so you can work this out. Tell him. Otherwise, he'll never know."

A few minutes later, he stepped out with a towel around his waist to hide his nudity, and found Clarissa where she remained at the pool's edge, staring out the windows, lost in thought. He stood there for a moment, admiring how the last rays of sunlight cast a golden aura around her. She was gorgeous, and if he played his cards right, she'd be all his.

"She's right angel," he said softly. "If you don't tell me I'll never know. I might be part human, but no matter how hard any of us try, we could never think like you. At least not completely. Our animal is always within us, and they play a part in how we think."

"What do you mean?"

He sat down beside her, getting comfortable. "Take for example the fact that all of us are adults, but not one of us moved away from home. Austin did time in the military, but when he was discharged, he came home. To you, that might seem odd, but to us it's normal. Even though some of our animals are solitary creatures, as shifters we band together. We'd spend our whole lives together if possible. We add mates and children into the mix, but most of us never leave our pride unless it's to join another. There are a few who live alone, but they're rare. Those are usually the ones causing the issues that expose us and make our presence known."

"So, the wolf shifter who killed all those people didn't belong to a clan?"

The headlines from the news flashed before his eyes. People had been eaten alive. He recalled human authorities hunting for the killer, while the shifters banded together, conducting their own manhunt. Knowing only a shifter could be behind the murders, they'd hoped to find the killer first. They were too late. In Washington D.C., cops stumbled upon him in the middle of his feast, two victims dead and another one barely alive.

"Patrick?"

He slid his legs into the water, and adjusted the towel that covered him.

"He was a loner, that shifter. The loneliness made his sanity snap, and the wolf within him gained control."

"Did you know him?"

He shook his head. "But if the Alpha of his pack had known his mental stability was in question, it was his duty to do something."

"Even though he left?"

"The pack leader would have still felt the connection to him because he hadn't vowed himself to another pack. So, yes."

"Why do you call them a pack, but yours a pride?" She tipped her head back to look at him, leaning on the palms of her hands.

"Every group of animals is technically called something. For wolves it's a pack, for bears it's a sleuth, lions a pride, but with leopards it's a leap. Some instantly understand what a pack or a pride is, but few know what a leap is. It's just easier for some to be considered a clan instead. We've considered calling our group a clan instead of a pride since we will be made up of other shifters besides lions, but calling ourselves anything other than a pride is a hard habit to break. It's not just a name, but who we are."

She stared at him for a moment before letting out a deep sigh. "Jade said you need to embrace your Alpha more if you're going to bring others in. Are you sure this is a good idea?"

"I do. In the end, it will give us more power. I've got my inner Alpha under control, and if they're going to come here they will have to vow their loyalties to me, severing all their former ties." He placed his hand on her thigh and gently squeezed. "This isn't the reason you rushed off before. Don't you think we should discuss that?"

"First, one more question. Why do prides make that much of a difference? I mean, you said before that the wolf snapped, and his beast took control. How does having a pride keep that from happening?"

"An Alpha has a connection with every member of his pride, so they'd have known long before the murders started and they could have redirected his mental instability into something else. It's an Alpha's duty to make sure things like that never happen, no matter the price."

He'd already had to think about the price of his duty. When Jade was captured, he wondered what condition they'd find her in. Every day that passed, he hoped she could keep her sanity. He was grateful the scientists who tortured her hadn't been able to break her spirit. She was still their Jade, despite the lingering scars and nightmares. Those were things they could overcome.

"How does this connection work with human mates?" Clarissa wondered, breaking him from his reverie.

"When one of my members mates, it lights the connection between the two. If the mate is a shifter, it would be the same as any other. They'd have to cut any ties with their previous pride or clan and vow themselves to me. If they mate with a human, the connection would still be there, but not as strong. My connection to the human mate would flow through the shifter. The shifter who vowed themselves to me would be the link joining the human to me and the pride." He tried to explain how it all worked but it was so much more than that. Until she was fully a part of it, she couldn't truly understand what it was like to experience the bond with the pride members.

"What about for *your* mate?"

With a raised eyebrow, he glanced at her. "For you, it's different. Unless I shield you from the connection, you would feel the members of the pride. As my mate, your voice is like mine. They'd be expected to follow your orders just as they'd follow mine."

"If our mating is going to work, you need to be straight with me," she said, her voice firm. "That means telling me *everything*. I won't put up with the old 'protect the woman' crap. I understand you have to safeguard the pride, but if I'm going to be your mate and I'm supposed to do my part, that means we're equals and I refuse to be treated as anything less. I won't have you hiding shit from me just because you think it's best. You're going to have to be up front with me, or we're going to have some serious issues."

"You know what they say about teaching an old dog new tricks? Well, it's worse with a lion. Us big cats are set in our ways." When she started to say something, he held up his hand. "But I'll try. That's the best I can give you."

"When the mating is complete, won't I know it when you're hiding something from me?"

"Who told you that?" When she smirked at him, he shook his head and gave a light chuckle. "Jade, I should have guessed."

"Is it true then?" she pressed.

"Yes. The connection would make it harder for me to hide things from you, even at a physical distance. That's one of the reasons the mating should…well, it would help if it happened before I leave." He paused for a moment, questioning his decision to be so forward about the topic. "Even with miles separating us, I would still be able to feel you as if you were there by my side, and my lion would be calm. Without the bond, my lion would be like a cat pacing a small box, searching for a way out, constantly on edge, and growing more and more distracted as our time apart stretched on."

She pulled her legs out of the water and stood. "Who were you to decide I wasn't ready?" There was an edge of irritation to her words.

"I was trying to give you time to adjust to all of this. You've been dropped into it, and it's a lot to take in, to accept. I didn't want to rush you into something you weren't completely sure about. There's no going back from a mating, and like I said before, there's no divorce or separation. You

FOREVER'S FIGHT

have to be completely ready to jump in with both feet and hang on tight because it's going to be the ride of a lifetime."

"You couldn't have known if I were ready without asking me."

He stepped out of the pool and went to where she was standing. "Well, are you?"

She took a step back and raised an eyebrow at him. "If I say yes, are you going to take me right here on the cold tile?"

"Oh, angel, I'll take you any way I can have you, but I think we can find somewhere better than the floor."

The door pushed open and Luke hovered in the doorway. "Sorry." He glanced from Patrick to Clarissa before continuing. "It's important."

"I'll be there in a minute."

Luke nodded. "My office."

As the door closed, Patrick took her hand in his. "I'm sorry, angel."

"Don't be. Go. But when you're done, come find me."

"There's nowhere else I'd rather be." He leaned in and pressed his lips to hers in a sweet, tender kiss. His lion surged him forward, demanding a taste of her, but he restrained himself. There would be time for that later.

Clarissa had spent much of the evening in the lab analyzing LUNA and working out her calculations. She had only taken a brief break when Jade brought her a plate of food since she had skipped dinner. Now she was curled up in bed waiting for Patrick, her notebook and pen in hand as she ran through the calculations. Something about LUNA was amiss, but she couldn't put her finger on it.

With each minute that passed, her eyelids grew heavier. Focusing was difficult, as the need for sleep pressed on her. She glanced at the bedside

173

clock and found that it was just before two in the morning. Whatever Luke had to talk to Patrick about kept him occupied for hours. She had been tempted to find him after she left the lab, but she didn't want to interrupt.

Promising herself she wasn't going to fall asleep, she let her eyelids drift shut and tried to run through the possibilities again. Something had to come to her, and sometimes ideas arose just as she was drifting off to sleep. She had very little time left if she was going to come up with a counteragent by the time Patrick and the others departed, but she couldn't give up hope.

The bedroom door creaked open and she forced her eyelids open to find Patrick standing in the doorway. "You're still awake?"

"I've been waiting for you." She scooted up in bed and set the notebook aside. "Is everything okay?"

"Luke found some files I needed to look at before we left. If I'd have realized it was going to take this long, I'd have let you know. You didn't have to wait up." He stepped into the room and shut the door behind him, surprising her because he normally left it slightly open.

"I was working on LUNA, so it's fine. Did you find anything interesting?"

"Enough that we're leaving tomorrow."

"That soon?" As he came up to the side of the bed, she could see the worry weighing on his shoulders. "What is it?"

"There's something missing from the files. Luke found signs of something more sinister, but that was it. If he can't find it, it's not there. After all, he's the best of the best. So, we're moving on the place tomorrow."

"What signs, what did he find? It's a work day tomorrow. What about everyone who will be there?"

"Blake, Chase, and I are leaving mid-afternoon, but we won't hit the place until evening. Andrew's on the nightshift again so everything will be fine."

She pulled her legs under her and reached out to lay a hand on his arm. "But you're not fine. Something's wrong. Tell me what he found."

He tensed under her touch but didn't move away. "You need to get some sleep."

"The way I see it, we have a lot to do tonight. If you're planning on getting any rest before you leave on this mission, you'd better start talking." She took her hand away, pulled back the comforter, and moved over. "Get in here and talk to me."

Silence and moodiness were draped over him like a second skin, but he untied his boots and slipped onto the bed to lay fully clothed beside her. She scooted close to him, and he lifted his arm to wrap it around her shoulder. Still, he remained silent.

She ran her hand over the thin material of his long-sleeved t-shirt. "We can sit here all night waiting for you to open up, or you can tell me and we can move to the fun portion of our night."

"Fun?"

She nodded, and when he realized she wasn't going to say anything more, he sighed.

"You were right about the threats against the children," he continued. "The files suggest they might have followed through. I've got to get into the offices, and find the file that's referenced in the email. Otherwise, we have nothing. If there had been enough time tonight to get there and deal with the situation before the employees came, we would have, but there isn't time."

"They didn't. Please tell me they didn't experiment on a child." Her stomach roiled with the very thought, and she was certain she might vomit. She covered her mouth, forcing down the bile. What gave someone the right to hurt an innocent child?

"We don't know anything for sure, but if they did, we need to find out what happened to the child."

"Could they have lived through it?" She wasn't sure she wanted to know the answer to that, but the question had been asked before she could stop herself, and there was no taking it back now.

"I don't know, angel, I just don't know."

She tried to stop her thoughts from heading in a dismal direction, but it was nearly impossible. All she could picture were the shifters in the labs and the tortures that were done to them. How could a child live through that? He told her that shifters were only born, never bitten, but could this child shift if the scientists were able to get things right?

"We don't know anything about the experiment or the child at the moment. It's possible that it never happened and was only discussed."

"It's unlikely. If I learned one thing about Hathaway Medical, it's that they like to put fear in people, but they also follow up on the threat if they're given an opportunity." She tipped her head up to look at him. "Would the child become like you? Would they even survive?"

"I've never tried to produce a serum that would change someone's physical chemical makeup…and I'm not even sure it's possible. I do believe that with some time and the proper equipment, a person could be given some of our characteristics. As for surviving the experiment…that would be questionable. More than likely, the first ones that were experimented on would die either from the process or from the changes within their bodies. The impact the drug would have on the body would be the killing factor."

Her thoughts turned in a new direction, giving her a mixture of hope and fear. "If the child is alive, the family will need protection."

"If there's a child who needs our help, we'll give it to them." He leaned his cheek against the top of her head. "We need that file, not only to help the child, but also to expose Hathaway Medical for what they've done. We can't stand by and let them hurt innocent children, ruin the lives of families. Do you see now why we must stand up against them? They won't stop until we're completely under control. There are too many at risks. Not just shifters, our mates, and children, but also civilization. They have already begun to see if they can recreate us from others. Maybe the goal is to recreate us into something they can control."

"Every time I think things couldn't get worse, they do. These actions make me ashamed to be human."

"Not all humans are bad, just a handful are doing this. That's the same with shifters. One lone shifter caused this outrage, and now all of us are paying for it." He squeezed her tighter against him and kissed the top of her head.

"We're going to get through this." She held tighter to him and tried to banish the fear rising within her. As life became more dangerous day by day, she worried about him leaving on the mission.

"I know, angel." He ran his hand along her back. "We *will* get through this. But at what cost?"

She couldn't answer that. Actually, she could but she didn't want to think about it. She had a feeling the cost would be high. The very thought of all she stood to lose if things went wrong made her stomach roll and heart beat faster.

It dawned on her that in the short week she'd been there, she had come to care about the O'Reillys, but more than that she had begun to fall in love with Patrick. He was the man who'd come to her rescue, and who hadn't left her side since. He was just like the man she had always dreamed about, except she'd never thought her dream man would be able to transform into a lion. Even now, it didn't bother her the way she'd thought it would. Love was more powerful than anything, and they'd get through this. *Together.*

Chapter Fourteen

Clarissa took a deep breath, pushed her nerves aside, and leaned close to him. It was time to show him just how much she cared about him. To live each moment like it could be their last. With the impending mission, no one could guarantee what would happen. She wanted—needed—the mating connection, joining them through all of it. She needed to give in to what her body craved.

She slipped her hand under his shirt and ran her fingers slowly up his chest. She caressed the contours of his abs and dragged through the small patch of chest hair near his heart. She remembered the night he came to her, waking her from the nightmare, and holding her tight. That night, his chest had been bare, and now she wanted to see it again. To see and explore it.

"Patrick, I want you."

"I have the unfortunate need to ask you if you're sure." He tipped his head toward her, and their gazes locked. "Though if you change your mind, I might ravish you anyway."

"You'd never do that. Unlike some, you would respect my decision." She pressed her lips to his, kissing him softly before drawing his bottom lip between her teeth and nipping lightly before letting go again. "Ask me if you must, but my answer won't change."

"You're beautiful." He tangled his fingers in her hair. "I can't get you out of my thoughts. Nearly every thought I have is about you."

She could feel her cheeks heat with embarrassment, but before she could say anything more, he closed the distance between them. His lips held just the faintest traces of saltiness from a beer he must have had earlier. Wanting more of him, she let her tongue slip into his mouth. They kissed as he slid his fingers under the hem of her nightshirt, gently pulling it up. When he'd tugged it as far as he could, he broke the kiss and pulled it over her head.

The warmth from the fireplace hit her as he tossed the shirt aside. Now that she was naked, she was more eager to get his clothes off. She started to pull at his shirt, but he stopped her.

"Don't look at me like that, I'm as sure about this as I've ever been about anything," she said, caressing his smooth stomach.

Seeing her honesty, he hopped off the bed and stripped. She suspected he was also overcome by a deep yearning. She tried to memorize the sight of him naked before he crawled onto the bed beside her. "Eager?"

"More than you know." He caressed his hand over her hip, ever so slowly sliding down her leg. "I won't give you a minute longer to question what we're doing. No doubt allowed because once I start there's no stopping."

She stared at him, running her hand down his chest until she found his shaft. She wrapped her fingers around it and rubbed down the length, painstakingly slow. She applied just enough pressure that he arched toward her. She loved the soft moan escaping his lips. "I have no doubt," she whispered.

"Good, because I'm going to make sure that doubt doesn't return." He pulled gently away which forced her to let go of him.

"Get back here," she ordered, unable to keep the smirk off her face.

"Later. I want to take in all of you. Oh, what a beautiful sight that will be." When she leaned forward, he placed a hand on her shoulder and lightly pushed her back down against the bed. He pressed his lips to hers with such desire that she moaned around his unrelenting kiss.

When the kiss ended, leaving her breathless, he whispered, "Beautiful. Truly beautiful." He kissed down her neck and chest until he feverishly claimed her nipple. With that went her last shred of reservation.

"Please…" She reached out, placing her hand firmly on his chest. His shaft pressed tight against her thigh. In his arms, she felt safe and desired for the first time in a long time. She ran her nails over his chest, her need escalating.

He slipped his fingers between her legs, sliding over her clit, pulling the pleasure from her inch by inch. He thrust his fingers into her as his thumb continued to pull more pleasure from her core.

"I need you. Please…"

He rolled over, taking her with him, making her squeal. With her on top, he slid his hands over her hips. "Mmm." He caressed her clit one last time before returning to her hips and lifting her gently.

"I'm normally shy, and I've never…I mean," she stammered, unsure how to say it. It had been a while since she had been with a man, and even then she had never been on top. Most of the men she'd dated needed to remain in control of every aspect, and would never allow her to ride them like this. Excitement shot through her like an electric current. She was nervous but there was something about being on top that made this extra special.

"I want to see you above me," he said. "But don't worry…we'll take it slow, and I think if you give it a chance, you'll enjoy it."

She tucked a lock of hair behind her ear and nodded, giving him the permission to continue lifting her gently. Once he got her into position, he slid his shaft along her folds, teasing her until she arched her back and a moan escaped her lips.

"Please!"

Without further delay, he slid his length into her until he buried himself to the hilt inside of her. He kept his hands on her hips, helping her work his shaft up and down. With each pump, she began to find her own way. As she became comfortable, she picked up the pace and drove herself up and down, the pace increasing with each thrust.

He moved his hands away from her hips, leaving the pace up to her, running his hands along her body. He reached up to fondle her breasts, sliding his fingers over the hard buds of her nipples, teasing them.

"Oh, Patrick!" She tipped her head back, growing closer to ecstasy.

He grabbed hold of her hips and drove his shaft into her harder and faster. The frenzy had her moaning until she called out his name and groaned as her climax sent her over the edge. His own followed moments later as he buried himself deep within her one final time.

Kissing her neck, he stayed buried deep within her. "My beautiful angel, Clarissa." He kissed a line along her neck, working his way to her ear.

"If you keep doing that, we're going to have a double feature," she teased.

As if agreeing, his shaft twitched, hardening against the walls of her core. "I think we can arrange that."

"Mmm." She moaned, teasing her fingers along his sides. Without moving off of him, she arched her back and looked down at him. "I don't feel any different."

"You will." He put his hands on her hips and gently guided her off of him. When she was stretched out on the mattress, he brought her tight against him and pulled the blanket over them. "It will take a minute while your body begins to absorb my fluid. Then, the changes will begin."

"Will it be painful?" she asked, needing the answer even though there was nothing she'd be able to do about it.

"No. You will feel a burning sensation tingle through you as your cells are rewritten to slow down your aging to match my lifespan. It will tie us together and you'll feel my...emotions, I guess is the best way to put it. If you focus, you'll feel my beast move within, and you'll sense how it sways my moods. Within minutes, you'll feel the connection with my brothers and Jade. Then it will be over."

"You make it sound like there's nothing to it, when actually this mating is changing my complete cellular make-up."

He turned his head to look at her. "It doesn't take away your personality or anything like that. It makes you better. You'll be tougher, you won't get sick any longer, but most importantly you will be harder to kill. You won't age like the average human, but who wants to do that when you can live so much longer. You'll always be active and full of life. Instead of barely able to get around, in some assisted living home."

"Oh." She rubbed her hands down her arms. "Flames. It feels like soft, warm, flames are licking over my skin and there's a heat burning from within."

"The heat is from the transformation of your cells. They're dying and being born again as new ones, stronger ones. It will pass in a minute." He rubbed a hand down her back.

"It wasn't until just now that I realized I won't be completely human, but I won't be a shifter either. I'll be in between, not really fitting into either group." There was no regret in her tone.

"You'll be a mate, and that makes you one of us. Whether you realized it or not, when you ran from Hathaway Medical you gave up on humanity. They'd have considered you a traitor. It was the first step on your path to me. You chose to make your new life with us, with me, and for that I'll always be thankful."

"There's nowhere else I'd rather be than right here with you." She leaned closer and pressed her lips against his, giving him a quick kiss before pulling back. "Promise you'll come back to me?"

"I promise, my sweet angel."

Patrick dropped his bag by the door where it landed with a thump, and turned toward the main staircase as Clarissa came down. His mate. He still couldn't believe he had convinced her to tie herself to him for all of eternity, but she was his. For now and always.

The mating had done wonders for her. The exhaustion, the dark circles around her eyes caused by her escape, had dissipated. Her pale skin had a healthy glow as if she had spent time in the sun. She was more beautiful than she had been only hours before. All he wanted to do was take her back upstairs, but he had to leave. He wanted to curse his luck, but he knew there were shifters in Hathaway Medical's lab that needed his help, and that had to come before his libido.

"All ready, then?"

He nodded and met her at the bottom of the stairs. "Chase is bringing the SUV around so we'll be ready when Blake is done gathering the explosives he put together this morning."

"I want all of you to be safe, to come home to me." She leaned into him as his arm slipped around her waist. "Especially you."

"We will, don't you worry. We'll be back before you know it." He kissed the top of her head and caught a glimpse of the SUV coming around to the front of the castle. "I hate to leave you while you're still adjusting to this mating."

"I'll be fine. It will take me time to adjust to having the connection with everyone, but it's not so bad. There's like a rope connecting us, channeling your thoughts and emotions to me. It was nerve-wracking at first, but now I can see the positives of it."

"If you focus, you can build walls to help block out some of it. When I get back, I'll help you learn how to channel it. Until then, I'll do my best to help block some of it for you."

She tipped her head back to look at him. "It's fine, I'm fine. I just want you to focus on this mission, so don't worry about me. I knew what I was getting into, and I wouldn't change it."

"I'm ready." Blake came strolling through one of the archways into the main living area, with Jade, Luke, and Austin only a few steps behind. "Sorry, need a few minutes?"

"No, we're just saying our see you soons."

"See you soons?" Jade leaned against the arm of the sofa.

"To say goodbye would make it too final. My family always believed that you should say 'see you soon' instead." Clarissa stepped back and looked up at Patrick. "Because I know he's going to come back to me, uninjured."

"Chase and I will keep him safe." Blake headed for the door. "I'll see you outside."

"I'll be there in a minute." Patrick didn't even turn to him. Instead, he slipped his hand around Clarissa's.

"By the way," Blake called over his shoulder, "Welcome to the family, Clarissa."

"Thank you," she replied, as he shut the door behind him.

"Don't worry about the home front," Austin told Patrick. "You know we'll take care of things." He waved his hand toward the door, urging him out. "Luke has everything backed up from the system, and the CEO of Hathaway Medical, along with two others, have opened their email. Their computers are now infected, so he'll see about gathering more from them while I begin working through the other stuff."

"I'm here if she needs anything," Jade said. "We'll have some girl time while you're gone." She gave Clarissa a huge smile. "It's nice not being the only woman here for a change."

"I have no doubt that each of you will make my mate feel like part of the family, and will keep her safe while I'm gone." He looked down at his mate, and for the first time in his life he felt the pain of leaving. "I'll be back soon, but while I'm gone, if you need anything you let Austin or the others know."

"We'll be fine. Now, the sooner you go, the sooner you'll be home."

"Don't wait up. I'll come find you when I get back." He leaned down and kissed her one last time. Before he pulled away, he wrapped his arms around her, placed his mouth next to her ear, and whispered, "I love you, Clarissa."

After he left, Clarissa made her way up to the lab. She needed something to think about, to get her mind off his last words. He loved her. She knew it wasn't just the connection that was between them, because she had been falling in love with him before the mating took place. Her only hope was that he knew she loved him, too, because before she could respond he had turned on his heels, grabbed his bag and was out the door. She remained stunned by his words.

He'll be back soon, and I can tell him then. In the meantime, she needed to find a countermeasure for LUNA. They had hoped to have one before this mission, but there was no doubt they had to have one by the next one. The world was becoming too dangerous for any of them to go out without something they could use to defend themselves.

A light tap on the door had her looking up from the latest calculations, and she saw Austin standing in the doorway. "Nolan found this in the supply boxes when they delivered LUNA, and he thought it might be of use to us." He strolled toward her with a folded piece of paper in hand.

"Where is Nolan, anyway? I haven't been able to talk to him about LUNA yet."

"He's been trying to locate another Ranger shifter and bring him to safety. All we've gathered so far is that he took off from the base two days before LUNA arrived, but no one has seen or heard from him since."

She took the paper from him and unfolded it. "Do you think this Ranger he's looking for is still alive?"

"I doubt it. He was too much of a live wire." He frowned. "But he was a good Ranger, and he was a pride mate of Nolan's, so he feels honor-bound to find out what happened to him."

"I'm sorry." She glanced down at the paper. There in black and white was the equation she had been trying to work out. The missing piece of the puzzle. "Wait, how did he get this?"

"He just said it was in the supply box. Why?"

"Find him. I need to speak with him."

"You'll need to come downstairs to speak with him," Austin reminded her.

"That's fine." She shoved the pen she had been using in her ponytail and rose from the desk. "Then do you have some time to help me?"

"I'm not a scientist by any means, but I'll do what I can."

She smirked at Austin. "I promise it won't be more than you can handle. I just need additional hands in order to get this done."

"My hands are all yours for as long as you need." As they headed toward the door, he turned toward her. "Am I to assume that whatever was on that paper can help you with LUNA?"

"I believe it just might. Which is why I need to ask him how it came into his possession. The government wouldn't have sent it to any military base. There had to be a reason, and I need to find out why." Even though she could feel the siblings and knew where each of them was, she couldn't stop herself as she glanced down the hallway to make sure they were alone. "Would there be any way a shifter could conceal their real intentions from an Alpha?"

"Do you suspect Nolan is a traitor? That he could have been sent here to spy on us or to lead us into a trap?" Before she could answer, he added, "I've known Nolan for years. He wouldn't do a thing like that. He wouldn't betray his own people for the government. No matter what they offered him."

"You didn't answer my question. Is it possible?"

"Maybe. If an Alpha weren't paying close enough attention to the new member or *any* member for that matter, things could slip past. However, not with Patrick. He's too careful, especially with everything the family has been through." When she took a step away from him, he took hold of her arm to stop her. "If you don't believe me, look for yourself. You're connected to Nolan now, just as you're connected to the rest of us."

"Maybe, but the connection with the rest of you is stronger."

"That because we're of the same blood, now that you've mated with Patrick. But just focus, and you'll know Nolan isn't here to betray us."

She stared pointedly at him, her brow furrowing. "It wasn't me who questioned Nolan's motives, it was you. Is there something you're not telling me, something Patrick and I should know?"

"Shit." He cursed softly enough that she almost questioned if she'd actually heard him.

"Whatever it is, tell me."

"Nolan is a good man and one hell of a Ranger."

"Why do I feel like there's a *but* coming?"

He let out a deep sigh. "He needs a leader. That's why he joined the military. His former Alpha was killed, and the pride went into chaos. They fought amongst themselves. No one took over as Alpha for very long. It was a continual struggle throughout the entire pride before the pride eventually disbanded."

"I'm not sure I follow."

"The trauma that can create is something that can stay with someone. He's seen his family being torn apart, many of them killed...brutally. I don't worry about him right now as much as I will if he finds this former pride mate. We will have to keep a close eye on him to make sure he stays on the straight and narrow. He needs the structure the military gave him, but he needs it from us now. As long as he knows his place, I don't believe we'll ever have any issues with him. But if he ever suspects he can get away with something, I believe he'll take that opportunity. He doesn't have the same moral commitments that most members of a pride have. If he ever steps out of line, I won't give him the chance to take us down. I'll kill him, and he knows that."

"Then it's our job to make sure we give him what he needs so that doesn't happen."

He nodded. "I see you're stepping into your role as the Alpha's mate quickly. It will be one less thing Patrick will have to worry about. He needs a good woman by his side. One who can handle the pressures of his role."

"I'll do my best to make sure he has what he needs, and I will support him in any way I can. I just wish I'd had that formula before he left. I might have been able to give them something so they were more prepared if…" She forced herself not to think about the danger he could be facing. She knew she could drive herself crazy thinking about *what ifs*.

"We'll have it next time. That's when we'll need it. Right now, they shouldn't run into too many issues if any at all. It's when we go after those camps that we really need to worry," he said. "Come on, let's see what Nolan has to say about that document."

She followed after him and tried not to think about the camps. The first one was just outside of Bangor, Maine, but since that memory had returned to her she hadn't had a chance to study the map and recall the rest. It still bothered her the camps had taken a backseat to the labs, LUNA, and everything else. The shifters imprisoned in those camps might be safe, but it did little to ease the guilt of not being able to get them out.

Dean had told her long ago that she cared too much, and that she couldn't save everyone. He had been referring to how hard she worked to find a cure for illnesses, but she could see how it impacted her life now. Her caring might be a downfall in some ways, but if she could save just one person, it was all worth it. The information she had brought to the O'Reillys was about to do that, and more. They were about to take down yet another lab, saving countless lives. Not just those who were already imprisoned there, but those who might have been.

One life saved…so many more to go.

Chapter Fifteen

Clarissa and Austin found Nolan sitting behind a computer in the library. Dark circles shadowed his eyes, clear indicators he hadn't slept in a while. The growth along his chin seemed to suggest he wasn't himself. After over ten years in the military, she highly doubted Nolan could just fall back into a routine of not shaving daily. She suspected it was more likely due to the search for his former pride mate. Everything about him suggested he was on edge, and that one push might send him over the brink. They would have to watch him closely.

"Nolan, we need to have a word with you concerning that paper you gave me."

"Not now," he snapped, not bothering to look up at Austin. "I'm busy."

"Yes, now. I don't care what you're doing, it's not as important as finding a protection against LUNA. None of us will be able to leave this castle if we don't find something…and soon."

Clarissa felt a hint of rage from Austin as she sat down across from the desk. "I understand you're looking for a friend—"

"A brother," he growled before she could finish.

"We've opened our home to you, supported your decision to search for him, and we've asked very little from you so far," Clarissa pointed out.

"Now, I just have a few questions, and we'll let you get back to your search."

With a huff, Nolan leaned back in the chair and stared across the desk at her. She recognized the challenge in his eyes and refused to back down. She met his rock hard gaze with one of her own, leaning slightly forward in the chair to let him know she was serious. If he thought he was going to intimidate her, then he was wrong.

When his gaze lowered, she smirked and leaned back. Win one for her, but there was no doubt in her mind it was the first of many more to come. "We appreciate that you were able to access the LUNA samples, especially since you brought us multiple injections. It will help us find something we can use against it."

"So you said."

"Nolan," Austin growled.

She crossed her legs and just watched him for a moment. "I'm quickly growing tired of your attitude. This is not how you treat someone who has opened up their pride and home to you. You treat them with respect, and you respect those who are in charge. With all the years you've spent in the military, I would have thought you'd understand how the chain of command works. However, if we need to go through an update on just what is expected of you, I'd gladly arrange it."

"I believe you're straying from the point." Nolan adjusted in his seat.

"Actually, that's part of the point. I'm Patrick's mate, and I demand the same respect you'd give him if he were sitting before you."

His eyebrow rose in question. "For a human you seem to have our customs down pretty well. Especially a human who only a short time ago stood against us. How Patrick could accept this mating is beyond me. He should have had more sense and fought it instead of being tied to you." Every word he spoke was laced with disgust, but it didn't faze Clarissa.

"Patrick and I are mated, so it entitles me to his knowledge." She let out a deep breath, and tried to stop herself from reaching over the desk and smacking him for his last comment. Neither did she give in to his baiting, instead, she let his comment slide off her and marked it up to his stress.

Austin stepped up next to her chair. "I brought you here because I believed you would be an asset to us and our fight. I don't know what's happened over the years since I left the Army, but you have changed. I won't have you insulting Clarissa or my family. Unless you know what you're talking about, you should just keep your mouth shut."

"I know plenty."

"You know gossip, and you judge me based on what my former employer did. You don't know who I am or what I've done. How would you like it if I judged you against all the military and blamed you for the deaths of your comrades? Not really fair, now is it?" She paused for a moment, but he didn't answer. "My point is, I never had any part in what went on at Hathaway Medical. At least, not like you believe. I was there as a scientist, but I never took part in any of the experiments they conducted. I only worked there for two weeks."

"When she found out what they were doing, she left," Austin added. "Patrick and Blake found her while she was running from them."

"A scientist, huh?" The disbelief was clear in Nolan's voice. "Then what did they recruit you for? Because I know for a fact that the military was trying to get you to work for them, and instead you went to Hathaway."

"You're right. I had entertained a job offer with the military, but I thought I would be able to do more at Hathaway Medical. When I accepted the position, I was supposed to work on finding a cure for cancer." She crossed her legs and leaned back in the chair. "All these years, we've been able to cure this disease or that one, but never cancer. It was the one thing I worked toward, and it's the reason I became a scientist."

"Then you were with the wrong company."

She nodded. "Hindsight, but I didn't know at the time. Not everyone who works at Hathaway Medical knows about what happens in the lab, or about the shifters who are hidden away down below. If I had taken the position with the military, I wouldn't have witnessed what I did, but…then again, I might not have met Patrick and the rest of the O'Reilly family."

He shook his head, seeming disbelieving of her claim, his arms folded on the desk. "How could you not know what goes on in there?"

"I worked there for two weeks," she said. "I was just settling in, working, making friends, and basically enjoying it." Uneasy, she fought the urge to adjust her positioning in her chair. She didn't want him to see how uncomfortable she was. "It wasn't until they wanted me to take part in an experiment that I found out what they were doing. I was appalled. Part of me wanted to run down to where they were kept, and do something about it then and there, but I knew it would only get me killed. It wouldn't help them. After giving my boss an excuse to get out of it, I made it back to my office to gather what I could. I wasn't sure who I was going to go to with the information I had, but I knew there must be someone out there trying to stand against what was happening, and I decided to find them."

"See what I mean?" Austin placed his hand on her shoulder, giving it a reassuring squeeze. "So, before you go judging someone, maybe you should take a few minutes to actually find out their story. Not everything is as black or white as you'd like to think."

"She still worked for one of the companies that are torturing our kind." Nolan defended his stance, but now his argument seemed halfhearted.

"And you worked for the government," Austin pointed out. "They're the ones who are behind this. Your branch might not be playing an active role in it now, but turn on the news and you'll see soldiers guarding the camps, capturing shifters. If you're going to blame her just because of her association with Hathaway Medical, then you're going to need to look in the mirror because you'd be just as guilty."

It was clear they weren't going to get through to Nolan just yet, and they were wasting time. When Patrick returned, he'd have to have a long conversation with him and make sure Nolan understood his place if he were going to stay there. Otherwise, it was better to cut their loss before he did something stupid and got them all hurt. "Due to your attitude, we got off track," Clarissa said. "I came down here to speak to you about that paper you gave Austin. How did you get it?"

"How?" He shrugged. "I grabbed it from the box."

"You know that's not what she meant," Austin growled his impatience showing. "That's a confidential file. How did you get your hands on it?"

"Why was it sent to your base to begin with?" she added before he had time to answer.

"Because they're one of the bases that will begin production on the stuff," Nolan said as if they should have already known.

"What?" Austin stepped forward and placed his hands on the desk. "You didn't think this was something you should have told me when you got here?"

"Sorry if I was preoccupied trying to save someone that actually needs my help, instead of thinking about fucking LUNA."

She spent the next twenty minutes gathering every bit of information she could about what the base was doing, and how LUNA was going to be produced and distributed. She repeated her questions in different ways just to make sure she was getting everything she could from him. In the end, Nolan seemed to know very little about any of it, only that they were starting production the following week, and it would be round the clock.

Even after questioning him with Austin's help, she still couldn't stop the nagging feeling that he had some other nugget of information they hadn't been able to get out of him. Neither of them wanted to find out there was something else he was hiding. By the time they stepped out of the library, she was ready to throttle the man. He had worked his way under her skin until she thought she was going to climb over that desk just to get at him.

"You handled that well," Austin told her once they had put some distance between them and the library.

"That's so unlike me." She waited until they were past the kitchen where Jade was busy making something that smelled truly delicious. From the hints in the air, Clarissa would have guessed there was a roast in the oven and fresh apple pie cooling on the counter. The scent had her stomach yearning for a bite. "He tried to dominate me with his gaze," she added as an afterthought.

"You didn't let him."

"I know. But I've always been more of a loner, doing whatever I needed to avoid fighting with someone. Submissive, if that helps you understand what I'm trying to say. But now…"

"You are an Alpha's mate, and that changes you. A submissive mate would be no good to a pride. I know you can feel his beast within you, and that's giving you the strength to be the woman he needs by his side." He touched her arm. "I don't think there was ever anything submissive about you."

"I ran when I knew what was happening at Hathaway Medical. Isn't that enough proof?"

He shook his head. "That's only proof that you're smart. You knew you couldn't handle it on your own, and that you were no help to anyone dead.

You're a strong woman, and you're becoming stronger because of the mating. That's what all of us need. Especially Patrick."

Hathaway Medical was just like all the other medical buildings Patrick had been in. The first floor had all the labs one would expect, with offices on the top floors. But this building had a secret lab hidden underground. That's where the danger and horrors waited for any unsuspecting person who happened to stumble upon it. They had done their best to keep those unwanted intruders out, with high-tech security at every door. Luke had given each of them a security card, and a homemade jammer to guarantee they'd get through every layer.

Blake was outside setting up the explosives, so they could blow the place sky high when they finished. Chase had continued farther down the hall with Andrew in search of any surviving captives. Meanwhile, Patrick had headed to Doctor Songborn's office. He was in charge down here in the basement, and he was also the one referenced in the file concerning the experiments on children. If they were going to find anything, it would be locked away in his office. Patrick only hoped he could do it in time.

Entering the office, he glanced around at the clutter. First impressions said a lot, but the biggest thing he noted was Doctor Songborn didn't like technology. Even though there was a computer sitting on the desk, there was a thin layer of dust coating it, and stuff stacked on top of it. The half empty cup of what had once been coffee, but now appeared to be sludge, sat on top of the ancient desktop. There would be nothing on the computer worth wasting time on. Anything of interest would be on paper.

Behind the desk was a lone bookshelf, mostly holding medical books, but there were a few personal articles. As Patrick rifled through them, he discovered nothing that shed any light on a life outside the office. This guy appeared to be a workaholic, and Patrick had less than twenty minutes to go through the mess in order to find the file he needed. Anything that might be important, he'd stick in his bag to examine later, but the file on the child they'd experimented on was the most important thing.

He rubbed his hands together and dug into the stack of papers on the desk. It was unlikely the file was there, but the mess before him was what the doctor had been working on recently, and therefore it was important. He'd scan it quickly before tossing it into the bag he had on the chair while he got into the man's head and figured out where he'd have put such confidential files. This was information even someone with the highest level of clearance wouldn't have access to. Experimenting on a child would be something they'd want very few people to know about.

He skimmed through most of the stuff on the desk when a line on the wall caught his attention. It was almost like a seam. Without scanning the final stack of papers, he tossed them into his bag and stepped toward it. He ran his finger along it, tracing the outline of the seam as he tried to determine if there were any booby-traps waiting for him if he opened the hidden door. If he had Blake down here with him, he would have known for sure, but he just had to take a guess that anything behind this door was too important to risk blowing up.

He placed his finger in the groove near the top and in one quick step backward he pulled it open. If anything was going to explode or fall on him, he wanted to make sure he was back a few paces. It might not save him, but it sure as hell would help protect him somewhat.

When the door swung open and nothing happened, he stepped forward. Inside the narrow doorway was a filing cabinet. This was what the doctor wanted hidden, and it was most likely what Patrick was looking for. If he were going to find the file, it would be here. Now he just had to find it.

He stepped forward and grabbed hold of the handle on the first drawer. It was locked, but instead of wasting time looking for the key, he just pulled harder and the drawer slid from the cabinet with ease. Sometimes it paid to be a shifter and have superhuman strength. He skimmed the tabs to each of the files, but nothing jumped out at him. But what was he expecting it to say, *child shifter experiment one?* No. Doctor Songborn would have been smarter about it. He'd have used a code word that meant something to him.

"I'm set up out here. How's things going?" Blake's voice came through Patrick's earpiece.

"I believe I found his hidden files. Shouldn't be long now." He might have sounded a little more optimistic than he felt, but he wanted to be done here and get back to Clarissa. After they toasted the place, they still had to get the captives somewhere safe since they had agreed none of them would be coming back to the castle. There was still a lot of work to do. Austin had set up a safe house for them, but they'd have to transport any survivors there before Patrick and the others could return home.

"Chase?" Blake called for an update when none came.

"Umm...I..." Chase's words trailed off, leaving a hint of horror echoing in Patrick's ears.

"Update now, Chase," he ordered as he dug through the files. He tossed most of them in the bag as he realized they weren't what he was looking for.

"They're dead...every one of them. Dead." Chase paused before adding, "We were too late."

"This isn't our fault. You know that." Blake tried to comfort him.

"We had to wait until we got everything off their system. It's going to help us save others." Patrick grabbed the next drawer and found journals. Instead of looking at them, he tossed them directly in the bag and moved on to the last drawer.

"Yeah, but…at the cost of those who were here." The repulsion in Chase's tone had been replaced with an unmistakable melancholy.

"How did they know?" Blake asked. "There's no way they could have known we were coming or we'd have walked directly into a trap."

"There's an order form," Chase said. "Shit, I can't believe I just said that—for more shifters. They've classified the ones held here as no longer of any use and…they were to be disposed of." Fury heated Chase's words. "It's not like taking out the trash. You can't just dispose of one of us, we're fucking people. With families who care about us and lives we want to live. Hopes and dreams—"

"Focus, Chase," Patrick ordered. "We knew what they were doing here, what the government is doing. That's why we're doing what we're doing. Now, keep it together."

"Does it say when the new batch is supposed to arrive?" Blake questioned.

There was a shuffling of papers before Chase answered. "No. Hell, what are they going to do with the ones they've captured for here? Kill them, too?"

"I doubt it." Patrick grabbed the last handful of files from the drawer when something caught his attention. "I suspect they'll send them to another lab or back to one of the shifter camps."

Blake picked up on what Patrick said first. "Back? You believe they're taking shifters from the camps and bringing them to the labs?"

"It's a possibility, one Luke and I have found little to confirm, but we're trying." He pulled out the file that caught his attention, and he didn't like the fact the folder was easily an inch thick. It hinted at too many experiments. Too many deaths. He pulled back the cover and a blonde infant with the bluest eyes he'd ever seen stared up at him from the first page. Bile rose in his throat, and he repressed the urge to void his dinner. "Chase. Finish looking through things down there, and then I want you and Andrew to get up here. I need some help with what I've found."

"There's not much here. I've grabbed the hard drives from two of the computers and a laptop just in case there's anything on it Luke didn't find. Other than that, there's nothing."

"Drug cabinet?"

"Yeah, why?"

"Empty it into a bag and bring it. We might need something that's here if we're going to find something to counteract LUNA. Anything you find that might help, take it, but do so in the next five minutes." Patrick rose from the floor and leaned against the edge of the desk, clutching his stomach. "Blake, we'll be there within ten. Stand by."

"You found it, didn't you?"

He didn't answer Blake as he flipped through the pages. The little girl he'd seen when he opened the folder hadn't been the first, but she had been the only survivor. "I got what we came for and more."

"Tell me it's not true." The sound of glass shattering as he broke the medicine cabinet followed Chase's heated words.

"I'll know more once I've had time to go over things. Now, get a move on." Patrick's stomach churned, and he wanted to kill Doctor Songborn. To make him pay for what he'd done to these children and their families. His lion wanted to tear him limb from limb and bathe in his blood. Instead of letting his anger bring his beast forward, he rose and shoved the file into his personal bag.

Once he had time to go over the information, only then would he tell the others what he'd found. Until then, he'd keep it safely hidden away. He'd protect his family whenever he could. It wasn't just his role as Alpha, it was the bond and love they had for each other. While his brothers knew about the possibility of a human child being experimented on, he had decided to shield Jade from it until they were certain.

Especially Jade. Because he knew it would break her heart.

Chapter Sixteen

The castle was quiet. Everyone had gone to bed hours ago, but Clarissa remained in the lab. With Nolan's information, she believed she had been able to find a counteragent to LUNA, but the only way to test it was to inject it into someone. She stared down at the vial of pale blue liquid and almost wished she hadn't found it. The endless possibilities of things that could go wrong rushed through her thoughts, each one worse than the last.

How could she let one of them test it? She couldn't risk it, especially now that she had come to care for each of them. They had accepted her into their family, and for that she would always be grateful. She knew right away that if she were wrong, this drug could kill. That was a risk she wasn't willing to take.

"What are you still doing up?"

She shuffled her papers to cover the vial and glanced up. Austin stood in the doorway, slipping his coat on.

"Thinking," she said, hoping her anxiety wasn't clear in her voice. "What's going on?"

"They're pulling up the driveway now. I was heading down to carry in the stuff they brought with them. Care to accompany me, or would you rather wait here for Patrick?"

She hopped off her chair. "I didn't expect him until closer to morning."

He smirked. "It's just before five. Please don't tell me you've been in here all night…"

"I haven't." She tried, but the lie failed. "Okay, maybe I have."

"Did you actually get something done, or were you just worrying about what will happen when one of us takes that drug of yours?" he asked as they headed for the steps.

"I'm so glad they're back." She sped her pace a little, but Austin matched it, keeping in stride with her.

"That would be the worst sidestep around a question on record. You know Patrick isn't going to be very happy that those circles under your eyes are showing again. He worries about you. You haven't been together long, and if you're looking like this on his first trip out, he'll only worry more next time."

"This had nothing to do with the mission," she insisted, even though it wasn't completely the truth. She had tried to sleep but when she climbed into bed it felt so lonely that she'd gotten up and gone to the lab. "I knew he was safe."

"Knowing he's safe isn't the point. It's only natural for you to worry about him." He paused as they neared the front door. "Don't tell him, but I do, too. He's our Alpha, but no matter what he thinks he's not invincible. The rest of us should be the ones leading the missions. His place is here, ruling the pride, not out there risking himself."

"He's not a man who would ask someone to do something he isn't willing to do himself." She turned to look at him in the faint glow of dawn. "Can you honestly see him ruling from the safety of these walls? As much as it frightens me, I know he needs the action."

"I'm glad he found a woman like you. You'll keep him grounded, support him, and yet still knock some sense into him when he needs it."

The front door swung open, and Patrick entered. "What happened, Austin? I thought you were going to meet us outside." When he caught sight of her, he dropped the bag he was carrying and took two steps forward before sweeping her off her feet. "My beautiful angel, how I've missed you."

"I'm so glad you're back."

"Oh, angel, I'm back and ready to roar." He held her tight, only tipping his head slightly toward Austin. "Go help the others with the bags, then tell them to get some rest. I want all the bags in my office upstairs. I'll begin working through them in the morning."

"Did you find…"

He nodded. "I've got it in my bag. I'll look over what I found once I have a proper reunion with my mate. I'll touch base with you on it later, and have Luke standing by in case I need him to begin a search."

"I can wait if you need to…" Before she could finish, he pressed a finger to her lips.

"No, it's time I get reacquainted with my mate and her divine body." He loosened his grip on her and stepped back to grab his bag before taking her hand and leading her up the stairs. "Before I get carried away, you can tell me what has you so stressed that you've stayed up all night. Was it this mission?"

"No, but I'm glad you're home." They climbed the steps and she smiled as she considered her comment on *home*. She had been on her own for years. A small loft was all she could afford as she worked her way up the corporate ladder. But now, for the first time in a long time, she felt like she was home, especially in his arms, and damn did she love it.

"LUNA?" His voice held a twinge of doubt. "You couldn't have found anything. I wasn't even gone twenty-four hours."

"Nolan handed me the answer, but we can't use it. What if it's wrong?

What if I screwed up? It could kill someone. We need to test it, but I can't test it. How can I use something I can't test?" She wanted to scream and fight. After all the hard work they'd done to find something to use against the government, she had the answer but refused to use it.

"Let's go upstairs and discuss it later. But I promise you, it's going to be okay."

"How?" she demanded. "To know if something works, it has to be tested, but we don't have a test subject."

He remained silent until he climbed the last staircase and punched in the code into the keypad to open the door to the family's personal floor. "I'll test it."

"You'll what?" With her hand still in his, she balked as he tried to lead her forward. "Tell me you didn't…"

Since she gave him no choice but to pause or drag her down the hallway, he stopped. "As you said, we need someone we can test this on. That will be me."

"No way. Absolutely not. I won't allow it." She kept shaking her head as if her words were not enough to get her point across.

"There's no other option. If we don't have something we can use, then we're defenseless against LUNA every time we go out. There would come a time that we wouldn't be able to go out at all. Think of all the people we could save but wouldn't be able to."

"No…not you." She didn't want him to risk himself. Not when she wasn't sure what could happen. "What would Austin say? The rest of your brothers? Jade?"

"I'm Alpha here, not them. It doesn't matter what they say. It's my job to protect them. I won't have one of them testing this. If we're going to use it, then I'll test it to make sure it's safe first."

206

She pulled her hand from his. "Then lead them. Don't go getting yourself killed."

"What's this about you getting yourself killed?" Luke stepped out of his room, a pair of loose pajama pants slung low on his hips, his chest bare.

"Nothing, go back to bed," Patrick snapped without even looking back at him.

"No, Luke, stay," Clarissa said. "Maybe you can knock some sense into your brother since I can't."

Luke's gaze slid over both of them before shaking his head. "A quarrel already? He just got home, shouldn't you two newly mated lovers be in bed making up for lost time?"

"Patrick is planning on testing the LUNA counteragent on himself." She could tell from the way he glared at her that he hadn't wanted her to tell Luke.

"You should let one of us do that." When Patrick turned to glare at his brother, he paused before adding, "You might not be happy with what I'm about to say, but here it is anyway. You're our Alpha, you don't take risks like that."

"Actually, it's just the opposite. I won't risk one of you until I know it's safe. Now that's the end of this discussion." He turned on his heels and headed down the hall toward his room.

"Patrick, wait," she called after him, but he barely slowed his pace.

"I'm going to take a shower."

"We need to talk about this." She glanced at Luke when Patrick didn't stop.

"Go after him." He nodded down the hall. "Just like for you, this is all new to him. He's our Alpha which means no one questions his orders. But you're his mate, so make him understand. If anyone can get through to him, it's you."

"I doubt I'll change his mind." As she strolled the rest of the way down the hall toward Patrick's bedroom, she debated hiding what she'd found, but the consequences of that were almost as disastrous. Without the counteragent, if one of them were caught out in the open by someone who had gotten their hands on LUNA, they'd stand no chance. They'd be captured or killed and that would be her fault. She couldn't live with that any more than she could live with putting the man she loved in danger by letting him test the drug on himself.

She pushed open his bedroom door only to find a trail of clothes leading to the bathroom. Making her way across the room, she couldn't stop herself from picking up the garments. Her thoughts remained on how she could convince him that it was too dangerous to turn himself into a test subject. She loved him, so she just couldn't stand by and let him put himself in danger.

As she neared the bathroom's open door, she could hear the rainfall shower head, and the faint scent of his woodsy body wash drifted toward her. There was something about the scent that fit him perfectly. The rough, manly aroma suited him on more than one level.

Through the glass enclosure, she could see him. His back faced her as he dipped his head into the water and soaked his shoulder length hair. He dragged his fingers through the wet strands and grabbed a bottle from the tiled wall along the back of the shower. Before she realized what she was doing, she was out of her clothes. Her fingers closed over the cool metal door handle as her desire rushed forward, rising within her, urging her to touch him.

She slipped into the shower without waiting for an invitation, and still he stood with his back to her under the shower head, soap running down his body. Even though he didn't turn around, his back muscles tightened. For a moment, she stood there wondering if she shouldn't have waited until he had emerged from the shower. It would have allowed for both of their tempers to cool. Her gaze trailed down his body, watching the way the soap bubbles slid along his skin before racing down the drain. Finally, she threw caution to the wind and stepped closer, giving into her temptation, running her hands up his slippery back.

"I knew you'd see reason and join me." He leaned back, letting the water run through his hair. Then he turned to face her. "Damn, I believe you've gotten more beautiful since I left."

"I didn't join you because I've seen your reasoning and changed my mind. I joined you because I missed you."

He advanced on her and pushed her against the cool glass wall, grasping her wrists with one hand and holding them above her head. "I'm Alpha here, and my word is law."

"You turn me on when you go all dominant on me." She wished her hands were free so she could run them over his body, feel the tight muscles as he barely held on to his temper.

"It's who I am."

"No, Patrick, that's where you're wrong." Unwilling to back down, she stared into his heat-filled eyes. "You're so much more than that. You're a lover, a brother, a fighter, and you care."

"You have no idea…"

"You're right. I might not have any idea how the shifter world works, or the hierarchy, but I know you. I know your family." Since his grip loosened, she pulled her wrists free and slipped away from him. The scalding water hit her full blast, but she didn't step out of the spray; instead, she took it as her heart cracked. "While you might be a natural leader and an Alpha, you're more than that. If you don't realize that, maybe I made a mistake." She placed a hand on the shower door to push it open, and he stopped her.

"I told you before that mating isn't something you can go back on. You can't file for a divorce or dissolve it once it has taken place."

"I never said you could. But if you can't see that you're more than just an Alpha and that your family needs you as more than just their leader, then I don't really know you."

His hand dropped away from her wrist. "What do you want from me?"

"Maybe this happened too fast for both of us because it doesn't seem like you know me either." She started for the door again, but he was on her within the blink of an eye. He wrapped his arm around her waist, stopping her from moving away from him.

"Oh, angel, I know you." He slid his free hand down her body, then between her legs. "I know if I touch you…" He paused as his finger glided between her folds and the tip of his index finger brushed over her clit. "Just here, that you melt into my embrace."

"This is more than us being sexually compatible." Even as she said it and fought against it, her body responded. He knew just where to touch her to make her feel like her world was exploding.

"It's important." He nibbled along the curve of her collarbone. "I've missed you."

"This fight isn't over."

"I have no doubt, angel. No doubt at all." His teeth grazed along the base of her neck, applying just a little pressure before easing back. "Right now, I want you. I don't want to fight with you about anything. Remember, you're supposed to be welcoming me home."

She pushed her thoughts away and just let herself feel. She gave in to the temptation of his touch. They'd make the most of the time they had, and deal with everything else as it came. "Oh, Patrick. I've missed you."

"Me too, my angel." He crushed his mouth to hers.

As his tongue explored her mouth, he thrust his finger into her, heat erupting at his touch, spreading through her like lava after a volcano eruption. She felt his lion come forward, moving within both of them as if they were one, purring within her as if she too was a shifter. Her legs weakened, but he braced her against the wall, keeping her on her feet, as he continued to pound into her until fierce desire poured through her.

"Take me," she murmured against his mouth, holding onto him as wild delight streamed through her.

He grazed her lower lip with his teeth and pulled his hand away. She cried out in frustration and arched toward him, but he ignored her demands. Gripping her hips, he lifted her until she was off the tiled floor. The only thing keeping her upright was his body pressed against hers.

"Wrap your legs around my waist."

Not that she needed to, but she used her hands on his shoulders to keep her balanced while she did as he asked. His body shielded her from most of the scalding spray of the shower, but he was warming her in other ways.

He leaned forward and claimed her mouth while he adjusted his shaft and drove into her with one powerful thrust. She moaned against his unrelenting kiss, her fingers tangled in his hair, as she pushed against him to meet his body. With every thrust, he increased his speed, slamming his shaft home with each pump. Her body arched toward him, propelling his shaft deeper and harder within her. All the while she could feel his lion purring within them, the vibrations from it sending a whole new wave of desire through her.

Where their last lovemaking had been sweet, this was hot and full of need. It sparked a new sensation inside of her that she had never experienced. She had grown in confidence and knew what to expect, so she was as eager as him, meeting each thrust and kiss with passion and need instead of hesitation.

He left her mouth, feathering kisses along her collarbone. She locked her arms around his neck as every pump of his hips sent pulses of pleasure exploding throughout her. She tightened her legs around him as he groaned and shoved himself deeper inside her. The pressure built within her until her body trembled and another orgasm rushed through her. She held onto him as he slammed home in a frenzy. A climax tour through her with such force her body shook. Her inner muscles clenched around him as he continued to drive into her. He bit the fleshy part of her shoulder, applying just enough pressure that there was pleasure to it, as he thrust into her one final time and he too climaxed.

She held onto him as they both tried to regain their bearings. Her head rested against his shoulder, and she realized how much she loved him. It wasn't just the mating, it was so much more than that.

"My mate." He growled. "I love you."

She smirked, and he rose an eyebrow in question. "I was thinking the same thing."

"Really, now? Maybe you just love me for my body."

"That's just a bonus." She cupped the side of his face. "Oh, Patrick, I want you for more than just the amazing sex. I love you."

Laughing, he kissed her once more and held her there for a long while until the water cooled.

Chapter Seventeen

Patrick stood by the picture window, looking out over the grounds. The sun hung low in the sky, casting a warm glow, as the wind blew the snow around, making it dance across the icy ground. At least there was no precipitation forecasted for the next twenty-four hours. Austin had a chance to give Andrew a training lesson. Like everyone else, Andrew would be expected to pull his weight now that he was at the castle. That included day to day activities as well as missions that required their attention.

He rolled his shoulder and tried to calm the rage coursing through him. The mission had gone better than he'd expected but now he was thankful to be home and back with his mate. He had looked over the file he found on the human child experiment, and it angered him enough that he wasn't sure he could keep his beast in check.

"Patrick." Clarissa called to him, her soft voice laced with sleep.

"I'm here. Go back to sleep."

"Come back to bed." She leaned up on her elbow and glanced toward him.

"I can't sleep. I need to talk to Austin."

"What's wrong?"

He turned back to the window and tried to banish the images he conjured in his thoughts. He didn't need to picture the little girl Hathaway Medical had used. Or the pictures of the girl's mother as she held her daughter. The pleading letter she'd written to Doctor Songborn, begging him to spare her daughter.

"No." She glared at him, begging him to deny it. The look in her eyes was enough to make him realized he hadn't shielded her from their connection enough. She *knew*. While he automatically shielded his siblings from his thoughts, he hadn't considered their connection and how she would pick up on it. The mating bond was still so unfamiliar to him. "Please tell me they didn't. After I left? I could have stopped it."

He stepped away from the window and went to her. "No, angel, you're not to blame."

"I should have stopped them."

"They had already begun testing on her when you were hired, and by the time you found out what Hathaway Medical was doing, they had already finished."

"Is she…" She took a deep breath before finally finishing her question. "Dead?"

"I don't know." It angered him to admit it, but it was the truth. He'd have Luke search for them but until they found something it would be a question that clung to him. He couldn't get the little girl out of his thoughts. Every time he closed his eyes, he could see her and those blue eyes that seemed to jump from the picture and pierce his heart.

"Then call Austin and Luke in here and get them started. If she's alive, then we need to find her and her poor parents."

"Mother. The father was the one who worked for Hathaway Medical, and when he threatened to expose them, they killed him and used his daughter for their twisted experiments."

"All the more reason to find them now." She slipped out of bed, pulling the sheet with her, to keep the chill from her naked body. "Go find them and get them started on the search. Then maybe you can get some sleep."

"No sleep for the weary." He pulled her into his arms and was tempted to tug the sheet away but stopped himself. "I'm going to look over your discoveries on LUNA, we're going to test it, and then I'm going to help the others working through some of the files I brought back with us."

"I thought we had the discussion about LUNA last night."

"We did, but you're stubborn and wouldn't listen." He ran his hand up her back. "I'm testing it, and there's nothing more to say about it."

"I can't let you."

"Why, because you doubt the counteragent you've come up with?" When she just looked at him, he shook his head. "I didn't think so. You're scared, and I understand that, but it's my duty. You can fight me if you wish, but it won't get you anywhere. I'll have Austin help me with it, but I would prefer if you were there."

"So I can see you die if I'm wrong?"

"There will be no dying." He leaned back to look down at her. "Everything is going to be fine. I have complete faith in you and I don't doubt for a minute that you've already checked the results under a microscope. This is the next phase, and we both know that."

"Why does it have to be you?"

"Can you really see me standing aside while one of my siblings risks themselves?" He answered the question with his own. "I would not let Austin or one of the others do this in my place."

She tucked a lock of hair behind her ear and shook her head. "I just don't want anything to happen to you."

"Nothing will." Before she could argue, he leaned down and kissed her.

If Clarissa thought the day before had been long and stressful, it was nothing like the day she was having now. Patrick, Austin, and Luke had been locked away in Patrick's upstairs office most of the day, searching for the child while she had been in the lab. Over and over she checked LUNA and the counteragent, but every time she came up with the same results. *It should work.* Even with the same test results each time, it didn't ease the rising terror within her.

"It's time." Patrick leaned against the doorframe.

"I'm begging you to reconsider."

"Everything is going to be fine." He stepped farther into the lab, and Austin entered a second later.

"What's Austin doing here?"

"To guarantee your safety." Patrick came to stand next to her, brushing his hand along her arm. "It's just a precaution. None of us have ever been shot with LUNA before, so we don't know how our beast will react to it. If my beast becomes out of control, you're to get out of here and he'll administer the counteragent."

"This just becomes more and more dangerous." She placed the syringe she had prepared aside. "Austin, could you give us a few minutes?"

"I'll be in the hall whenever you're ready." He stepped into the hallway and closed the door, giving them a little more privacy.

"I don't want to argue with you about this again. It is what it is, and if you can't do it then Austin will."

She forced herself to take a deep breath. "That's not why I asked him to give us a minute. Shit…" She rose from the chair and strolled toward the window. "I'm trying to be understanding, to accept the fact you're used to ruling and having everyone just fall in line. But this…" She paused, trying to decide on the best word for what was between them. "This relationship…it's more than just you ordering and me falling into line."

"I never doubted you'd be a challenge far beyond anything I could imagine. You're a feisty, free spirited woman and that's part of why I love you. You'll make sure all the years ahead of us are never dull."

"As much as I don't want you to do this, I understand why you must, but if anything happens to you…"

He cupped the side of her face while his thumb traced the curve of her cheekbone. "My sweet angel, I love you and everything is going to be fine."

"You say it, but I can feel the undercurrent of concern. Your beast is on edge, pacing within you. You're as nervous about this as I am."

"I've looked over everything you have and I don't see any reason this shouldn't work. I have confidence in it, and in you. This is going to work." He pressed her tight against his body and held her. "I realize this is all still new to you. It's a learning curve, but we're going to get through it. You'll come to accept and love my dominant ways."

She couldn't stop the rumbling in her chest as it quickly blossomed into full-fledged laughter. "I don't know about that."

"What do you mean?"

She tipped her head back to look at him. "A relationship is supposed to be give and take. If you're thinking you can control me like one of the members of your pride, you're delusional. You're going to need to learn how to take my feelings, my wants, and my needs into consideration."

"Angel, I already do. Part of being an Alpha is doing that. Anything I do is always in the best interest of you and our pride."

She tried not to think there might be times when her wants came second to the pride. He'd have to please the majority, and hopefully she wouldn't get tossed to the side in the process. Every relationship had sacrifices. Maybe this one was hers, but as long as he tried to balance things between his duty to the pride and to her, she'd accept him. There were always other ways he could make it up to her.

Before her thoughts started to turn erotic, she nodded toward the door. "Go get him and let's get this over with."

"Tonight I'll reward you for being brave and for your work in finding this." With a quick kiss to the top of her head, he stepped away.

She'd hold him to his promise…if they managed to make it through this in one piece. He'd be spending a lot of time making her forget the fear that had settled into her shoulder muscles since he announced that he'd test the counteragent. He'd have to show her just how much she meant to him, and then maybe she could put this behind them. At least, that was the reason she'd use to get some quality alone time with him. Just the two of them.

Clarissa was right about one thing, Patrick was concerned about the testing—more than he'd let on. His beast wouldn't settle and had been restless since he'd made the decision. Now he just wanted to get it over with, and quickly. The doctor side of him knew things would be fine, that the trials she'd done and the figures were all as good as they could get. Unlike a new drug, there wasn't a lab rat they could test it on, so he had to be the test subject.

"What do you need from me?" Austin leaned against the corner of a desk.

"Clarissa's got LUNA in a syringe." He placed his hand over hers. "The announcement about LUNA says that it will force a shifter to transition within sixty seconds of the dart. So, I'll have the second syringe with the counteragent in hand. I'm going to do my best to wait as long as possible to inject myself so we can determine how long we'd have in order to do it."

"If this was happening in public and we were being given LUNA by the military, police, or everyday citizens, we're not going to be able to give ourselves an injection to hold off the effects," Austin pointed out.

She nodded. "Good point, but I believe this will work for approximately twenty-four hours from the time of injection. Patrick wants to test it this way so that we'll know how long you'd have before you would have to take the counteragent."

"Also, since none of us are sure how LUNA will affect us, we'll test it completely. Once we know it works, we can test it at different intervals after we've taken the counteragent."

Austin nodded. "There's no way you can put your beast through all of this. You'll have to let us help."

"We'll see." When Austin continued to stare at him, Patrick nodded. "Once we know this works and there's no danger to anyone else, we can test on you, Luke, Blake, or Chase to see how long the drug would withstand the effects from LUNA. However, Jade will have no part in this, and until we know how well this works, it stays within the family. Not a word to Nolan or Andrew."

"She won't like that you're protecting her and not allowing her to do her duty for the family."

He nodded, knowing Austin was right, but it didn't change anything. "I'll deal with her if need be. She's been through enough. I won't put her though anything more. We won't use her to test this, end of story."

"I agree. I'm only saying that she's going to be livid." Austin rubbed his hands together. "Well, let's do this."

"If anything happens, I want you to make sure Clarissa gets out of here." He squeezed his mate's hand. "I don't know how LUNA will affect the beast, and I don't want her hurt if things get out of hand."

"She'll be fine."

She pulled her hand from his. "I'm right here and I can take care of myself."

"No doubt, my angel, but I'm your mate and it's my job to protect you. Now, you promised you'd listen to Austin if things don't go as planned. If you're going back out on that, we can do this without you and you can join Jade downstairs."

"I'm not going to back out of anything, but I'll be damned if I'll stand by while you treat me like a wilting flower. I'm not breakable." There was a fire in her eyes as she glared at him.

"Angel, you're very breakable when it comes to an out of control shifter."

"Don't sweat it too much, Clarissa, even other shifters are rarely a match for Alphas." Austin shoved his hands into the front pockets of his jeans. "They have a power, strength, and will unlike the rest of us. It's what makes them who they are. They have the pride's strength within them, and those with large prides will have more of it behind them."

"It's not so much about the size, but the unity and harmony of the pride. If the pride is divided, even slightly, it can break that connection the Alpha has, and make him more vulnerable."

"That might be the case, but either I'm a part of this...family...pride...or whatever you want to call it, or I'm not. If I am, then you need to treat me as if I am." She crossed her arms over her chest.

"That's what I'm doing. Didn't you just hear me tell him that we'd protect Jade from this as well? Do you even see her here? No. Because she's downstairs, safely away from anything that could happen."

"I understand you have a different idea of relationships than shifters do when it comes to mating, and that's understandable considering your upbringing." Austin's gaze traveled from her to Patrick. "Maybe talking to Jade would help you understand things better. There are going to be areas that will be harder for you. As the Alpha's mate, you're held to a different standard and will require different protection. Even so, Jade might help you understand why females are protected and sheltered, especially now."

"He's right." Patrick nodded toward his brother. "Our relationship is going to be different than what you're used to, and she can help you adjust to that."

"What if I don't want to *adjust* to it?" Anger heated every word. "Maybe by accepting this mating, I've denied myself things I could have had with a human. I thought when the mating had taken place, it would make things easier, but I can't help but wonder now."

Patrick ignored the first comment because he knew it was out of anger. There was no real option but for her to adjust to how their relationship would work. He'd do what he could to give her everything she needed and wanted, but in the end he couldn't stop his lion from wanting to protect her. The two of them would have to balance this out between themselves and come to a mutual understanding. "Can't help but wonder what?"

"How will I ever know if what's between us is because of some chemical reaction within you or actual love?"

"You can feel it." He stepped toward her, closing the distance she had put between them when she took her hand from his. "The mating is like an attraction between two people. It gives you the desire to be with that person, but doesn't make you fall in love with them. While it bonds us together for eternity, that's all. Your emotions, the love you feel, that's you."

"Many humans believe in love at first sight, and this is pretty much the same thing," Austin added. "There's the instant lust and emotion, but the love is something the two of you build together. The way you look at each other, that's not the mating, that's your love for each other. Don't let the word *mating* scare you, or let the mating bond intimidate you from what you're feeling."

"That's not as easy as it sounds."

"That's because you're overthinking it. Stop analyzing every move, and just feel." Austin rubbed his hands together. "If we don't get started, we're going to miss dinner, and Jade's going to be pissed."

"Are you okay?" Patrick asked her.

"Let's get this over with." She grabbed the syringe from the desk, and his hand closed over hers.

"I love you, Clarissa, for the woman you are." He brought their joined hands to the front of her chest, just above her heart. "Feel it in here and you'll know the words I say are true."

"I wish I knew what I was feeling. Ever since this mating, it seems as though all of the other thoughts and emotions have overrun my own."

"Tonight, I'll help you with that. There are tricks to sort them into compartments." He raised his free hand to cup the side of her face. "We'll get through this."

"Tonight, I had other plans." She tipped her head and kissed his wrist. "I know I sound so unsure, but I do love you."

"My mother always said that with love you can overcome anything, and you can climb the tallest mountain." He was tempted to pull her tight against his chest, but he knew that would only delay things further, and they'd all be in hot water with Jade if they were late for dinner.

"If we're finally going to do this…" Austin paused for a moment as if he expected one of them to back out. "Then I suggest you step away from her."

"What?" Her voice was low but the surprise was evident in her eyes.

"My angel, he's only protecting you. We don't know how LUNA will affect my beast." He plucked the syringe from her hand. "Austin will administer this."

"What am I supposed to be doing then? Just stand around watching the man I'm supposed to spend the rest of my life with suffer?" Fear tainted her voice as she clung to his shirt.

"Everything is going to be fine." Austin cleared his throat, and Patrick turned to look at him. "You have something you'd like to add?"

"We need Clarissa here because if anything goes wrong she's the best we have. Your medical skills will be no good to us right now." He turned and looked at her pointedly. "That leaves you."

"I'm not a medical doctor," she reasoned.

"No, but you're the best we have if anything goes wrong." He stepped forward and looked at them both. "You'll know what to do if anything happens. Trust me."

"What do you mean?"

Patrick took his hand from her face and rubbed it down her arm. "The connection between us will let you know if I need something. It won't be like you'll hear my voice, but you'll just know."

"Hey." Blake peeked around the door. "How did it go?"

"We haven't done it yet." Austin nodded toward them. "These two have been cozying up to each other instead of getting some actual work done."

"Better hurry. Jade sent me to give everyone the thirty-minute notice." With that, Blake disappeared, most likely heading over to tell Luke about dinner.

"Maybe we should wait until after dinner."

"Oh no, angel, we're going to get this over with now." He kissed her forehead before stepping back and handing the syringe of LUNA to Austin. "Shifting works up an appetite, so I'll be able to enjoy Jade's dinner more than usual."

He stepped into the open space they'd cleared for him to shift and began undressing. He tugged his long-sleeved black t-shirt over his head and dropped it to the floor before his fingers began to work on his belt.

"Don't be surprised if you hear him roar or even growl. It's normal for a vocal performance, especially after an Alpha's transformation. We're vocal creatures, but an Alpha always feels the need to warn others. Think of it as a way of saying, 'look at me,' if you'd like. Patrick sure seems to think so." He smirked at his brother.

"Pot and kettle." Patrick stripped off his remaining clothes.

"Pot and kettle?" She leaned against the desk, her gaze traveling over Patrick's naked body with more interest than she should have considering what they were about to do.

"You know the pot calling the kettle black? They're both black. Same here. Austin is very vocal when he shifts as well. You find that with the more dominate shifters. Whereas Chase is less vocal because he doesn't want to attract attention or draw unnecessary problems. He'd just rather exist and enjoy letting his lion free."

"Every day I learn something new about you and your species." She shook her head. "Next thing I know I'm going to wake up next to you and you'll be in lion form."

"Not me, angel. Chase, maybe, but I prefer to cuddle next to my mate in human form."

Austin uncapped the syringe and stepped forward. "Ready?"

"As ready as I'll ever be." Patrick took a deep breath, his gaze locked on Clarissa's.

If this didn't go as planned, he wanted the last thing he saw to be his mate. That alone would give him the strength he needed to fight whatever happened. Love was stronger than any other will. It would bring him back to her.

Chapter Eighteen

Clarissa stood on the sidelines, her gazes completely on Patrick as he fought against LUNA. Inside, she could feel the fight as if it was her own. The burning frenzy, his lion's growls vibrating within her as the beast was pulled forward with incredible might. His beast was ready to shift and rip out the throats of anyone in its way. The anger that LUNA caused poured through him until she thought he'd lose it. His beast pushed forward, demanding to be on top, to be in control. It took all his will to keep a rein on the lion within, and she could only imagine the struggle of a lesser shifter.

He let out a deep roar before gaining a little control, holding back his beast. "Must find a way to…use before LUNA."

She felt the anger he had over not being able to completely relay his message. Those words had taken all of his effort, and anything more would have his beast surfacing completely.

"What?" Austin asked as he stood mid-distance between Patrick and Clarissa.

"He means we must find a way that we're able to use the counteragent *before* you head out on a mission. LUNA is too powerful, and lesser shifters won't be able to stand against the drug long enough to inject themselves with the counteragent," she explained.

"How did you get all of that?"

"I can feel it." She took a step forward. Remembering the danger, she stopped. "I can't explain it, but with his lion so close to the surface it's like the connection is stronger. I can almost feel his lion purring within me."

"It's amazing the bond between mates. See, I told you it would be good to have you here." A roar from Patrick cut Austin off.

"Take the counteragent," she told Patrick, but his beast was already too near the surface. "Austin, do something, he can't hold it off any longer. We need to complete the test."

Austin reached back to the desk and grabbed the second syringe with the anti-LUNA in it. She wanted to go to her mate, to pull him through the torment he was enduring, but she promised she'd say back until it was over. It left her standing there watching the horrid effects of LUNA taking its toll on his body and beast.

He began to shake, while his human eyes faded away to be replaced with the eyes of his lion, all warm gold like fresh honey. Gold fur spilled through his skin. His hair lightened a few shades as his mighty mane spouted along his face just seconds before his transition into his other form began. LUNA was forcing the shift. He wanted to think, to let his mate know it wasn't as bad as it looked, but all he could do was focus on keeping his beast from ripping completely through his skin.

"Hold on," she urged Patrick as Austin stepped toward him, but it was too late.

His lion was about to burst free before the shot was administered. Bones cracked and morphed, he fell forward to land on four large paws. He shook out the fur that ran the full seven-foot length of his body, not including his tail, making sure to shake his mane out, until it fell around his face without issue.

Even at nearly five hundred pounds, he normally felt light as a feather and ready to do anything despite his bulkier size. Now, he could feel every ounce of his weight, and his head felt full of stuffing. His paws seemed as if they were glued to the floor. All of it aggravated his beast more, and he had to fight to keep control instead of giving in to his lion's unease.

There he stood, staring down at his paws for a moment before tipping back his head and letting go of the roar that had been building within him. He roared as if his life depended on it, letting every shifter in the area know he was king. There was an anger hidden within the vocal display that was completely due to LUNA.

It even had Austin stepping back from him for a moment before calling his name. "Patrick."

"Is he okay?"

"Stay back, Clarissa." Austin neared Patrick but kept his movements slow and steady. Nothing jerky or fast. "LUNA has affected his beast more than we expected. Just look at his eyes. Patrick is trying to keep a close leash on it, but his beast wants to attack."

"I can feel the struggle." She never took her gaze away from him. "This isn't my Patrick. This anger isn't natural, and I can feel it coming off him in waves."

"It's still him, but there has to be something in LUNA we're missing. Something that would provoke the beast to attack. I've been drugged before, it's nothing like what's happening to him now." He uncapped the syringe and took a final step toward the lion. "Patrick, remember yourself because I have a feeling your beast isn't going to like this."

"My love, focus on me." She tried to pull his attention away from Austin. "Don't let your beast gain control and do something you'll regret. Just focus, it will only be another minute."

As she talked to him, Austin shoved the needle into the fatty part of

Patrick's shoulder and pushed the plunger, sending the cool blue anti-LUNA coursing through him. The lion's paw swiped toward Austin, but he had managed to step back in time. Thankfully, the swing was halfhearted or Patrick would have been up and on Austin before the drug had time to course through his system.

"Austin, get out of the way," she hollered, worried Patrick would hurt him, but he was already coming to stand beside her. "Damn it, Patrick, he's your brother!"

"Don't be too hard on him. He's not thinking clearly," Austin said. "Watch the way he keeps shaking his head, it's like he's trying to clear the fog that's over his brain." He tipped his head to Patrick, who was now stretched out on the floor, his large paws before him. "LUNA has more of an impact on a shifter than we suspected. Can you see if you can figure out what the additional compound is? It might give us an advantage."

"I can still feel the connection to him, but it's as if there's a heavy fog over it." She continued to stare at her mate. "If it does this to a five-hundred pound lion, what would it do to a smaller shifter? A leopard? A wolf?"

"A little closer to home…" Austin shook his head before continuing. "What will it do to weaker shifters?"

"You say that like you have someone in mind you're concerned about. Do you mean Jade? I thought we weren't going to test this on her."

"Chase. His lion has always been more sensitive, picking up on the vibes from all the other shifters in the area, especially family. While he can hold his own in a battle, he doesn't like confrontations. If there's one person in this family who might not have the strength and willpower to fight for control over his beast, like Patrick is doing, it would be Chase."

"What would happen if you don't control the beast, but let it control you?" she asked as Patrick stumbled to get back onto his paws and stand. "I thought it would have counteracted LUNA by now."

"You can see it work. His head isn't tipping to one side. Now that he's getting off the ground, he should begin to shift." Austin took a step to the side, now completely blocking Patrick's path to her. "He's still fighting with his beast, but once he shifts back to human form, it will help put his lion back where it needs to be."

Just like that, the air had begun to swirl around Patrick and the hair that had grown was starting to recede back into his body. The fog that had tainted their connection was beginning to dissipate, and the anti-LUNA pushed the remaining drug from his system. He fought to shove his lion back into the darkest corners of himself, but something about the fight told her it was harder than ever before. He was focused on her, and it was clear he was battling his way back for her. *Come on, Patrick, you're stronger than this drug.*

"Patrick." As he completed his shift, she moved toward him, but Austin put his arm out to stop her.

"Give him a second to get himself together."

"I'm fine, Austin." He growled, but Austin held tight to her arm. "Damn it, I said I was fine."

"Listen to yourself, Patrick. You're not fine. I won't have her hurt because I didn't take every precaution. My Alpha or not, you know you're not ready yet. Get your beast under control and I'll let her through."

As if to show just how out of control his beast was, he started to get to his feet to go after Austin. "It's okay Patrick, deep breaths." Her voice seemed to calm him, and he lowered himself back to the floor. If his heart wasn't slamming against his ribcage, his beast would relax a little.

"You okay, Clarissa?" Austin asked.

"It was almost as if I was the one fighting. I felt the anxiety and adrenaline that rushed through him. LUNA had some nasty side effects that were more mental than physical but it was the fog that settled over his beast that had him threatening to attack. He fought to keep a tight rein on it, because he knew that once he let his control slip, his beast would cause havoc. That was the closest I've ever been to understanding what it is that you go through, how much the beast is within you. It's not that you can change your shape, but the beast is always there, lingering under the surface even when you're in human form." She grabbed the knitted blanket off the small sofa and moved forward. Austin took one step ahead of her as she neared her mate.

Patrick glanced up at her, and then at the blanket. "Being naked doesn't bother me. Does it bother you, my angel?"

"On the contrary, I enjoy you naked very much. But right now, you're shivering." She didn't wait for him to take it. Instead, she wrapped it around his shoulders. "I believe it's a side effect. The counteragent is working with your system, speeding LUNA out of your body, and therefore it's limiting the other functions, such as body heat. This could be dangerous in the field."

"Less so than shifting." With the blanket secured around his shoulders, he grabbed her wrist and pulled her onto his lap. "I guess little brother still questions my sanity," he added when Austin flinched.

"Not your sanity. We just aren't sure how these drugs will affect you, and you should be more cautious. I only allowed her to get this close because you were freezing and didn't seem to be in a hurry to get up or get dressed."

"Stop it, you two. He's fine," Clarissa said. He slipped the throw around her, and she wrapped her arms around him. "Instead of questioning this, why don't you answer the question I asked before?"

"What's that, angel?"

"Before you shifted back, I asked Austin what would happen if you failed to control the beast, but let it control you instead."

"That would be almost as dangerous as becoming a true rogue. The beast would have nothing to keep it in check. We'd truly be the animal instead of the animal just being part of us." He placed his cheek on the top of her head.

"Are you saying you'd be like a true lion?"

"Possibly worse," Austin answered. "Unlike the natural born lions who are born knowing what was expected of them, how to act within a pride, our lion would not have that same knowledge. They'd be wild in every sense of the word. We would no longer be a civilized house cat, with our human manners. If our beast gained complete control of us, it would lash out at anyone and anything, out of fear."

"As unhappy as I was about it, that's why Austin kept you back until I had complete control over my beast. LUNA is unknown to us, and he wasn't willing to take any chances." Patrick smoothed a hand down her arm. "A lesser shifter would be at the drug's mercy. They could lose themselves to their beast and might not find their way back, especially if they don't have a pride's backing."

"The government must not know what they're doing. The risks they're taking with LUNA." She tipped her head up at Patrick, and there in her eyes he could see the need for reassurance. "Right?"

"My sweet, innocent angel, I'm afraid they know exactly what they're doing."

"What do you mean?"

The pain was clear in her eyes as he explained that her race was guiltier than she wanted to believe. "They had to have tested this in the labs. They would have seen the shifters who had given up, who were letting their beast gain more and more control, and would have witnessed just how dangerous this drug could be. But they're administering it from afar, with dart guns, and they're armed through the teeth. Once a shifter starts the transition, they have the right to kill. They're in very little danger while we're shifting, but if they hesitated even for a second it could mean their death."

"Americans always complain about the suffering that is happening in other countries. But look at how much our own country is responsible for. We're torturing our own citizens. What about the suffering right outside our front doors? It's time people start doing more for those who are already here, instead of sending money to other countries. What makes what happens here any less important?" The first tear rolled down her cheek. "I'm ashamed to be part of this country."

"Clarissa." Austin placed his hand on her shoulder. "It's happening all over the world. Not just here in the States. We're leading the pack, but we're not the only ones who are dealing with the war on the shifter population."

"Soon, there will be nowhere that is safe. Jade and I were discussing that not long ago because she suggested we return to Ireland, our father's homeland." Patrick wiped the tears from her face. "If we're going to survive this, we have to stand up and fight."

"I'm not backing down."

"None of us are, my angel." He squeezed her tight against him.

She let him hold her tight. As much as he needed it, she needed it more. There was no doubt the future was going to be dangerous for all of them, but she wouldn't go down without one hell of a fight.

Clarissa sat on the small sofa in the lab with Patrick's arm snug around her shoulder. After barely picking at her dinner, Jade had sent Austin up with a mug of warm tea for her, but even that was sitting to the side, untouched. She should have been relieved that Patrick came out of the counteragent testing without any issues, but now she was questioning their future. There was still a lot to do for the counteragent, but what if the government came up with something new in the future? They had a whole lab of captives to test on, and no conscious. She had the O'Reillys…her mate and her family. More important, she had a conscious. She wouldn't torture someone in the name of science.

"Mate, you're stressed." He placed a gentle kiss on her temple. "Let's go to the bedroom and let me relax you."

"I've got to work. See if I can figure out what else they're using in LUNA. I was too preoccupied trying to find a counteragent, and I wasn't looking closely enough at the compounds. Maybe I can find something now. Maybe it will give a lesser shifter a better chance against it. We can't risk Chase until we know he can withstand it. We can't lose him to his beast, not if we can help it."

"Angel, you're more stressed than you let on. Chase is going to be fine. His connection to me is strong, and I can pull him through it. But you're right, for now we're not using him. It's a draining test, both physically and mentally." He stood, pulled the blanket from her lap and tugged her up until she was standing. "Neither of us will be any good to anyone if we're exhausted. Let's take a few hours to ourselves, and then we can get back to work with fresh eyes."

She nodded and let him lead her out of the lab and toward what she had started to think of as their bedroom. He preferred to be in the room that was his before she arrived because it gave a better view of the grounds and was in between his siblings. She didn't care what room they were in as long as they were together, so she had started to stay there. All she had to do was move her things in, and everything would be official. Somewhere along the way, she had accepted this mating.

"Glad I caught you." Luke stepped out of his office and strolled toward them. "Andrew's gone."

"What?" Her stomach flipped. After everything that happened at Hathaway Medical, Andrew shouldn't have been out. They were probably after him, or the very least they'd want to know why he hadn't protected the building since he had been on duty that night.

"When he didn't show up for dinner, Jade and I went to check on him. She wanted to talk to him about searching the Shifters Underground for his niece, but he was gone. There was a disk on his bed."

"What's on it?" Patrick questioned.

"Information on the camp outside of Bangor, Maine." Luke dragged a hand through his hair, out of nervous habit. "His sister's name is on the list of the dead brought there. He believes his niece might be there."

"Shit. He's going to get himself killed."

"Should I get Austin and go after him?"

Patrick shook his head. "No, we need you here. There are a lot of files to go through from Hathaway Medical, and I need you looking for that little girl."

"What about Austin or Chase? Someone should go after him," Clarissa said, holding her breath as her entire body tensed up. Andrew had warned her to record what happened there, otherwise she might have never considered infecting the computer system, and bringing all the information to them. She might not be there without him, and she felt she owed him somehow.

"No."

"What?" She couldn't believe she'd heard him correctly. He had been willing to help people he hadn't even met, but he was willing to let Andrew walk into a concentration camp, where he might be captured and killed.

"I promised you I would send someone to check out the camp, but not like this. I won't send my brothers to their death."

"How do you know it would mean death? Why is this different?"

"Andrew won't be thinking clearly. He'll be out for blood for his sister's death, and for the kidnapping of his niece. Anyone who's with him could end up dead as well. I won't send them to be slaughtered." When she stepped out of his embrace and turned to him, he added, "If Andrew had come to me, given us time to put together a mission, we'd have gone…but not like this."

"He's right, Clarissa," Luke said. "It will be a blood bath if Andrew storms the gate to rescue his niece. An attack on the camp will send everyone in a fifty mile radius on alert, and any shifters in the vicinity will be killed on the spot. They won't risk the chance they could get the upper hand. If they're not killed, they won't just be imprisoned in a camp. They'd be sent to a lab."

"I've seen what they did to one of my siblings because I didn't protect them," Patrick said. "I won't have it happen again."

"What happened to Jade wasn't your fault." She tried to reason with him, but even as she said it she knew he'd never believe her.

"I'm not just her brother, I'm her Alpha. That gives me double the responsibility. Instead, I let her go out on that mission and she was captured because of me. She suffered endless torture because I didn't protect her. I cannot stand by and let that happen again, nor can I suffer along with them through it again."

"Suffer with them?"

"He could feel everything that happened to Jade because they started to break her spirit," Luke explained. "She didn't have the fight or the will to keep the barrier between them, and because of that Patrick had to deal with it. It wasn't just the physical pain, but the emotional and mental aspects of what she went through." Luke glanced at Patrick. "It broke something within you that I wasn't sure you'd ever get it back, but Clarissa has given you that spark again." With that, Luke turned on his heels and went back to his office.

"I'm still going to our room, but if you don't wish to join me, you don't have to." He stepped around her and had nearly made it to the door before she gathered herself enough to realize what had happened.

"Maybe you're right, and maybe you're wrong about Andrew. I don't know him enough to tell you what type of mind frame he's in, but what I do know is that you'll have to live with your decision. If it's anything like the guilt you carry around about with what happened to Jade, I'm not sure how you'll get through the days."

"I'll get through them knowing I kept my family safe." He spun back to her. "It would be a different story if my pride were just members, but they're my siblings. I won't risk them. Would you rather I go after him instead of working with you on LUNA? Because I can do that."

"Damn it, Patrick, that's not fair. Don't ask me choose between Andrew and you."

"Why? Isn't that what you're asking me to do? Choose between him and my siblings. Do you think I'm not worried every time I send them out? The same thing that happened with Jade could happen again, but I have no choice. Sometimes the greater good outweighs the risk, and each of them realize the risk when they leave the castle. We do this for our kind, and to protect the ones we love."

"I'm sorry." She closed the distance between them and placed her hand on his chest. "Andrew was there for me on my last day at Hathaway Medical, and to stand by doing nothing when he might have finally found his niece is hard for me. I do understand your reasoning. You know I never thought of my life as simple before, but now part of me misses those days. Each day I realize what kind of world we live in…a war zone. The best part is you and your siblings. I wouldn't want anything to happen to them, either. I love you, Patrick O'Reilly, nothing will change that, and that's *not* the mating talking, it's me."

"I'll protect you and get you through this war zone I dropped you into, I promise."

"This wasn't your fault. I chose this path the moment I ran for my life, away from Hathaway Medical. I chose this life and this mating. I'm in this with everything I have because I want to be."

He pushed the bedroom door open the rest of the way and wrapped his arm around her waist. "I love you, my beautiful mate, for now and for always."

Chapter Nineteen

Days had passed without a word from Andrew, but they had bigger issues to worry about. LUNA testing had begun. News reports flashed on the screen announcing what Patrick had already read online. Now that LUNA was taking its full effect, thousands of jobs were vacant. On-the-job testing for any government, military, and first responding employees was the first stage, and the impact of shifters walking off the job was becoming clear. Other companies who weren't in the first string of testing were just beginning to feel the impact. Humans had to leave their employment to follow their shifter mates into hiding.

There were no figures to check, but he suspected that over a third of the United States population were shifters or had mated to one. There were some who had left their jobs to support their mates, or simply because they disagreed with what was happening, allying themselves with the shifters.

He only hoped that those who hadn't shown up for work had somewhere safe to go because the military had already begun to rally and track them down at their homes. If found, they'd be tested, then killed—or worse. What it meant for the human mates, no one was sure of yet.

His thoughts returned to Andrew. Had he made it to Bangor yet, and what happened to him? Even as he searched the news, he knew there'd be nothing about the camp. They might never know what had happened there, or if he'd found his niece, but now more than ever he was glad he hadn't sent anyone after him. Things were too dangerous to risk anything. With the military and police out patrolling and subjecting everyone they saw to LUNA, there was no chance of getting anywhere safely.

The intercom on his desk crackled to life, and a split second later Blake's voice came through. "Patrick, pick up line two."

"Who is it?" He sank into the chair behind the desk. It wasn't his usual work station since that had been moved up to the family floor, and he was using the office on the main floor while Clarissa worked in his personal office upstairs.

"It's important, just do it," Blake retorted.

The intercom faded out and Patrick glanced at the phone before finally picking it up. "Hello."

"Is my sister still with you?" Dean asked.

"She is, and she'd like to speak with you. Are you safe?"

"Safe enough for now. Does that offer still stand?"

"Yes, of course."

"Good." A siren cut Dean off for a moment. "I'm in trouble, so consider me on my way."

"You need help? I can get backup to you quickly if you let me know where you are."

"It'll be faster if I just make my way there. I'll stick to the shadows and stay out of sight. Seems like all hell has broken out, but I'll get there because you'll want what I've found." Dean cleared his throat. "If I'm not there in two days, consider me dead. She'll know where I put the information I had. Otherwise, wait for me. It will be easier to explain if I'm there. If I'm dead, do your best to make sure she doesn't only remember my screw-ups."

He hurriedly gave him the details on how to get to Forever Creek, then added, "Please, tell me where you are, and let me send you some backup."

"Two days, I'll be there. If I stick around here, I'll be dead anyway."

The line went dead before Patrick could say anything else. He wished he had traced the call, but knowing Dean it would have been blocked. Whatever mess he'd gotten into, at least no one would be able to trace this number. With no choice left, he hung up the phone. He'd have to find his mate and tell her that her brother would be arriving soon. To keep her from worrying about his journey would be next to impossible. The next two days, he'd have to balance the needs of his mate with that of the pride. Each day presented a new challenge.

What could he have found that changed his mind from the hatred he had before?

He scooted the chair back from his desk and stood. There was no point in putting it off. He knew she'd be upstairs working, and now that he'd gotten caught up with what was happening in the world, he had no excuse not to be helping her. Heading toward the family room, he passed Chase in his lion form and Jade camped out in front of the television. She was talking about whatever show was on and every once in a while, Chase would purr in agreement. As he caught a glimpse of them, he was reminded of what their lives had once been like. None of the missions, death, danger, labs, or LUNA. He wanted that life back.

He was tired of all the shit they had to go through each day, every threat that surrounded them any time they went out, and the danger his family was constantly in. He wanted his siblings to be able to live in a safe world, and most of all he wanted Jade to be safe. She deserved it after everything she had gone through. All the future generations deserved a safe world to live in as well. They needed to have a bigger game plan, not just eliminating one lab after another, because there was always another willing to take its place. They needed a battle plan on regaining their freedom.

By the time he'd climbed the steps, he had mentally started a list of things they needed to do in order to get back the life they once had. It wouldn't happen overnight, but no longer would he be willing to just do the minimal. In the coming days, he'd sit down with Austin and go over some of the strategies.

He punched in his code and opened the door to their floor. He stepped through and made sure the door closed tightly behind him before continuing toward the lab. Even as he neared the room, he heard Clarissa mumbling to herself, and he couldn't decide if she was on to something or the rambles were of mere frustration.

"Angel, you got a minute?" When she looked up at him, he knew she was lost in anxious thought. There must have been a piece to LUNA she didn't like or couldn't figure out.

"What's up?" She scooted the laptop to the side and leaned forward on her elbows. "If you're coming here to see if I've found what we need, I told you earlier I would let you know. Don't bother me."

"No, I came with other news." He placed his hands on her shoulders, and gently massaged the tight muscles. "You're stressing too much. We'll figure it out."

"We need the answers now."

"No. We can test it again without knowing. I'll take the anti-LUNA first, give it a few minutes, then have LUNA injected. We'll see how my beast can handle it. That might be all we need. If we can take it beforehand, there might not be any issues on how LUNA affects our beasts."

"But we don't know it will work. If it doesn't, we can't risk injecting you with the counteragent a second time. You'd have to suffer the consequences of LUNA completely. There'd be nothing to stop the way it tried to bring your beast into full control. I don't want you to risk yourself until I figure out this second compound."

"I'll control my beast, don't you worry about that." He wasn't excited to inject LUNA again, especially if there wasn't something he could do to stop the effect, but he'd do it if he had to, and he'd get through it. Though, the next time, he'd make sure she was safely in another room. There was no reason she should watch if LUNA had him fighting with his beast for control.

"If you didn't come up here for an update, what did you want? I know it wasn't to give me a shoulder rub. So, what's up?"

"Dean called and he's coming."

"What?" She nearly shot off the chair. "Is he in trouble? He wouldn't succumb to defeat unless he's in serious trouble."

"I don't know any of the details, only that he'll be here within the next forty-eight hours. He mentioned that he found something we'd be interested in. That's all I know."

With closed eyes, she rubbed her temples. "What kind of trouble did he get himself into now?"

"You don't know he's in any trouble." He tried to reason with her before her fears took over.

"He wouldn't be coming here if he weren't in trouble. Not yet, not after the anger he had toward you and Blake last time we saw him. He'd need time to cool off."

"Maybe he realized he's a wanted man. Even if he hadn't left his job, they'd want him for his connection to you. You knew he'd be in danger if he didn't come with us, it's why you begged him to come. He needed time, but now he's coming, so you should be happy."

"I can't trust it. Something is up. He found something that got him into more trouble. I don't know what, but something isn't right."

"We'll know soon enough. Until then, there's no reason to upset yourself. He wouldn't tell me where he was, so I can't send anyone to get him out of whatever mess he might be in." He ran a hand down her arm. "It's going to be okay."

"You'd send someone after him?"

"Yes, my angel. Didn't you think I would?"

"I guess I'm surprised, after the way he treated you and Blake." She bit the corner of her lip as she thought about something. "Plus, what happened with Andrew…"

"The situation with Andrew is different. Whatever the outcome will be, it's already in the works. If Andrew hasn't made it there by now, he should be close. Even if I wanted to, there's no chance I could get a team there before he did whatever half-brained scheme he's devised." He tucked a strand of her hair behind her ear. "Dean is different. He's your brother, and you have to know I'd do whatever I could to make you happy. Family and mates are everything."

"But he was so rude to you before."

"He came a long way to protect his sister, and then suddenly someone else was there to do it. That had to hurt his ego. I'm willing to put everything aside and start over. Hopefully, he's willing to do the same."

She leaned toward him and wrapped her arms around his chest. "Did I ever tell you how much I love you?"

"My angel, I think it would be better for you to show me later. Right now, what can I do to help you?"

"Magic ball? You don't happen to have one, do you?"

"No, but you have me and I'm almost as good. Let me see what you've come up with. Maybe a new set of eyes will help you see something you've missed." He hooked another chair with his foot and scooted it toward them.

"We can figure it out together."

A gentle shake of Patrick's arm pulled him from a deep slumber. At first he thought it was Clarissa, and started to snuggle against her warm body, but then he caught sight of the figure standing by the side of the bed. His senses kicked in, preparing him for attack, but his lion smelled Luke's scent before it sprang into action.

"What the hell?" He growled.

"You need to see this."

Patrick sat up, agitated. "You need to answer the phone, you need to see this, that's all I've heard in the last twenty-four hours." He tossed back the covers, careful to not uncover his very naked mate, and slipped out from her embrace. "This better be important."

"It's about Andrew."

Patrick grabbed the shirt he'd tossed on the nightstand and slipped it on. "Shit, tell me they didn't capture him. He knows where we're located."

"They didn't give him enough time to squeal our location."

He didn't like the sound of it, but instead of asking questions, he just followed Luke from the bedroom to his office. He'd find out soon enough what happened to Andrew, though he suspected he was dead by now. *Wonder how many others will suffer for Andrew's lack of planning?*

Luke waited until Patrick entered, and then shut the door behind them. The action itself piqued his curiosity because it was a definite sign something disastrous had happened. None of them ever shut their doors. "They executed him on live television."

"Fuck!" He sidestepped the sofa, turning his attention to the television mounted near the fireplace, and watched as the news reporter's camera zoomed in on a figured as it moved through the tree line. Even with the low quality of the video, he knew it was Andrew.

"They're replaying it over and over with a message."

"What message?" He leaned against the sofa's arm and watched the television, knowing he wasn't going to like what he saw over the next few minutes.

"That this will be the first of many shifters exterminated until the world is free of the scum." Luke handed him a computer printout. "This was officially conducted by Shifter Free World, SFW. They've vowed to exterminate any person who they believe is a shifter and anyone known to associate with our kind."

"As if the government wasn't bad enough, now we have our own hate group determined to eliminate us."

"You'll see from the paper I handed you that they're determined to free the world of our *disease*. Right now, they're still small, but they won't stay that way for long. There will be people joining their ranks by the droves."

"But there will be others who will remain neutral or will throw their support in our direction. This just makes things more desperate. Remember us discussing emailing the president…are you *sure* it won't be traceable?"

"I'm positive. Why? What are you up to?"

Before Patrick could answer, the camera adjusted, getting a better view of Andrew strapped to the bed of a truck. He fought hard against the restraints, but even with his shifter strength, he was no match to the heavy chains. SFW had done their research on what would hold a shifter—or maybe this wasn't their first kill.

Light glistened off a blade as it was brought down between his pecs, quickly slicing through his skin as it was drawn in a downward motion to his navel. Growls echoed through the speaker and there was no doubt the bear within Andrew wanted to come out. Something was holding it back.

"Why hasn't he shifted?" Patrick leaned forward, trying to get a better look at Andrew's face. He needed to see his eyes to know how close the beast was to the surface.

"What I found online is on that paper. SFW claims the chains they are using are special ones that have been cursed to encase the beast within the body. The chains won't let him shift."

"You believe this?"

Luke handed him another page, but this time it was a closer look at Andrew's face. There was no doubt the beast was upon him, but he'd been unable to shift. There would have been no way Andrew could have held it back on his own, probably not even with the aid of an Alpha. He was just too close to the transition. It *had* to be the chains.

"Centuries ago, there were said to be chains that would encase a demon, making it impossible for them to use their powers." Patrick tossed the papers on the sofa. "I never believed it before now since nothing was ever discovered but…"

"This seems like proof chains like that exist. But we're not demons."

Patrick nodded in agreement. Unlike what some people thought shifters were cursed, or demonic. Their roots could be traced many centuries back, and their second nature was the result of a spell cast by witches who were captured to be put to death. Those witches would cast spells to try to escape their fate, turning themselves into animals and taking off before they could be held accountable for their so-called sins. Only, they didn't know their spells would become a permanent feature of their lives. Whatever animal they chose would be passed on through their future generations.

"The question is…how…how did they come up with these chains?" Patrick couldn't take his gaze away from the screen as they continued to slice

Andrew to pieces. His chest was spread open, exposing his heart, but they hadn't taken the final blow yet. Shifters were harder to kill and it would take their bodies longer to shut down from the lack of blood, but once the heart stopped even a shifter would be dead.

"I'll see what else I can find out." Luke plopped down on the sofa and turned to face Patrick. "The government has been an evil we were expecting, but this…" He waved a hand at the television. "This is taking it another step. What are we going to do about this? It's another threat we're going to have to worry about every time we leave here. We have no protection against this. With LUNA, Clarissa came up with something that will work, but this…with this, we have nothing."

"We'll deal with it."

"Patrick, what are you considering? You asked about emailing the president again. I thought you didn't send the one you wrote before you went to look for Clarissa. You said you decided it was a bad idea. What changed?"

"We can't continue on the path we're on. We're going to have to do something different if we're ever going to reclaim our freedom. Our best bet is to take our demands to the highest authority because taking out one lab at a time does nothing for the overall problem. I don't know about you, but I don't want my children to grow up in fear. I don't want Jade or any of us, to have to live like this." As the final blow sliced Andrew's heart from his chest, Patrick grabbed the remote and muted the reporter. "This can't go on. Next time, it might be one of us."

"Think about this before you do anything. I don't want you to do something stupid and get us all killed."

"Don't you think I'd do everything I can to protect you and the rest of our siblings?" Patrick glared at him. He was beyond tired of having to defend his actions. "Every decision I make is to make a safer world for all of you, to protect each of you."

"That's not what I mean." Luke pushed off the sofa and strolled toward the window. "You don't need to protect us. We all know what's out there, what the risks are, and we're all willing to do what needs to be done." When Patrick started to say something, he cut him off by adding, "I know you suffered with Jade. The connection with you being her Alpha *and* her brother, made things worse. Not to mention the fact that you shielded the rest of us from it. But you can't do it all yourself, and like you said we can't live like this forever. All of us deserve to have a life again."

"Do you honestly think we'll ever be able to go back to our lives? That I'll be welcomed in any town as a doctor? Don't tell me you think you can go back and work for one of the top companies as their IT specialist again." Patrick didn't give his brother a chance to answer. "No, none of us will ever be able to reclaim the lives we had. Jade will never be able to finish her college degree or become a teacher. I might be able to use my medical training again, but I'll never have my own practice. The only patients who will come to me are shifters or their mates, and even then it will only be for wounds. We don't get sick and our bodies heal quickly. My training is of little value to shifters. The best I can offer is delivering babies. Each of us needs to start to accept that our lives will never be the same."

"We already know that. Maybe we do hold out some hope that we'll live normally again, and maybe it's just a dream, but when you give up hope you have nothing."

He rose from the arm of the sofa and looked at his brother. "Then do us all a favor and hold on to your hope. Hold on to it for the sake of all of us who have lost it."

"What happened to you, Patrick? You used to be the most optimistic one of us."

"Real life." He slammed his hand down on the back of the sofa. "I've made some horrible mistakes since I took over for Dad. He'd have never let Jade go out on that mission, and she'd have never been captured. I didn't send anyone after Andrew and look where that got him. Now I have a human mate who was in danger already, but by being mated to me, marked by me, it makes it so much worse."

The door pushed open and Clarissa stood there with a silk rope tied loosely at her waist. "Worse for who? You or me?"

"Clarissa, go back to bed."

"No, I want to know. Why is being mated to me so bad?"

Luke glanced at his brother before trying to stop the fight that was brewing. "That was taken out of context."

"Luke, I know you mean well, but I highly doubt it. So, *mate*...." She spit out the word like it left a bad taste on her tongue.

"Being mated to me has put you in more danger." He decided to be honest with her, to let her know just what type of risk she had taken. "If something happens to me, I won't be able to protect you."

"Protect me from what?" She wrapped her arms around herself. "From the government? Don't worry about that, because if there were no chance you were alive and coming back to me, I'd do what I had to do to ensure they never got their hands on me. Even if that meant taking my own life. I've seen what they're capable of, and I won't be at their mercy."

"My sweet angel, you have no idea how much they can make you wish you were dead and yet be nowhere near you." He reached over, grabbed the pocket knife that was sitting on Luke's desk, and flipped it open.

"This isn't necessary," Luke stated, taking a step toward Patrick.

"I think it is." He dropped the shields that were like a second skin to him, protecting her from the worst within him. The constant strain of decisions, fears, and worries. He kept up the shields protecting her from the rest of the pride. Those wouldn't matter now. He watched as the way she looked at him changed. The anger she'd held only moments before was gone, but before she could say anything, he turned the knife on himself. He drove the blade into his stomach, careful to miss his organs.

Even though it was a small stab wound, the pain exploded through him, shaking his knees. Clarissa curled forward, grasping the area on her own body where he'd stabbed himself. Even as she slipped her hand underneath her robe to check for blood, tears spilled down her face. It broke his heart and he quickly slammed the shields back into place, taking the pain from her.

With her breath back, her legs would no longer hold her, and she sank to the floor. "What the hell happened?"

"My shields protect you from me. Some mates aren't able to build shields like the ones I'm able to, but since I'm an Alpha it's practically mandatory. Otherwise, no one would survive the mating, especially not a human. There's too much turmoil going on within me to let it go unshielded. Even though I dropped the shields, you only felt part of it because I was focused."

"What was the point of that, to cause me pain?" She sobbed. "So I could see what's within you?"

"No, my angel, I'd never want to cause you pain." He dropped the pocket knife to the corner of the desk, careful to ensure it didn't drip blood onto any of Luke's papers. "I did it so you'd see what would happen if they captured me. Eventually, they'd tear down my shields and I wouldn't be able to protect you from it. I wouldn't be able to shield my siblings. Austin would step into the position of Alpha, and then he could take the brunt of the assault, as I did when it came to Jade's torture."

He closed the distance between them and knelt in front of her. "Even Austin wouldn't be able to help you. He couldn't protect you from the bond between mates. Do you understand the risk you took accepting this mating? Do you see why you're in more danger than ever before?"

"I see that you tried to scare me, but it's too late. If you wanted to scare me away from accepting what's between us, you should have done it before the mating. Now you're stuck with me."

"That wasn't the point of this." He took his hand away from the stab wound, revealing the blood that had seeped through his shirt and onto his fingers. "I wanted you to comprehend how dangerous things are. Each day I do my best to protect you and my pride, but with the way things are going I don't know what the future will hold."

"What are you talking about? What happened?" When he remained silent, she glanced up at his brother. "Luke?"

"Andrew was killed." Luke, who had remained silent, answered.

"Not just killed," Patrick said. "Fucking hell, he was tortured."

"Oh, hell." She rose up onto her knees. "Did they capture him when he checked out the camp?"

He quickly brought her up to speed on the situation, and what had happened before he grabbed her hand and pulled her to her feet. "Now, go back to bed. I'll be there shortly."

"We need to see to that." She glanced toward his stomach. "I can't believe you stabbed yourself. Come on, let me patch you up."

"I'll take care of it in a bit."

"Go ahead." Luke nodded to the door. "There's nothing more you can do here. I'll see what I can find on SFW, and I'll let you know when I learn anything important."

"Bring Austin up to speed, and if you need help, get him to help you," Patrick ordered Luke before putting his arm around his mate and leading the way out of Luke's office.

"You know, there had to be a better way than stabbing yourself," Clarissa said, not bothering to hide her annoyance.

"It brought home the point, but I'm sorry that it hurt you." Subconsciously, his hand returned to the wound. "Shifters heal quickly. The skin will be closed by this afternoon, and completely healed tomorrow."

"Forty-eight hours…all to prove a point," she bitched.

"You're worth a lot more than a little stab wound."

"If so, then you'll make sure you keep yourself alive and free. Remember that, mate."

"Yes, my angel." He'd do his best to ensure he was always there for her, and everyone who depended on him. He wouldn't be like his father and desert his family.

He didn't desert us. Even as he told himself that for the millionth time, he couldn't convince himself, because part of him believed his father had abandoned them. Even if it was subconsciously. *Not me. I'll stand for my pride.*

Chapter Twenty

Days had passed since Andrew's execution, and a gray cloud had settled over Patrick and the family. Even Nolan seemed to feel the unease and had stayed out of Patrick's way. Not that he was down on the main floors much. Patrick was up in his office working on strategies, in between the trial runs of LUNA's counteragent. He was working on a plan to take to the president. Something that would eliminate the threats, and hopefully destroy all the labs once and for all.

"Here's the information you requested on Parachute, Colorado." Austin placed the computer printouts on Patrick's desk, next to the keyboard. "What's this about?"

"I've got to have all my bases covered." He laid a hand on the file and looked up at his brother. "Do you think you could find me two or three other small towns that would be habitable for a large group of shifters?"

"You're not seriously considering suggesting to the government that we set up towns of shifters? How is that better than the camps they already have?"

"There's no way the government and the rest of civilization are going to let us just move back into our old lives. If we could establish laws of protection, homes, and employment again, maybe we can get some resemblance of our old lives back."

"What do you have in mind? Go through it step by step with me." Austin lowered himself into the chair across from the desk, crossed his ankle over his other knee, and settled back to listen.

"If we establish a land that is just ours, like our own country, maybe we can begin to live again. Establish a town of our own, set up security around the perimeter to keep outsiders out, law enforcement to keep everyone in line. We can have everything we need right there. Our people will be safe."

"What about the fact that more than a third of the United States is either a shifter or mated to one? There's no way we could put that many people in Parachute. The different animals won't live in harmony like you want. Not to mention that some just won't accept it."

"I've considered that, and I've laid it all out in the plan I've spent the last few days devising. Multiple towns will be required, many of them will have a dominant animal in charge. For those who are unwilling to live like this, I have no doubt the government will keep them in the camps, unless they can live under the radar. Though, once they're captured, law enforcement would have no choice but to either send them to one of the shifter towns or imprison them in one of the camps." He noticed that Austin didn't seem convinced, but it was the only way. "It's either this or we continue being hunted down like rabid animals. The camps and labs will continue to exist. If we present this in a way that makes it sound like it's to their benefit, we can get them to approve this. Think of how many we'd be able to save, how many we can free from those camps."

"It's going to take more than just you to make this happen."

Patrick nodded. "I need you on board. Your military experience will be an advantage, and if I get them to approve this, I'd like you to head up security for us."

"You think they'll let us stay here?"

"Why not? They haven't put anything into writing that a shifter cannot own land, and this is our home. We'll fight to keep it. I'd like to have them transfer some of the land around here or the town of Parachute for the other members. This way they're not in our home. It would be safer for us. It will also allow for families to have their own home and privacy, something they couldn't have here, and would give them a sense of freedom."

"It sounds like you have this all thought out." Austin leaned forward. "You're going to need a detailed security outfit for each of the towns, especially here. If we're going to do this, it won't be long before every shifter knows we're the ones behind this idea. You realize there will be death threats?"

"I know I could be digging my own grave with this. Especially if I can't convince the government." He dragged a hand through his hair. "I can't see any other way, though."

"Not just you. We're all in this together. We vowed to stick together, and we'll all have your back for this." He slapped his thighs and started to stand. "Send me what you have already, and I'll go over the security aspects, add my suggestions, and get it back to you."

"Thanks, Austin. I mean it. I couldn't do this without you and the others behind me."

"We're family. We'll always have each other's backs. That reminds me, when are you going to tell the others?"

Patrick glanced at the picture of his family on his desk, stared down at his father's smiling face for a moment, and hoped he was doing what his father would have wanted. "Let's get things ironed out more before we tell everyone."

Before Austin made it to the door, he turned back. "Have you discussed this with Clarissa? She might have some insight on aspects that should be covered in the proposal before we take our case to the president."

"She knows I'm working on something that will hopefully make our lives easier, but I haven't gone into any details with her. Though, you do have a good point. I'll speak with her and see if she can think of anything I've missed. Sometimes we forget what it's like to be human. All I can think about is how my beast is on edge with all the developments recently. SFW and those demonic chains aren't helping anything. All over the web, people are discussing the possibility of being able to make them and have them enchanted by a witch or a shaman. Others have tried to find their own.

"There's so much hatred toward our kind right now that it makes me sick. My lion wants to rip through and show the world what real dangers could await them if they continue on this path. More and more shifters will let their beasts gain control, and eventually there will be so many rogues the humans will be in real danger." Patrick leaned back in his chair and sighed. "The world is going to Hell, and this is our last effort to pull it back from the brink."

"We're going to be the saving grace." Austin smirked before growing serious. "I might not have been on board before, but you're right. There are no other options. We can't live in a world where we have to worry about the labs, camps, LUNA, SFW, and now public executions. We need a safe world for future generations."

Clarissa pulled off her lab coat. She needed a break, anything that didn't have to do with this lab and LUNA. She had been at it since daybreak, and now the sun was long gone. Patrick was still in his office, working on this secret project. She debated about going to him, to pull him away from his work, and slip back to their room for some quality time. Before she could, Jade burst through the door, out of breath, her face flushed.

"Where's Patrick?"

"In his office. Everything okay?"

"I found her!" she hollered, dashing toward Patrick's office.

Eager to know who Jade had found, she followed. *So much for quality mating time.* "Found who?"

"What's going on?" Patrick looked up from the computer screen, the pinch of skin between his eyebrows seeming to say he would have preferred not to be bothered.

"I found her…" Jade tossed the papers on his desk. "I found Andrew's niece. She wasn't at the camp after all. His sister sacrificed herself to save her little girl, giving her time to run. She's only eight, but she's smart enough that she was able to hide out, steal the food she needed, and find a place to stay warm. She was on the run for two weeks, moving from place to place, never staying too long for fear she'd get caught. She finally found a family to take her in."

"How did you find her, then?"

"The family who took her in are human. They didn't know what she was until Andrew's death, when MaKayla saw it on the news and got upset. At first the family thought it was because of what she'd seen, but she eventually told them the truth. I received an email through Shifters Underground from them this afternoon, and just got off the phone with them."

"Please tell me they aren't turning her over to the authorities," Clarissa begged. Needing his touch, she stepped around the desk to stand beside Patrick.

"They care about MaKayla, but the news announced that school children will now be tested with LUNA, and they're afraid for her safety.

They have a toddler of their own and have asked that we find a place where she'll be safe."

"How did they find out about Shifters Underground?" He pushed back from the desk and pulled his mate down onto his lap.

"MaKayla. Her mother had an account on the site, and that's how they contacted us. I told them we'd put together a plan and come get her." Jade took a deep breath and placed her hands on the desk. "I want to be the one to go get her."

"Absolutely not." He nearly pushed Clarissa from his lap before he caught himself. "You're more valuable here. You'll stay. Blake and Chase can manage this. Or Chase can take Nolan. Either way, you're staying here."

"She's scared. Having two burly lions show up isn't going to put her at ease." She stepped away from the desk. "Patrick, I know the risks, but we're talking about a little girl. She's terrified, and her family has been killed by these assholes. We need to put her at ease from the beginning. Chase isn't as intimidating, but he won't have time to comfort MaKayla."

"Not after last time, Jade. I want you right here where you're safe."

"It's not like I'm happy about it, to go out there, and put myself in danger again." Fear sparkled in Jade's eyes before she was able to blink it away. "Eventually, I'm going to have to go back out there. You can't expect to ask everyone else to go but me. You *know* I'm right."

"No, what I know is I won't put you back out there for something to happen to you. Things are too dangerous, especially now with SFW."

"We'd only be gone a few hours. She's a little over an hour away. If we go at night and stick to the back roads, we'll be okay. Send whoever else you want, but let me go to her."

"If you don't want Jade to go, then let me," Clarissa offered, knowing he didn't want Jade in danger again. Especially without him there to keep her safe. "I agree, having a female will help MaKayla."

"Don't you start." He growled at his mate. "You're not going anywhere, either."

"You know we're right," Jade added. "Put your worries about me aside, and think about that little girl. I need to do this for her."

"Then I'm going with you."

"What?" Both of the women asked at the same time. Clarissa turned in his lap to look at him.

"You heard me. If Jade's going, I'll be there to make sure she's safe." After last time, he wasn't ready to take any chances.

"We'll keep her safe." Austin drew the attention to him while Chase stepped up beside him, and the two of them strolled in. They must have heard the ruckus. "If she's going after MaKayla, let Chase and I go with her. We'll keep her safe, and you and Clarissa can keep working. We can leave tonight."

"We'll make sure she gets back okay." Chase leaned against the wall, his arms crossed over his chest.

"Shit, I don't like this," Patrick said.

"I know." Austin nodded. "You have more important things to deal with, and we'll be back in a few hours."

"Take Blake with you, too."

"Four of us, for one little girl?" Jade shook her head.

"Not just for her, but also to keep you safe," Patrick told her as he ran a hand up his mate's back. "I guess you're stuck with me tonight. Can't say I'll be very good company until they get back."

"Then how about I help you with whatever you were working on?" she suggested.

"I think that's a very good idea," Austin said, smirking before nodding to Jade. "Let's go. You contact them and let them know we'll be leaving in thirty minutes. I'll get Blake and Chase, grab the supplies, and we'll meet downstairs in twenty."

She waited until they were alone again before she looked back at Patrick. "What did Austin mean?"

"I'm working on a proposal to contact the president."

"You what?" She jumped off his lap to look at him. "Are you insane? Going to the man who's responsible for the labs and camps? He must have approved them, provided the funding, and his people are the ones demanding more."

"Come here, angel." He held out a hand to her but she didn't take it. She needed to move around. "I've considered all of this."

"Yet you're *still* considering this?"

"Because I see no other option on how to make us safe. Not just us, or the pride, our other contacts, but my species in general. If we don't do something, more than a third of the United States population will be wiped from the face of the Earth. I'm not talking about through a virus that will kill us quickly, but at the hands of the government or SFW. If we can get President Ashworth to agree to let us live in peace, it's possible that other countries will do the same."

"More than a third of the population." She shook her head in disbelief.

"Not all of them are shifters, but most. The others would be our mates. I'm not even counting the family members of the human mates who might be supportive of our kind." He rose, went to stand before her but didn't touch her yet. "It's amazing to think how this all happened because of witch trials all over the world, for centuries. They turned into animals to try to hide from their supposed crimes. We don't even really know how many witches worked the spell, and now look at the population of shifters."

"So you're going to what? Ask the president to just let you go back to the lives you had before?"

"No, we're going to ask to create shifter towns. It will be a few steps above the camps they have now. We'll request to be in charge of our own security, and monitoring the shifters who live within the town to make sure they're not causing any problems."

She shook her head. "With what they've seen the shifters in the labs do, the rogues, and those in camps, you think they'd actually let this happen?"

"We've got to try. I've put together a twenty-page proposal. It goes over everything from what we'd need in the towns, the security, the monitoring, to what we'd expect in return and can give them. As well as why they should approve this."

"And why should they?"

"If they don't, they're declaring war on themselves. We will make sure our women, and children are somewhere safe, but then we'll be left with no choice but to go to war. Even with the counteragent to LUNA, we don't stand a chance. Not with SFW and those damn demonic chains. I believe if we can't find a common ground with the government, war will be in the near future."

She stepped back and leaned against the chair. The thought of them going to war scared the hell out of her. They weren't just talking about a minor skirmish if such a large chunk of the population were shifters or related to shifters. They were talking a full-scale war. That didn't even count those who were human, but would ally themselves with shifters. There was no doubt that thousands would die. On both sides.

"Austin knew about this?"

He nodded. "I discussed it with him after he found the information I needed on a couple small towns we might be able to use. The first being

Parachute so we can stay here in our home. But we'd need other locations as well. Many shifters will prefer to mostly stick to their own clans. There will be some with mates of a different breed. Others who have been accepted into another clan. We won't make it mandatory to divide into breeds, but we need to make sure it's an option."

"Throwing different clans or prides together, won't that cause fights for dominance?"

"It could, but I believe I've covered that."

"How?" She eyed him, not at all surprised he'd thought of just about everything.

"Each town will have one Alpha, one who will be in charge. He'll have to monitor his own town, set up the security that would be needed to keep his members safe, as well as keep them in line. Each town Alpha will be directly responsible if the members are causing an uproar. They will be held accountable by the government if they let their members go wild and cause problems, especially if they have a shifter who goes rogue."

"You'd be willing to live under someone else's control?" She raised an eyebrow at him because she knew the answer.

"No, but my plan is to keep Forever Creek. Each town will have a maximum number of shifters allowed there. Hopefully, we can keep the castle for ourselves, and take over some of the surrounding areas and set up a shifter town. There's plenty of land around the castle that we can build on, but that will take time. Most of the other resort buildings need work, while some aren't even standing. Parachute has a lot of space, empty buildings and houses, since so many have left the area now that the ski resort has been shut down for so long. It would be the perfect place to use."

"What of the people who have remained? Would you evict them from their homes?"

"That would be the government's choice, however, we could live here in peace with the human residents. Just as we did before we were forced into hiding." He placed his hands on her shoulders and slowly dragged them down her arms. "My angel, I'm not saying this will be easy or even that there aren't serious dangers in doing it, but I have to do something to make a better world for us, for all of us."

"At what risk to yourself?" She placed her hand on his chest. "You'll be putting yourself in jeopardy. If the president doesn't approve this, he could try to eliminate you…all of us…before you could even start a war."

"I know." He pulled her tight against his body and held her. They clung to each other for a long moment before he pressed his lips to the top of her head. "It's either this or we're picked off one by one as the powers that be find us. We're out of options. Both are awful choices."

"A real rock and a hard place situation." She tipped her head up to look at him. "Until I started on my destiny to find you, I never really understood that saying. Now…now I wish I still didn't."

"I know, my angel. I'd shelter you from all the dark spots of my world if I could."

She gripped his shirt in her hands and admitted her greatest weakness. "I love you…and to think of what could happen to you terrifies me."

"I'm going to be okay." He used his index finger to draw her mouth up to his. "We're all going to be okay." With that, he kissed her.

She met his lips with an eagerness of her own. Letting her tongue slip between his lips, she devoured him and forced her fears back into the dark corners of her mind to deal with later. Right now, she just needed him. To feel his body against hers and meet the desire that was constantly rushing through her. Tomorrow, they'd deal with everything else.

Chapter Twenty-One

A few hours of quality time with his mate had Patrick energized, even his lion felt full of energy again as his beast paced within him. Now he sat in front of the fireplace in the family room with his arm around Clarissa's shoulders, waiting for Jade and the others to return with MaKayla. With every minute that ticked by, he tried not to worry. Even if his connection to her and the others let him know they were safe, he wanted Jade home. He didn't like taking risks when it came to her. She was the only sister he had, and even with five brothers, he took it as his personal mission to ensure her safety. Maybe he sheltered her, but with what had happened to her, no one could blame him. At least, that's what he told himself.

"I thought I relieved your stress earlier. Do we need a refresher course?" She snuggled into his embrace. With her eyes fluttering shut, she didn't look like she was up to another round of lovemaking, even if he carried her up to their room.

"I'm not stressed, just uneasy that Jade is out there. She might be getting her strength back, but she's still vulnerable. If she got captured again, she wouldn't survive it." He hated to admit it, but it was the truth. Even if they didn't kill her on the spot, she'd never survive being held in one of those labs again.

"I know you went to her the other night. Is she having nightmares often?"

He nodded. "Almost nightly. She tries to hide them, but when she wakes up screaming she can't deny them. At first she wouldn't let anyone in, but slowly she opened up to me. Our bond has become stronger. Even though I wasn't there, I suffered right along with her."

"For her to put this behind her, she's going to have to face up to what happened to her. She's going to need help to get through it. Possibly professional help."

"That's not so easy to do right now." He shook his head. "I've been trying to help her as much as I can. I know she's suffering from PTSD, but she's only willing to open up so much, and to push her will make things worse."

"Have you thought that maybe you're not the right person for it? Maybe she'd open up to someone else?"

He had thought about all of this before, but always came back to the same conclusion. There were only a handful of them who could help her. "She's only spoken to me about it. Austin and everyone else have tried, but she clams up. Chase has gone to her in his lion form, curled up with her, and that has helped her calm down from the nightmares. She tells him bits and pieces, but very little."

"We'll figure something out," she reassured him, as the front door opened.

Patrick didn't know what to expect as Jade led MaKayla inside.

"Welcome to Forever Creek," Jade was saying to her. "You've had a long night, so we'll get you settled and tomorrow I'll show you around." She turned as Patrick slipped out from Clarissa's embrace. "Patrick, I didn't expect you to be down here."

"Welcome, MaKayla," he said, offering a warm smile. Her bleached hair with pink and purple highlights were even more vivid in person. "I knew your uncle, and it's a pleasure to have you here."

"MaKayla, this is my brother, Patrick. He's the Alpha here." Jade nodded to Clarissa, who had climbed off the sofa and was standing a few steps behind him. "That's Clarissa, his mate."

The little girl seemed to close into herself more with Patrick standing before her. She shrank back at the word *Alpha* and fear poured off her. The poor girl was terrified, and seeing him before her was doing nothing to put her at ease.

"Jade, I've made up a room on our floor. My former suite." Clarissa tipped her head. "Why don't Jade and I help you get her settled?"

"Come on, MaKayla." Jade grabbed the bag that Chase had placed near the steps. Chase, Austin, and Blake stood near the bottom of the steps waiting.

With the women gone, Austin sank onto one of the sofas and let out a long yawn. "She hasn't spoken since we picked her up. The family said that since she found out about Andrew, she's spoken very little. She's having a hard time, but Jade was able to make her smile. Even if it was just a small one, it's something."

"With everything that's happened in the last few months, we can't blame her for being scared." Patrick took the seat he had vacated only moments before.

"Why'd you give her a room on our floor?" Blake leaned against the corner of the sofa, looking exhausted.

"Clarissa convinced me." He shook his head at his mate. "She was like a dog with a bone."

"Rumor has it that mates can be like that," Austin joked.

"With MaKayla being so young, Clarissa said she'll be scared being in a new place and having others close will help her feel safe. Plus, no one will be on the floor except us. Right now, Nolan's the only other person here, until more join us. It's just easier to have her with us now, instead of having to move her later." He picked up the mug of coffee he had set aside earlier. "There're no other children her age to play with, which is going to make it rougher for her."

"What about her hair?" Chase smirked. "That hair makes her unforgettable for sure. We're going to need to be careful with her."

"It's unforgettable, that's true, but she's not going to be leaving the castle." He set the mug aside and looked at each of his brothers. "We'll have to keep her hidden from anyone who could come our way. At least until we can make sure we can trust each of them. I'm sure that by week's end, the authorities are going to be spreading the news of a missing eight-year-old matching her description. I hope you've warned the family that it's likely they'll be tested with LUNA due to the timing of this."

"We have," Blake affirmed. "The husband is a teacher, so he'll be tested anyway. Thankfully, they've been using the story that it was a friend's child who was staying with them temporarily."

"One problem at a time. We need to focus on things here, so we can't worry too much about them." He leaned back against the sofa and decided now was as good a time as any to unveil his plan. "I know you're tired, but there's something I wanted to tell you before you retire for what's left of the night."

"Should we get Jade, Luke, and Clarissa?" Blake asked.

"Clarissa already knows, and I'll speak with Jade when she's done. Luke just fell asleep, so I'll talk with him in the morning."

Over the next twenty minutes, he went over all the details of the proposal he was sending to the president, the plans, and answered their questions. Even as he said it aloud for the second time, he couldn't shake the doubts that were lingering in the back of his mind.

He thought telling his brothers the plan would help confirm his desire to do this, but as he watched their faces he could see the doubt in their eyes. The only one who had remained neutral was Austin, since he already knew what Patrick had been up to the last few days.

"I know this is a surprise, and I know it brings more dangers to all of us. So, I'd like all of you on board before I do this."

"You have my support." Blake leaned his head back against the sofa. "But just in case this doesn't work, I'll make sure I'm ready for war."

"We're already living that way, the way we would in these towns you have in mind. So, go for it." Chase shrugged. "If they come after us, we'll be ready."

"I want to do everything we can to avoid a war with the humans," Patrick reminded them.

"We all do, but it might not be an option. In the end, it will be their choice. We can only do so much, put up with so much, before we have no choice but to strike back." Austin turned to Chase and Blake. "We all need some sleep, but after lunch we're going to increase the training sessions. There's more danger coming our way, and I want to make sure we're ready."

"You'll take the women as well."

"What?" Austin turned to Patrick. "I know Jade's always participated in the training sessions, and has even gone on some missions, but to involve them in the fight that's coming our way…you can't be serious."

"I would never want them on the front lines. Jade isn't ready, even if she wanted to be. But I want each of them to know how to defend themselves." Patrick leaned forward, placing his elbows on his knees. "I'll take Clarissa. Austin, I might need your help with her. My natural instincts are to protect her, so I know it will be harder to work with my own mate."

"She's human…" Austin started before Patrick's growl cut him off.

"She is, and even though she won't stand up in hand to hand combat with a shifter, there're other ways. She's a scientist, so it's unlikely she's spent much time in a gym learning self-protection. Her father and brother taught her some, but not enough."

"Very well, whatever you need." Austin nodded. "Has her brother arrived yet?"

"Not yet. He's still got a little more than twenty-four hours." He glanced at Chase and Blake. "I think right now MaKayla would feel better if with Jade or Clarissa were with her for these sessions. We're going to have to teach her, too. So, since she's a shifter, I want her with Jade. MaKayla doesn't know her own strength yet because she's still coming into her beast. It's growing and maturing with her as she ages, so you could say she hasn't completed her transition yet, and that will make it harder to determine where her true strengths are. I want the two of you to tag-team with Jade and MaKayla. Build on Jade's strengths, and do what you can with MaKayla."

"I'll pop in to oversee your session with MaKayla, maybe I can give you some pointers on what areas would be the best to work on with her," Austin added.

"Just remember to take it easy on her," Patrick ordered. "I don't want her to suspect anything, because we're not telling her the plan yet. It would be best to divide Jade's training so that only part of it is with MaKayla, then you can work Jade harder."

"Jade relies on her beast too much. If you can show her that she can defeat someone even without her beast, it will give her more confidence," Austin suggested. "Now, if Patrick's done, you two can go get some sleep. I'd like to have another word with our Alpha."

The younger brothers rose when Patrick nodded. "Get some rest."

When they were alone, Austin leaned back against the sofa. "When are you sending the proposal to the president?"

"Not until after Dean arrives. He said he found something that I'd want to see, but wouldn't go into any additional details. It might be something that would be useful for this proposal."

"Are you going to tell him your plans?"

Patrick leaned back and thought about that for a second before he finally answered. "I haven't decided yet. I need to see his attitude when he arrives, and what he's found. Hopefully, he will see that his sister is happy and won't make an uproar."

"If he causes a problem?"

"Then I'll deal with him, and yes, even if that means removing him from the castle. Now, is that all you're concerned about?"

Austin shook his head. "Giving him our location and then forcing him to leave could cause issues, but that's not my only concern."

"I don't think he'd put his sister in jeopardy. Despite his faults and his attitude, he cares for her and would protect her with his life, just as I would. What else is on your mind?"

"Has Luke made any progress on the child they experimented on?"

"Not enough for a location. He believes the mother is alive, and thinks the child must be as well. He's still a few steps behind, and will most likely need a few more days before he has anything solid."

"Jade wanted to go get MaKayla. Instead of two of us going, four of us went. You need to be ready for her to fight again. I don't think you should let her go on missions yet." Austin let out a deep sigh. "She's not ready. The whole drive to pick up MaKayla, her nerves and fears clung to the air like a sickly gas, putting all of us on edge. She's hiding it, but she's still terrified, possibly more than before, now that the nightmares are more frequent."

"I knew she wasn't ready, but she needed to see it for herself. The mission was only a few hours, so it was the best chance to give her the opportunity to see it for herself. Hopefully, she'll accept her limitations now, and stay here."

"Until MaKayla got into the SUV, I think Jade had to bite her tongue to stop herself from demanding we turn around. I hated to see her like that, but like you said, she needed to know what it would be like. Otherwise, she wouldn't have faced it." Austin slammed his hand onto his thigh. "Hell...she's pushing herself too hard and too fast."

Patrick nodded in agreement. According to the calendar it had been months, but to him it only seemed like days ago. She had come a long way in the weeks since she had been back home. Being surrounded by her pride had helped her heal, but there were times when she didn't think anyone was looking that he could see her deep sadness. She was starting to remember more than he had hoped she would. He'd have to decide whether or not to reveal what he had found in her file. She might need to know everything in order to put it behind her.

That was a decision for another day. Instead, he rose from the sofa and glanced at Austin. "I'm going to find my mate. I suggest you get some rest as well."

"In a bit. I want to do my pass on the grounds and make sure nothing has come by."

"Since you weren't here, I did it earlier. All is well, but knowing you I just wasted breath by telling you." Patrick shook his head. "Careful out there, the fresh snow has made the mountains hard to trek through." With that, he headed toward the stairs, determined to find his mate, and get a few precious hours of sleep. It would help pass the time until Dean arrived, and resting would keep his thoughts from wandering to unanswerable questions.

Clarissa shut MaKayla's door all but a few inches, and walked down the hall with Jade. As they moved out of shifter hearing range, she whispered, "She hasn't spoken since you retrieved her?"

"We were told that she's spoken very little since she saw Andrew's death, and not at all since she found out they were forcing her to leave. She seemed to accept their reasoning, even contacted us, but you can feel the despair pouring off her."

"I never realized the connection Patrick had to all of you until the mating was complete. Even though she's not in the pride, I can still feel a connection to her. Why's that?"

Patrick stepped onto the floor, locking the door behind him, just as she finished her question. "Because she has no sleuth."

"Sleuth?"

"It's the bear's form of a pride, like I mentioned before," he explained. "She's without the sleuths backing, so any Alpha who comes into contact with her would feel some connection to her. That is until she commits to an Alpha. As another shifter, Jade could feel her emotions, especially since MaKayla's beast is still maturing within her and she can't shield like she needs to, but she wouldn't feel everything you're feeling."

"Can she commit to a pride even though she's a bear shifter?"

"She's free of all her connections, so she can. Once she feels safe here, she might decide she wishes to commit herself to our pride. However, until she makes the decision to commit or to seek out another Alpha, we must protect her. She's been entrusted to my custody, and I won't have her pressured to pledge herself to someone else until she's ready. Some wouldn't be as willing to allow her to make the decision on her own. They'd pressure her until she felt she had no choice but to agree." He slipped his arm around his mate's waist. "How is she doing?"

"She's resting now, curled in a tight ball." Jade's lips twitched down in a deep frown. "There's so much sadness within her."

"You want to heal her because you cannot heal the hurt within you."

Her eyes widened as she stared at her brother. "That's not true. I'm fine."

"If you can't be honest with me, at least be honest with yourself." Patrick waited a heartbeat before he shook his head. "There will come a time when you're ready to face what happened and the nightmares will cease. Only then will you truly be able to heal. When you're ready, you know where to find me. We will all have your back, no matter what's down that road."

"If there's one thing I've learned since I've joined this family, it's that the O'Reillys stick together." Clarissa glanced between the two, a ray of happiness sparking within her because she was a part of their family. "If you ever need to talk to someone besides one of your burly brothers, I'm always here." She smiled at Jade, who was becoming like a sister to her. They had bonded, and Jade had help Clarissa adjust to shifter life. The least she could do was be there for her when she needed someone to confide in.

"I'm going to bed." Jade turned and took a step toward her bedroom before glancing hesitantly at Clarissa. "Thanks…I mean it."

"Actually, Jade," Patrick began, "I need a minute before you turn in." His tone held more of a serious note than it had only moments before.

"If it's about what happened before, or tonight, I'm not up for it right now. Can't it wait until morning?"

"It's not about that. Let's go to my suite, it will only take a few minutes."

"I can go to the lab, and you can come get me when you're done,"

Clarissa offered.

"No need, we're just going to discuss the proposal." He kept his arm around her waist as they made their way down the wide hallway.

She leaned against his chest and tried to quell the rising fear within her. The government could send out a team of elite military to eliminate all of them before things could go any further, and the O'Reillys could start getting the other shifters in an uproar. She knew the government would go to great lengths to keep the shifters in check, and to stop a war that would be on their own soil.

I won't lose Patrick or this family. She would fight for them just as they'd fought for her.

Chapter Twenty-Two

Patrick's eyelids flung open as his lion caught the scent of someone moving outside. He slipped his arm out from under Clarissa, causing her to let out a soft moan, but she didn't wake. When he was sure she'd stay asleep, he moved quietly to the window. Outside, everything seemed just as it had been hours ago when he had climbed into bed with his mate, but someone was coming. His lion sensed it. Whoever it was, they were at least a ten-minute walk away. It gave him just enough time to get Austin, and prepare before their guest—or their intruder—reached the castle.

He grabbed the jeans he'd discarded at the edge of the bed and slipped them on. He slid the zipper home just as she began to stir. She slid her arm across the bed to where he should have been, but when she didn't find him she shot upright on the mattress.

"Patrick." With her voice full of sleep, she fought to open her eyes.

"I'm right here, angel."

"Come back to bed."

He tugged a black long-sleeved shirt over his head. "I've got to deal with something, but I'll be back as quick as I can."

Half-heartedly, she scooted toward the edge of the bed. "I'll come with you."

"No, angel, it won't take long. You stay here and keep the bed warm."

He grabbed hold of her ankles as she lowered them toward the floor and quickly pulled her back into bed. As her head pressed against the pillows, he pulled the covers around her. "I won't be long. Rest, my beautiful angel."

"The bed's so lonely without you." Her eyelids fluttered shut as she tried to stifle a yawn.

"You won't be awake long enough to be lonely." He smirked as she tried to pry her eyes open to look at him, which she barely managed. "You're exhausted, so stay in bed. I promise I'll make it up to you."

A soft moan warmed the air. "Now, that might be worth a few lonely hours in bed by myself."

He shook his head and hoped it wouldn't take hours, but there was no telling. Instead of denying it, he leaned forward and placed a gentle kiss on her forehead before rising off the mattress. He curled his hand around his jacket, but then stopped and stepped toward the closet. From the top shelf he pulled down a locked box and took out his handgun. He kept it in the holster and slipped it into the waistband of his jeans. It wasn't comfortable, but at least he'd have other means besides hand to hand combat or shifting if things got out of hand with this stranger.

"Patrick," Austin called softly from outside the door.

"Coming." He placed the box back on the shelf, closed the closet, and grabbed his jacket. With Austin waiting outside the bedroom for him, having picked up on the approaching intruder as well, at least he didn't have to waste any time. As he stepped out of his room, he found Austin, already wearing his coat and ready to go outside.

"It couldn't be Dean, could it?"

He hadn't considered Dean. One would have thought he'd have more sense than to go stumbling through the woods in the middle of the night, to a castle full of shifters. All of it was a recipe for disaster. If he were smart, he'd wait until first light to make the final journey to the resort. "Could be, but it's a good way to get himself killed."

"Maybe whatever he found is worth the risk," Austin offered as they descended the stairs. "Or, whoever was after him could be hot on his trail."

"If he brought trouble to our door, he won't live long enough to regret it." His growls mixed with his words as he considered whether Dean could be stupid and selfish enough to bring trouble straight to his sister's doorstep. Would he risk her to save himself? Or did he figure the shifters would protect them? If that was the case, he was about to learn a harsh lesson.

"She wouldn't like it."

"He'd have risked our pride, and that's punishable by death."

"Shifter logic," Austin pointed out, and Patrick wanted to deny it, but it was the truth. Humans didn't go around killing each other for such things.

"That's true, but she needs to realize she's not in the human world any longer." He glanced at Austin as he stepped to the bottom of the stairs. "Even if it is Dean, he might not have trouble hot on his heels, and if he does we'll deal with that, too."

"So, are we going out with guns blazing?" Austin nodded to Patrick's waist.

He smelled the gunpowder. Any shifter would, but they didn't have much fear when it came to guns. The bullet would have to be well-placed, centered on the heart or the brain for a shifter to die from it.

"Whoever's out there is human. So, if it's not Dean, then we have a trespasser." Each turn of the lock echoed through the quietness as if announcing their departure. "Keep the guns hidden until we know who it is, and then only if needed. If it's not Dean, maybe it's a lost hiker."

"This time of year?" Austin chuckled as the last lock slid away.

Patrick pulled open the door, only to be hit full force by the bitter cold wind. A human had to be crazy to go out in this. Crazy or desperate. Instead of debating it any longer, he stepped outside, Austin right behind him, and headed in the direction the smell was coming from. There was something familiar about the scent, but even now, his beast wasn't convinced it was Dean.

They trekked through the snow in silence. Neither of them bothered to head downwind to keep their scent away from the intruder. Since he wasn't a shifter, it didn't matter. Instead, they just marched straight toward the scent, which was just beyond the trees now. If it were a trap, they'd be open targets, but the only scent of gunpowder was their own. Whoever was out there was unarmed and alone. It had to be Dean.

The figure stepped out of the trees, and the scent of fresh blood invaded Patrick's nostrils. Even with the smell and the heavy parka, he instantly recognized Dean. His scent was different because not all of the blood on him was his own. "Fuck, what the hell happened to him?"

"I'd say from the blood that's coating him, whatever happened, he won."

"At what cost?" He increased his pace because Dean was bleeding heavily. If he died before Clarissa was reunited with him, she would be heartbroken, and Patrick wasn't sure how he would deal with that.

Dean staggered and started to fall forward into the snow. Austin and Patrick each caught one of his arms just in time to keep him upright. "I thought I'd never make it." Exhaustion clung to his every word.

"What the hell happened to you?" Patrick questioned as they tried to move him forward, toward the castle.

"Long story…good news is, I won."

Dean felt heavier the closer to they got to the castle. They had to get him inside so Patrick could look at him. He had lost too much blood and was quickly going into shock. They didn't have a supply of blood on hand, so hopefully they'd be able to handle this without taking him to a hospital, which was out of the question anyway.

"Dean…" Austin shook him until he looked up. "Did anyone follow you?"

He shook his head. "Dead…all dead."

By half carrying, half dragging him they were able to get Dean inside. On the sofa, Patrick began to pull off the layers of clothing and ordered Austin to fetch supplies. "Get my kit, some hot water and towels."

"Drink." Dean let his head rest against the back of the sofa.

"Get him some water after you bring the other stuff." He pulled the jacket off and tossed it to the floor. "Where are you injured?"

"Where am I not?" He tugged up his shirt to reveal a rather nasty stab wound. His attacker must have pulled up on the knife, making the wound worse. "Where's Clarissa?"

"In bed. I'll get her once I've looked at you." He didn't want her to see her brother in the condition he was in. She'd have a fit that he'd risked himself and wouldn't let them send backup. It was best to get him cleaned and patched up first. He didn't even question what Dean had found. Not yet at least.

Commotion in the hallway woke Clarissa. She stretched her arm out to touch Patrick, but he still hadn't returned. As the events of the morning flooded back to her, she slipped off the bed and grabbed a robe. She stepped into the hall just in time to see Austin dashing toward the steps, carrying what appeared to be medical supplies.

She went back into their room and shoved her feet into a pair of slippers before jogging after him. If someone was hurt, she might be able to help them. As she hurried down the steps, she noticed that none of the connections within the pride were disturbed, so none of them were injured. Could someone have shown up while she was asleep? Dean? She sped her pace until she was running down the steps at full speed.

The last staircase opened up to the family area, and she saw her brother on the sofa. His bloody clothes had been stripped from him and tossed aside. His pale, unconscious body was stretched out on the sofa as Patrick attended to his wounds.

"Dean!" She cried out even though she knew he couldn't hear her, while tears streamed down her cheeks. She felt as though she were on the verge of hysteria. "What…what the hell happened? What did…what did you do to my brother?" Her breaths came faster, her anger spiking.

Patrick didn't even glance up, which only enraged her further. She came to the bottom of the staircase, but Austin stepped in the way.

"Let me through," she snapped.

"No." Austin looped his arm around her waist to stop her as she tried to slip past him. "His injuries are bad. Let Patrick attend to him."

"What happened to him?"

"I don't know." Austin still didn't let go of her. "It happened before he got here, but he's been stabbed multiple times. Patrick is stitching him up now, but we had to sedate him, so he's going to be out a while."

"You thought we did this." Patrick's statement was so soft she wasn't even sure she'd heard him, but she could feel the sadness tugging along the invisible strings that connected them.

"Oh, Patrick…" She wept, unable to control herself. "I'm so sorry, I didn't…I know you couldn't have done it, but that doesn't explain what happened." The anger that had coursed through her dissipated, just like that, because she knew in her heart that her mate would do everything he could to save her brother.

"Come sit over here, and let him finish." Austin let go of her waist and took hold of her hand.

"You don't have to worry that I'll go after the good doctor." There was a tremor in her voice. She was shaking.

"Just come over here."

She shook her head but followed. "I didn't mean it like it sounded. To see him so badly beaten…and all the blood."

"You jumped to the conclusion that I did this to him," Patrick accused.

"No. Actually, when I said it, I didn't realize how badly he was injured. I only thought…" She let out a deep breath and decided it was better to be honest than for him to think she didn't believe him. "I thought you heard someone sneaking around the property, and instead of finding out who it was first, you hit him over the head, knocking him unconscious. Precautionary measure, nothing more. Patrick, I know you…I know you both, and neither of you would have hurt him unless he attacked first. If he did, I'm not sure you'd be over there healing him right now."

Patrick stopped mid-stitch and looked at her. "So, even though, I'm a doctor and your mate, you actually think we'd let him die even if he attacked?"

"Well…" She tried to stand up, but Austin stayed in her way so she couldn't. "Why would you? If he attacked you, then he betrayed us all. He betrayed not only you, but also me. His own sister, same flesh and blood." She leaned back against the chair Austin had led her to and realized that was part of the issue. She felt betrayed by her brother because he hadn't come with her in the first place. He let her go with Patrick and Blake while he went off on his own somewhere.

"Because of you, mate." He spit it out like it left a bad taste in his mouth. "If I had to knock the senses out of him, I'd still patch him up so I could send him back to town. Killing your brother wouldn't bring our relationship anything but trouble."

"You'd leave a standing threat out there, one who knew your location, because of me?"

Patrick didn't answer her, so Austin finally did. "There's very little we wouldn't do for our mates. In time, you'll find that out, but tonight I'll tell you he had nothing to do with this. We were checking out what we believed was a trespasser when Dean stepped through the trees. Patrick recognized him immediately, so there was no rough and tumble. The condition you see him in is the way we found him."

"Did he say who did this to him? Why?"

"No, only that they were dead. Since then, he's been unconscious, but we're as eager to get information out of him as you are." Austin looked at her and then at Patrick before his gaze finally stopped on her. "If you're going to behave yourself and let him work, I really need to check the land. Make sure there's no fresh blood spilled that will lead anyone here, or draw the attentions of any animals."

"Go ahead, I'm not going to interrupt him."

After a long moment, Patrick nodded. "Go on, Austin. He said the men were killed two towns away, just outside of town limits, so I suspect if you find anything it will only be his blood."

"Then there should be very little." Austin grabbed his jacket from the back of the sofa where he had discarded it. "He bandaged his wounds enough to keep from leaking a trail of blood everywhere."

She waited until Austin was gone before she adjusted in the chair. "Patrick, I'm sorry. I didn't mean it like it sounded."

"Don't worry about it."

There was a hint of disappointment in his voice that made her stand and go to him. She was careful not to interrupt him as he stitched the last of Dean's chest wound. "I never thought you'd do this to him. I was only scared."

"I know what it's like to find one of your siblings injured to the point you're not sure if they'll make it. Or, if they do, what kind of condition they'll be in." He grabbed a towel, wetting it with water from a pitcher before wiping his hands.

"When you found Jade, it had to have been worse." She squeezed his shoulders. "But she's fine."

"Dean will be, too." He began to clean up his supplies. "He'll have to take it easy for a few days because of the blood loss, but there's nothing I can do about that. I don't have blood on hand, and if he killed someone, we can't risk taking him to a hospital. We also don't know how much danger he's in because of whatever he found. So, he'll just have to wait it out."

"What about his other injuries?"

"He might always walk with a limp. He put the knee they dislocated back in place, but didn't get it completely into the socket, so I had to adjust it again. The rest will heal in time."

She grabbed hold of his wrist. "Will we?"

He stilled under her touch. "We're fine."

"Are we? Because it doesn't feel like it." She squatted next to him, careful not to hit her brother's leg or any of the supplies. "It came out wrong, and I'm sorry. I know you'd never do this." She blinked away the tears. "Oh, Patrick, I thought he was dead."

He let the towel drop onto the table and rose, taking her with him. "Come here, angel." With his arms tightly around her waist, he pulled her to him. "He's going to be okay. I cleaned, treated, and stitched his wounds. Now you just have to wait for him to wake up, though hopefully not until we get him upstairs. Once the drugs have left his system, moving him is going to cause him agony."

"Thank you." She held a finger to his lip. "Did you find out what he thought was urgent enough to risk his life for?"

"Not yet, but he should wake up soon. I only gave him enough to sedate him, and I can give him more for the pain once he answers a few questions." He let his hands slide down her body before he stepped back. "Let's get him upstairs. His clothes are ruined, so just leave them, but grab his bag and I'll carry him."

She tossed his duffle bag over her shoulder and watched as he lifted Dean into his arms as if he weighed nothing. There was an ease to his movements that made her want to run her hands over his body to feel the tautness of the muscles under his shirt. Seeing the attention he used in caring for her brother made her heart swell.

"Why are you looking at me like that?"

"Like what?" Without meeting his gaze, she strolled toward the stairs.

"Like you're seeing me in a whole different light."

"Maybe I am." She caught a glimpse of him out of the corner of her eye. His eyebrows were raised in question while he waited for her to explain. With a deep sigh, she nodded. "I've seen how much you care for others, but I can also feel it within me because of this bond between us. The way you are with your siblings…I know it's not how some Alphas could be."

"You know that how?"

"I just do. I can't explain it, but I know things are different in your pride than in others. You take into consideration their needs, wants, and feelings. Take Jade for example. Another Alpha would have just flat out denied her request. Not you. Instead, you sent four of them to pick up one little girl, leaving the castle more vulnerable. You can't tell me you don't run things differently here."

"You've been talking to Austin."

"Not about this." They paused outside the door to their floor as she punched in the code to unlock it. "I've watched how you are with your family, your interactions with Nolan. Mind you, there's been very little of those because of this proposal and LUNA, but it's different than the way you are with your family. He's committed himself to your pride, to this operation, and you act only as an Alpha with him. I'm not sure I'm explaining this very well, but there's a difference."

"I've heard it all before." He entered the room across from MaKayla's and waited while she pulled down the covers on the bed before he placed Dean on the mattress. "I've had this conversation with Austin several times."

"I know." She tucked the covers around her brother's still unconscious body. "Jade mentioned it, but that's not why I'm bringing it up."

"Then why?"

"My brother was an ass when you first met him, and yet you have let that go because of me. The hatred in his words and the way he looked at you…" She went to him and slid her arms around his waist. "You cared about him because he's my brother. To you, that's the same thing as your own family. He was unconscious, so he'll never know what you've done for him, but I'll always know. Thank you."

"Maybe I did it because of whatever information he found." He smoothed his hand along the small of her back.

"Not a chance I believe that. You care more than you want people to know, and that's one of the reasons I've fallen in love with you."

"My angel, when you say that, it makes me want to pick you up, carry you to our room, and show you how much I love you." He leaned down, pressing his lips to hers.

A throat cleared behind her and the kiss broke as quickly as it started. "What happened?" Dean's voice was groggy.

"You're awake," Patrick announced as if she couldn't already tell.

"Awake, and stopping you from shagging my sister."

"Who even says *shagging* anymore?" She shook her head and went to stand next to the bed. The wound along his face that was fresh the last time she'd seen him was nearly healed, but now he had more all over his body to take its place. It was as if he was seeking out trouble, to see how much he could push his limitations before he ended up getting killed. "If we wanted to *shag*, as you so kindly put it, we wouldn't be standing in your room. Now, why don't you tell me what the hell happened to you?"

"Mom."

"What?" She glanced back at Patrick. "Did he hit his head? Was he making sense before you sedated him?"

Dean cut him off before Patrick could answer. "Your first question. It was Mom who always said *shagging*, and I don't know, it just popped out."

She didn't want to think about her parents, or how each of them had been snatched away from her before she graduated college. First her mother to cancer, and then her father in a car accident. Until she met the O'Reillys, Dean was the only family she had and they stuck together. "So, you didn't hit your head?"

"No, I believe my head might have been the only thing I didn't injure this time." Dean glanced past her toward Patrick. "I think I told you before I passed out…there's no threat to your home. I was careful I wasn't followed, and this happened a few towns over. The man's dead." His words came out groggy from the medication and his eyes fluttered shut.

"Why were you attacked?" Patrick asked.

Before answering, Dean glanced at her. "Sis, why don't you give us a few minutes?"

Patrick's arm tightened around her waist, holding her there, not that she had tried to leave. "She's staying. Anything you have to say, she needs to know. This will affect her as much as the rest of us."

"He's right, I'm not leaving. So, why don't you just come out with it? Tell us what information you found, that was important enough to risk yourself for."

Dean's gaze never left Patrick. "I've done a lot of research on your kind. You've mated with her, haven't you?" When Patrick nodded, he added, "I was afraid so."

"What's that supposed to mean?" The first flickers of rage started to burn within her.

"I only want to protect you, and mating with a shifter will bring you more danger than anything else. I've got contacts, and I might have been able to clear your name for what happened at Hathaway Medical, but if you're mated to him…"

"Dean." She sat on the edge of the bed and took his hand into hers. "You're my big brother, and have always tried to protect me, and for that I'll always be thankful. But this isn't something I need or want to be sheltered from. Patrick and the pride have opened my eyes to new things, to a love I've never known before, and to what's wrong with our world. I'm staying here not out of some duty, or because their battle is the right thing, but because I love them. Not just Patrick, but all of them. Honestly, I don't have any desire to clear my name. What's the point when I know it will only be tarnished again? There's a war coming, and I know which side I'll be on. Do you?"

"Now I do." He nodded. "I didn't know before, and when you went with him and the other one I was angry. I said some nasty things and acted like a complete ass. For that, I'm sorry. You, little sister, deserved better from me. They didn't deserve my hatred because of the scar on my face. They had nothing to do with it."

"Which side?" She forced herself to swallow the lump that was forming in her throat.

"This one."

"What you've found changed your mind?" Patrick asked.

"It's in my bag." He started to move until his face became distorted with pain, and his hand shot toward his stomach wound. "I've done a lot of research on your kind," he gasped. "That was my job before all of this happened. Unlike Clarissa, I wasn't anywhere near the experiments." He took a deep breath, seeming to work through the pain. "I was a technical manager. It wasn't until a few days before she called me that I knew what they were doing. That's when I really dug into the computer systems so I could duplicate them for Brazil. Before that, I never realized the torture they were doing, only that they did have shifters in those labs, but I thought it was legit." He paused for a moment, relaxing against the pillows. "I was preparing to leave, put in my vacation request. I had to do it by the book or they could have hurt Clarissa before I even got back to the states."

"What did you find that made you ready to give everything up?"

"Before, all I had was bits and pieces, but now I have evidence." He glanced at her. "I'm sorry, but what happened at Hathaway Medical went deeper than you think. They tested on humans, not just shifters."

"I already know." She reached up to cup Patrick's hand, which was resting on her shoulder.

"Oh, then you might already have the information on Mallory Barrow and her daughter."

"Who?" Patrick's hand stilled under hers, and her heart sank. *Was this the little girl they'd experimented on?*

"Mallory has a daughter who is a year old, and she's the only known *human* survivor of the experiments. All the others are dead. So, I take it from the looks on your faces you didn't know about them. Well, the information I was able to gather is in my bag."

"We knew of a child who was used, but a name wasn't in the files, only an identification number. Luke has been working on it. Do you know where they are?"

Dean shook his head. "I haven't found their current location, but after I broke into Doctor Songborn's house, I had someone on my tail."

"You went to his house?" She couldn't believe what she was hearing.

"You know him, then?" He didn't wait for her to answer. "Yes, and he's dead. Before you even ask, it wasn't planned. I knew he was connected, but I didn't know how. I broke into his house, found the files he kept and the few things on his computer. That asshole kept video recordings of it. He'd watched them over and over again, like he was getting off on the torture he put the Barrows through. When he stumbled into the house after a few too many drinks, I couldn't stop myself. My rage got the best of me, and I killed him." He leaned his head away, his cheeks reddened. "His son had come home with him that night, and he was the one who followed me. We got into an altercation, and I ended up with a few stab wounds, but…he's dead now. I think I got the better end of that deal."

"Get what he has in the bag, and I'll take it to Luke," Patrick said. "He can get started on it, and maybe it will bring us closer to a location. At least now we have a name. Meanwhile, you need to rest. I'm going to grab some medication, and I'll be back."

When Patrick left the room, instead of going for Dean's bag, she sat there staring down at her brother. All she wanted to do was hit him, or scream at him for risking himself. He could have told them about what he knew when they first met Patrick, or at least told her. Instead, he rushed off on some errand, nearly getting himself killed in the process.

"You're angry."

"Damn right I am." She withheld the rage that was threatening to escape. "You could have told me."

"I didn't know anything would come of this. Even if I would have told you, or them, I wouldn't have been able to let it go. What was the point of telling anyone until I knew if the Barrows were even alive? Why should anyone else have to carry that knowledge with them if there's nothing that could be done? I was trying to protect you."

"I could have lost you." She squeezed his hand and tried not to think about it.

"You didn't, and you seem to be in good hands here." He glanced at the door as if checking for Patrick. "You love him, but if he ever mistreats you, I'll kill him."

"Oh, dear brother, he'd have you for dinner." She smirked. "Don't worry, he's a pure gentleman and he loves me in return."

Chapter Twenty-Three

While everyone tried to busy themselves with whatever they had on their agenda, Patrick had put the final touches on the proposal to send to the president. Rather than sending it just yet, he went over things numerous times with Austin and Clarissa, debating whether they should mention what Hathaway Medical had done to Mallory Barrow's daughter. Until they had solid evidence, he wasn't sure putting it in the proposal was the best idea. There was no reason they should show all their cards at once. This piece of information could be something that would help them later, give them something they could take to the media to show shifters weren't the only ones being harmed here. First, they had to find Mallory and her daughter.

While he tried to give Luke more time to locate the Barrows, Patrick spent the last two days with Clarissa in the lab, working on LUNA. They had done enough tests to prove anti-LUNA would be good for twenty-two hours once it was ingested. Lesser shifters would have forty minutes to get somewhere safe before they could no longer fight the change, and once the transition happened they'd be stuck in their animal form for an hour at the minimum. The timing could change for each shifter depending on their strength, willpower, and how long it had been since their previous transition, but it was the best they could come up with from the limited test volunteers they had.

Still, having something that could stand against LUNA gave them all one less thing to worry about. At least until she came up with something else, he wouldn't have to go through further trials, and for that, his beast was thankful. LUNA had been rough on his lion. If he never saw that stuff again, it would be too soon.

While they had been busy with that, Austin, Blake, and Chase had put MaKayla and Jade through their paces when it came to training. Even Patrick made sure that Clarissa got some much needed hours in the gym. Austin had also increased Nolan's training and once Dean was on his feet again, he'd join everyone in their training routines. Everyone who was going to stay at the castle would be able to defend themselves.

Things were starting to come together in order for them to put their plans into motion, and it was almost time to send the proposal. Even with Luke's assurance that the email wouldn't be traceable, he couldn't help but look at each of the people depending on him as the first sensations of doubt rose within him. If even one of them got injured or killed because of this, it would be his fault.

"Hey, Jade." He called to her as she strolled past his upstairs office on her way from the gym to take a shower. When she paused and looked in, he added, "How's MaKayla doing? Speaking yet?"

"Not really, but she's been working out in the gym, and she seems to be taking to Chase. They both enjoy being in their animal form, and they've seemed to bond over it. Blake seems to scare her almost as much as you and Austin do." She used the towel around her shoulders to wipe the sweat from her face. "She's downstairs with Clarissa now. They're bonding over ice cream, and she's telling MaKayla how Andrew saved her life. She knew Andrew longer than any of us, so I bowed out to let her try to connect with MaKayla. The poor girl is too traumatized from all she's been through."

"Things are only going to get worse, so we need to do what we can to make sure she's ready for it. We'll protect her as much as we can, but you know some of it's going to leak through."

"She's tough, even if she doesn't realize it yet."

"I just wanted to see how things were coming along. I've been trying to keep a little distance between her since every time I'm nearby, she clams up." He rubbed a hand along the five o'clock shadow he hadn't bothered to shave off yet. "Go shower."

"You know it's not you, right? She's scared, and you're the Alpha, so it's natural."

He nodded, but she was already gone.

He knew it wasn't best to wonder what might have happened had things been different. If he had known, he would have been able to stop Andrew from leaving. Once an Alpha started doubting themselves and their decisions, others would see it as a weakness and use that opportunity to attack. He rose from the desk, squared his shoulders, and reminded himself now wasn't the time to start doubting things. He had a pride that was growing, and each of them depended on him.

Instead of doubting himself, he headed to Luke's office, hoping for an update on the search for the Barrows. With the news coverage of the last few days about everyone who had left their jobs because of the LUNA testing, and the recent threats from SFW, he didn't want to put off the proposal much longer.

"Damn it," Luke's growl came only seconds before he slammed his hand on the desk.

Patrick turned just in time to see his brother arguing with the computer. "Is the computer fighting back?"

Luke glanced up from the computer screen and gave him a look that let him know now was not the best time. "Every bloody time."

"Huh?"

"Mallory Barrow has been moving around the country since she took her daughter and ran. Every time I pinpoint a location, she's already gone before I can gather the needed information. Bank accounts, everything. Just vanishes."

"That's not the information I wanted, but I know you'll find her." He leaned against the doorjamb. "I guess it's something to confirm she and the child must be alive."

"How many others were in the files who didn't live through it?"

"Five others." That churned Patrick's stomach. Five innocent children had been test subjects. "None of them survived, but some lived longer than others. Even with the information Dean brought with him, I can't figure out why some died nearly instantly and others might have lasted a few months. Another question is how the Barrow child survived. If I had all his research instead of just bits and pieces of it, maybe then I could figure out what changed from child to child."

"I can't help you there. I searched through Hathaway Medical's files, and there was nothing on their system. Anything Doctor Songborn had must have been separate. It's almost like he didn't want the brass to know what he was doing."

"Not surprising, after seeing his office. He seemed to be the type who didn't trust technology. His computer was from the stone ages, and all his files were handwritten." Patrick shoved his hands into the pockets of his jeans. "I'll let you get back to it. But if you don't have anything by tomorrow, I'm going to send the proposal. I can't wait any longer."

"Actually, I've been thinking about that. I know you've discussed it with Austin but…" Luke paused as if reconsidering his decision to approach the topic.

"Out with it. There's no need to pussyfoot around whatever's on your mind."

"Fine." Luke nodded. "I'd suggest you leave the Barrows out of the proposal. If the president knows about Songborn's experiments, there's no reason to mention them again. If he doesn't, it could reveal our hand too soon. We don't know what their decision will be, and if it's unfavorable they might send someone to capture or eliminate the Barrows."

"I've considered that, but I've also got to consider the other side of that coin. It could be just what's needed to get them to see how bad things have become. To see what's happening, not just to us but to humans as well. If they experiment on children, there's nothing they won't do. Children should be off-limits."

"You can't protect everyone."

Patrick knew that, but it didn't stop him from trying. He'd become a doctor for that reason, to protect and heal. It went against everything in him to sit back and do nothing when people were being hurt, tortured, or killed.

Instead, of debating things further, he turned and strolled back to his office. He needed time to think, to prepare for his next move. The time for decisions and planning was coming to an end. He needed to step up and lead this family. No longer could he be half-hearted about it. He'd have to step up and be the Alpha his father was. The Alpha, his father, had taught him to be. It didn't matter the time had come sooner than he had expected or wanted. What mattered was his family was depending on him.

The changes that were coming to the pride were numerous. Far more than just preparing to deal with the government, protecting themselves, or even preparing for a war. His siblings were about to be introduced to the new Alpha side of him. He'd respect the opinions of his siblings, but when it came down to it, he had to make sure they knew that even if they disagreed with an order, they had to follow it. Right now, he believed they'd follow him but they didn't fear him. Maybe it was time to make sure they feared him, too—especially now that Nolan was here, and they were beginning to bring others into their pride.

He pulled out the leather high back chair and took a seat. For the next hour, he was going to read over the proposal one last time and then he was going to send it. No more delaying. Once it was sent, it would be time to implement some additional changes. Tonight, after dinner, he'd call a family meeting to inform everyone how he wanted to proceed with the future of their pride.

For months, he had felt adrift, never completely in control, and always one step behind where his father would have been. But now, with his mate by his side, he could claim his role as Alpha whole-heartedly and lead his pride members as they deserved to be led. He could almost hear his father's voice. *I'm proud of you, son.*

With her wine glass in hand, Clarissa leaned back into the sofa, her gaze following Patrick as he moved before them. She had seen him in charge of the pride before, but not like this. There was something different about her mate. He was commanding instead of questioning his decisions and waiting for their reactions. He carried himself with more confidence, and she knew that if they were going to get through this, it would be because of him. She wasn't sure what happened earlier in the day, but whatever it was had brought out the man they all needed in order to prevail.

It wasn't just her who saw the changes. The others watched him with awe and pride. The knowledge and confidence they had in him had changed.

She could feel the approval that he had taken his leadership to another level and was finally ready to lead them in every way an Alpha needed to. She might be new to the shifter world, but she knew it was a huge step. She was proud of her mate, and when they were alone she planned to show him just how much.

"I've sent the proposal to the president, and now we just have to wait. Blake increased the security this afternoon. Every door and window has an alarm that we'll hear if anyone tries to get in without first disarming the system. It's on a frequency our ears will pick up, but humans won't, so they won't know they've alerted us until it's too late."

"Tomorrow, I'm going to break down a couple walls upstairs and create a family room there as well. Anyone who has free time, I could use your help," Blake added.

"Why, when we've already got all this space here?" Jade questioned.

"I want a secure place where we can relax. This is very open, and if the danger level increases, or the president denies our request, I want to make sure there's a safe place for everyone that isn't down here." Patrick placed his hands on the back of the chair he had been sitting on before he decided he needed to move around. "If our request is approved, we'll be able to move other shifters into their own houses, and that will give us more privacy and security."

"That will also mean we'll need to begin to restore some of the other buildings on the grounds," Blake added. "If Patrick gets what he's asked for, we will hopefully gain additional land and buildings people can live in. With luck, they'll be inhabitable with very little work."

"I'm ready for this to be over, for the labs to be a thing of the past." Jade pulled her legs up against her chest.

"Little sister, I have a feeling that even if the government agrees to all of this, the labs aren't just going to pack up and close. There might be less of them, and they might not be as bad as things are now, but they'll still be there." Austin took a long pull from the glass of whiskey he had poured.

"We'll be one step closer, and that's what counts," Patrick countered, glancing toward Clarissa. "You've been quiet through all of this."

"I've been watching you at work." She wiggled her eyebrows, hoping he realized just how much he turned her on when he was dominating. The Alpha side of him fit like a second skin and heated her to the core. All she could think about was finishing this meeting and getting him alone.

"Why didn't Dean join us? I mean, shouldn't he know what we're getting into?" Jade asked. "I understand why we waited until MaKayla went to her room to read, but Dean…"

"His body is fighting an infection. Patrick drugged him up, and he's resting," Clarissa supplied. "Patrick and I will speak with him, but I want you all to know that he's on our side. He's risked himself so much already, there's no way he's going to turn his back on any of us now."

As if trying to change the subject, Luke cleared his throat. "What did you decide about the Barrows? Did you include them in the proposal?"

Patrick shook his head. "I've left Mallory and her daughter out of it so far. We'll hold that card for now, and see how things go. Once we have her protected, if we need to, we'll expose Hathaway Medical and the other labs for what they are. That will take the government with them since these labs are operating on their backing."

"Are you any closer to finding them?" Austin set his glass aside and leaned forward.

"I've found the location she was at five weeks ago," Luke said. "So, I'm gaining on them. It's only a matter of time. Give me a little bit longer and I'll have a location for you."

"You seem to carry more urgency about this than other missions. Do you know something we don't?" Chase finally spoke.

"I can't explain it, but I know that child needs our help. The mother must be out of her mind with worry as well. We don't even know if she completely understands what's happening to her child. Think about it, at least our parents knew we were shifters. Mallory is human and most likely has very little knowledge on shifters."

"Wait, I thought you didn't shift until you were a year or two old?" She rose her eyebrows at Austin's suggestion that there were changes that were noticeable in their childhood.

"True, but there are still abilities that are noticeable at a young age," Austin started before Patrick cut him off.

"Each breed is different, but for lions and most cats, when we're young we purr. We do it in our sleep but also sometimes when we're awake and content. Some kids lay down and watch a movie with their thumb in their mouth. We might lay down and watch a movie but instead we purr. There are other signs, too. We're faster, even at a young age. We crawl, walk, and even speak before other children do."

"But the transition isn't complete until puberty."

Patrick nodded. "During childhood, the beast grows and matures with us and when we hit puberty it's finished. We're then able to shift at will and can control our beast better than ever before. That said, we don't even know the child will go through the transition. As I explained to you before, shifters can't be created by a bite or a chemical, they are only born. However, I believe it's possible that depending on their methods she might have some of our qualities. For all we know, she might only purr for the rest of her life. Or maybe she's faster than the average child."

"Has anyone been able to determine the child's name?"

"Not yet, angel. We wouldn't even have Mallory's name without your brother. All Songborn had in his files were test results, and he only referred to them by number."

Her lips curled down in a frown. "It would just be nice if we had a name or something."

"Soon," he reassured her.

"Anything else?" Jade asked as she stretched her arms above her head.

"One more thing. Clarissa, I've looked over the map you've been working on, with the highlighted areas where you remember the shifter camps to be. But until we have the government's decision, we need to lay low. That means no missions to scope out the camps, and we've got to put off going after any more labs." With an echo of growls from his siblings, Patrick sighed. "I understand, but if we demolish another lab right now, they might deny our proposal just out of spite. Hopefully, we'll know something quickly and can move forward with whatever the next step of the plan will be."

"I figured the camps would be put on the back burner right now. Particularly after what happened with Andrew and SFW, but I wanted to mark the map as I remembered."

She had come to accept they'd have to choose their battles. Their numbers were too small, and there was too much happening in the world. There was no way they could be everywhere. She had gone from living her life like everyone else to wanting to just survive the day, to live to see the next. Even so, she knew she would rather fight for every breath if it meant being with Patrick and the rest of her family. She didn't want to be alone.

Chapter Twenty-Four

Days had passed in quick secession, each one past slower than the last, as they waited for word from the president. Even as the days went by and no one showed up to kill them, it didn't put any of them at ease, least of all Patrick. He had been anxious ever since he clicked send, and as the days went by it only made things worse. With each passing hour, his doubts grew. Every time he hit the refresh button on his inbox, he began to expect a flat-out denial or no reply at all.

Clarissa had taken to pulling him away from the office, so he wasn't constantly stalking his inbox. Part of him had wished he had included a phone number in the email, but it was too late. He had to wait and see how things turned out.

One last check, then I'll go for a run and let my lion roam the grounds for a bit. His index finger slid over the mouse and clicked the refresh button. That's when he saw the email and his stomach dropped. All of a sudden he wanted those days of blissful ignorance back.

Lead the pride. He had a duty to his pride. Instead of closing the laptop and pretending he had never seen the email, he opened it and read it.

Mr. O,

I won't waste time on pleasantries, instead I'll get straight to the point. After all, judging by your very detailed proposal, I'd say you're a man who likes to get right down to business and for that I can admire you.

When I first came into office, most of this was already happening. I'm not passing the blame onto my predecessor but instead explaining the situation. I've met with a number of your kind over the years, and just like humans there's good and bad among both species. Many times I've considered the fact there seems to be more good than bad, and that fear is what got us into this situation. Those hired to keep this issue under control, and keep shifters away from humans, have gotten out of control. Some of that is my fault for not overseeing the project as I should have. Some of the blame must fall on the shoulders of your species for what has happened since this began. There was nothing peaceful about the way they've handled things.

While LUNA has both helped and hurt the situation, it was something that would give first responders a chance to determine if they could put the subject into handcuffs and be safe, or expect to have more dead bodies on their hands. The labs were never supposed to become what they are, and while the department has pushed for more, I have not granted them permission to expand. At least not until changes are made. As you so clearly pointed out, this should be done with volunteers as we do for human case studies. Instead, shifters are being treated like the animals you shift into and used like the dogs some manufacturers test their products on.

A change as great as the one you're asking for will take time. It will also take both of our efforts, a lot of work from everyone involved, and most importantly truth. Can I trust you, Mr. O? Trust is hard to come by, but when you won't even tell me your name, and your location has been untraceable, trust is even harder.

I'm making no promises, but we will discuss this further. I've started a list of negotiable topics that need to be covered for both sides of your proposal. Some are more for your benefit, while others are for mine. I think if we are all willing to compromise, we might be able to work out something that will keep your kind from being hunted. However, if you backstab me, I'll be sure that you and everyone you love are executed. Think about how much you are willing to risk before you go any further.

While you consider the things I've mentioned above, I'll finish my list of points and should have it to you shortly. Meanwhile, only those who need to know will be informed of this development, and I would hope you would do the same—that includes going to the media or any other scare tactic designed to expand your audience. I'm willing to negotiate, but I will not be blackmailed, or backed into a corner so that you can get what you want. Remember that when you look at your family and decide just how much you're willing to risk them. Don't forget you have a little woman to think about now...

We'll speak soon.

President S. Ashworth

Patrick read the email a second and third time, and each time it was that last line that tickled the hairs on the back of his neck. *A little woman.* Was he reading too much into it, or did President Ashworth know more about Patrick and his pride than he was letting on? Or, was it a bluff? Either way, it gave him an uneasy feeling. There had to be something in the proposal that hinted at who he was. How did he know about Clarissa already?

He had to fight the urge to pack up his pride and run again. Only, this time, he had no idea where they'd go. When they'd left their home, he knew they'd work their way west and eventually come to Colorado and the castle. They had no other such location to flee to. At least not like this, not where they had room for others as well.

"Hey, mate." Clarissa strolled into the office in a bikini that barely covered her body.

The lion within him growled, wanting to cover her before others could see how little she was wearing. He drank in the sight of her. Her long blonde hair fell down around her shoulders like a curtain, making him want to brush it back to reveal every inch of her. He had seen her naked, many times, but as she stood there barely hiding a thing from him, she was more beautiful than ever.

"Close your mouth and let's go."

"Go?" He blinked and tried to remember what plans he had with her.

"Swimming. You said you'd join me for my laps after lunch. Since you skipped lunch, I figured you were working, but you're not getting out of this. You've been stalking your email since you sent it. An hour, that's all I'm asking. Now, come on." She ran her hands down the curve of her hips. "You really don't want to miss it. I've threatened everyone here to stay the hell away from the pool. So, we'll be all alone, and I have a few ideas on how we can spend the time."

"What did you threaten them with?" He smirked at his mate and wondered just how much of a dark side his angel had.

"This and that." She winked. "Each of them will suffer immensely if we're interrupted and it's not an emergency."

"I've no doubt." He glanced back at the laptop screen and debated for a moment. "Umm…"

"What is it?" She came around the desk. "Did you hear something?"

She caressed his arm as he minimized the tab with his email. "It's nothing…let's go."

She didn't move. Instead, she used her free hand to bring back the minimized tab in his email. "Lying with this connection between us is impossible, so why don't you just tell me what's going on?"

"No reason to spoil our fun. Come on." He leaned forward and kissed his way up her arm, all the while hoping to distract her.

"Shit, Patrick." Her gaze was still on the screen and her body stilled under his fingers.

"It's going to be okay."

She leaned against the desk and watched him. "How do you figure that? He has to know who you are. Your family…the little woman. By the way, if

I ever hear you referring to me as that, I'll hand you your balls for your trophy wall."

"Maybe it's a bluff," he offered, but every cell in his body knew that was a lie. "Either way, there's no way he knows our location. Luke ensured it couldn't be traced."

She sat there silently for a moment before letting out the breath she had been holding. "I guess this is the increased danger we were concerned with. What are we going to do?"

"We're going to stick to the plan. Everyone on guard and ready if something happens, but most of all we stay here *together*. We're going to get through this and in the end things will be better." He took her hands into his. "I promise I'll keep you safe."

"I know you will." She shot him a half-hearted smile that didn't quite reach her eyes. "Do you think he'll be back in touch?"

"I do, but I'm not sure we're going to like all his demands."

"We knew there'd be cost for what we're asking for. It's got to be better than living in fear, right?"

He'd have loved to tell her yes, to eliminate any trepidation rising within her, but that would have been a lie. He didn't know what the future would hold, or what President Ashworth would ask for, and that was enough to bring his lion close to the surface. "Both sides will have to work together."

"What if the rest of the shifters aren't willing to go along with this?"

"I've no doubt there will be some, possibly many who are unwilling, but with some luck on our side, most will see this is better than how things are. As the government begins to trust us, they'll give us more and more freedom." He pulled her off the desk and onto his lap. "It's better than being hunted down for the labs, or camps, or even killed. The ones who refuse to live in shifter towns will most likely be imprisoned in the government camps, but that will be their choice."

"They'd have to be caught first."

He nodded in agreement. "There will be some who will want to live under the radar. I can't fix things for everyone, but I'm trying to make this better for those who want the life we once had. For us. It's possible many of us won't be able to return to the careers we had in the past. There'll be jobs within the shifter towns that will need to be filled. If the government stops hunting us down, some might be able to return to the jobs they left."

"What about you? Do you want to set up your medical practice again?"

"Maybe, but I suspect there will be other things that will require my attention. If we can set up a town here, then we'll have a lot to do. What about you?" He hated the concern the idea brought him. Fear of her leaving the castle each day for work, and the danger their connection caused, rose within him. She was his mate, and it was his duty to protect her, but to keep her stuck within the walls of the castle could suffocate her.

"I worked hard to become a scientist, and before I met you I didn't believe there was room for anything else in my life." She ran her hand along the curve of his cheek. "Now, I realize there's so much more to life. I'll do what needs to be done. If I need to go back to work, I will, but if I can stay here with you and do good, I would prefer that. I'm assuming you'd still be Alpha of Forever Creek, correct? Then, as more people come here, you're going to need help."

"This is my land, and yes I plan to remain in charge." He hugged her tight against his body and knew he could never submit to another's authority. Doing so could cost them their home.

"Then you're going to need my help. Unless…"

"Don't even say it, angel."

"Hmm?" She averted her gaze, a clear sign she knew what he meant.

"There's no one else I'd rather have by my side. You're my mate, and in this pride the only one who has more authority than you is me." He nuzzled her neck. Even though she smelled of him, his lion demanded to mark her to ensure everyone knew she was his. It was the lack of clothing that had sent his beast on the path to ward off all others. "I'm planning on officially naming Austin my Lieutenant."

"Your what? What would he do?"

"Lieutenant, he'd be my second in command. He'd help us with the pride, and deal with the government if we need to. Basically, everything he's already doing but this way he'll be officially recognized within the pride and the shifter town once it's set up. That way, no one else will try angling for the job because it would be officially taken."

"Is this like if they wanted to be Alpha? They'd have to fight to the death to take the job from him?"

His lips curled up into a smile. "Yes, unless the Alpha demoted him."

"He'd make you proud, and his military experience will be a benefit in that position." She wrapped her arms around his neck. "So, I'm assuming we're not going swimming. Call Austin up, let's bring him to speed, and you can promote him. Then, if you haven't received a new email, we'll find a better way to occupy our time while we wait."

He reached past her and hit the intercom button. "Austin, I need to see you upstairs."

A second later, Blake's voice came through the speaker. "He's on his way."

"Are you going to tell the rest of the family about the email?" she asked.

He leaned back and shook his head. "Not yet. I'm going to wait and see if we get anything more from him before the end of the business day. Otherwise, tonight, we'll let them know." His gaze traveled down her body.

"Did you bring a robe with you?"

"Why, sweetie, ashamed of my body?" She raised an eyebrow at him.

"The complete opposite. You're beautiful and all mine." He growled the last word as he ran his hands down her stomach.

"Like your brother has any interest in me, and even if he did, he knows you'd kill him for looking at me the wrong way."

"Never mind, stand up." He rose, taking her with him. "You can have my shirt."

"You can't be serious."

He was completely serious, but she just stood there shaking her head as he unbuttoned his shirt. He slid it down his arms and held it out to her. "Just put it on for me."

She took the shirt and shrugged it on. "I can see the way this outfit affects you. Your eyes are more of a warm gold like honey than normal, meaning your beast is closer to the surface. I've seen it before when you've shifted. Your voice has a trace of a growl. Protective and possessive. While some might not like it, I think it's somewhat of a turn-on. As long as you don't take it too far. Remember, you don't own me."

"My angel, I'd never want to stifle your spirit. It would change who you are, and that's never my desire. My beast wants you all to himself. I don't even want another man looking at you the wrong way. Dressed like that, how can someone not look? It makes me want to throw you over my shoulder, take you to our suite, and have my way with you."

"I'm going to hold you to that once you've finished with Austin."

"Oh, angel, you have no idea how much I want you." He closed the distance she had put between them as she slipped on his shirt. His hands slid under the thin material of the shirt and caressed the curve of her hip. "I'm going to rush this with Austin, and then I'm going to have my way with

314

you right here. I'll make you scream my name until your throat is raw. You'll forget all about our missed swim time."

"I was thinking…"

"I'm about to ravish you, and you've got something more serious on your mind?" He shook his head. "I should have known from the look in your eyes I didn't have your complete attention."

"You'll have my complete attention soon."

"I wouldn't have it any other way, angel. So, tell me what's on your mind."

"Maybe things won't be as bad as you fear." Her voice held a touch of innocence and hope that he was missing. "President Ashworth came into office after this all started. Those two months between the elections, and the time he took office, everything changed. Maybe he would have done things differently if it had happened just a few months later."

She had a point there, and although he had considered it, he hadn't given it much thought. President Ashworth had been in office for over a year, and during that time nothing had changed. It was possible he wouldn't have done things the same way, but Patrick couldn't hold out hope for that. He had to be prepared to convince the president there was another way.

"Everything we know, all the government work on the labs and camps, have been dealt with by the person the former president put in charge. Ashworth might not know the full extent of what is being requested, demanded, or even done."

"I'm not delusional enough to think shifters are top priority for him, and now that you've mentioned it, I don't believe he's come out on his stance on shifters. So, it's possible you're right, but he's had enough time to make changes if he wanted to."

"I think she's right. He probably would have handled things

315

differently." Austin strolled toward them.

"What?" Patrick turned to his brother, not at all surprised he'd heard them.

"There's a rumor that someone close to the president is a shifter." Austin took a seat across from the desk and watched them. "I've researched it but haven't been able to find a thing. Whoever it is, it's buried. No pride or clan backing."

"How did you hear this?"

"Military personnel talk." He shrugged. "Like I said, it's a rumor, but if he's willing to discuss your proposal, I'd have to think it's not just a rumor. So, you've heard from him?"

"Yes." Patrick brought him up to speed, wondering the entire time if the rumor was true. If there were a shifter close to the president, it could change everything. As long as the shifter hadn't gone rogue, of course.

"Waiting. That was always the worst part of the military. Hurry up and wait." He joked. "Too many military families have said that over the years, but until now I didn't realize what it was like to be on the other side. I always knew what I was waiting for…orders or deployments. Spouses and families were always waiting for us to come back home. Now, here I am again, sitting here waiting."

"Well, maybe this will be something to take your mind off of it." Patrick leaned against the corner of his desk, his arm around Clarissa's waist. "I…we'd…like you to be our Lieutenant. You've been unofficially acting as one since I took over the pride, but I want to make it official."

"Because of this proposal with the government?" Austin's expression gave no hint as to what he was thinking.

"No. I've been thinking about it for some time. When it was just the family, it didn't seem to matter as much since they had already accepted your role within the pride, but adding more members and mates makes it more important."

"What do you think about this, Clarissa?"

"I think there's no one better for the position." She fingered one of the shirt buttons. "I'm just getting used to the pride structure, but from the way things have happened, I've always had the impression you were second in command."

"If there's to be negotiation with the president, then I want you as my Lieutenant. It would give you a reason to be informed of what's happening, attend any meetings that might take place."

She spun toward him, her eyes wide with fear. "Meetings? You mean you'd leave here to go meet with him?"

"My angel."

"No, what if it's a trap? What if it's his way of eliminating you before you could start any problems?"

"We've got to take that risk," Austin spoke up.

"He's right." He ran his hand down her arm. "We'll do our best to make sure we know what side they're on before we agree to meet. We'll take precautions."

"Then at such time, I demand to go with you."

"What?" He pushed off the desk to stand.

"If it's safe enough for you, then it's safe enough for me. I want to go with you."

"Depending on the situation, it could be good to have her at your side," Austin added. "Having a human on our side, especially one who knows what's been happening in the labs, might not be such a bad thing."

"This is my mate we're talking about."

"What about our talk earlier?" she snapped. "The one where you mentioned not crushing my spirit. I'm not a possession. I'm a woman, with my own mind, and I want to go. If I'm supposed to help lead this pride, then I should be there."

"You already said it yourself, it could be dangerous," Patrick started, but she only cut him off.

"If so, then there's *still* nowhere else I'd rather be. I'd rather die by your side than have you hundreds of miles away being killed."

"No one is going to get killed." Austin rose from the chair. "If it comes down to meeting them, we'll meet on neutral ground and we'll take precautions. Remember, they're taking as big of a risk as we are. So, how about until the time it comes, we don't argue about who's going to attend the meeting and who isn't. Clarissa, I agree with you on coming along, but as a shifter I can also agree with Patrick. He's only trying to protect you, not lock you away here. Let's just wait and see how things progress with them, and take things one day at a time."

"And you wonder why we think you'll make an excellent Lieutenant." She smiled at him. "I agree to wait until the time comes, but don't think I'll give up."

"I'd never expect anything less from you." He pulled her back against him. "One thing I love about you is your fighting spirit. You'll always keep me on my toes."

Epilogue

Three weeks had passed since the negotiations had begun, and Patrick was beginning to question if they'd ever come to a mutual agreement. For each topic they managed to iron out, two more issues popped up to replace it. He'd spent more time in front of the computer than with his pride, or even with his mate. Work had begun to consume him until he wasn't sure there was life outside of his office.

President Ashworth had begun to push for a face-to-face meeting, but Patrick wanted more before they got to that step. He had wanted the meeting to be the final piece. They'd meet, work out some final details, shake hands, and things would change. He knew it wouldn't be that easy, but he could hope.

Even through his desperation, he knew that each day was bringing them closer to their goal. One day soon, they wouldn't have to live in constant fear. Then all the work and hours he'd put in would be worth it.

Through the process, he had only shared most of the details with Clarissa and Austin. Updates from Austin kept him informed of what was happening with everyone else, but it wasn't the same. He missed the family time they had together.

With Nolan gone, rescuing a friend in need, MaKayla had begun to come out of her shell. She had started speaking to them. She and Clarissa had bonded over their memories of Andrew. Despite this, she was still a very scared young girl. He had hoped she'd commit to his pride before the changes, therefore ensuring her safety, but so far that hadn't happened.

"I've brought you a sandwich." Clarissa strolled toward him with a plate in one hand and a glass of what appeared to be iced tea in the other. "You're working too hard and stressing too much."

"That's what it takes to be Alpha."

"Well, I'm also bringing the message that Luke found something. He said he needed ten minutes, and then he'd be over to tell you." She placed the food in front of him. "Turkey and cheddar with spicy mustard, just how you like."

"Thank you." He picked up half the sandwich, but his hunger wasn't for food. "Unless whatever Luke found changes things, I'll be done in an hour. I thought maybe we could go for that swim we never had time for."

"I think I could squeeze it in. I might even be able to find that bikini."

"Not that it will be on long." Images of her in the bikini filled his thoughts, but more to the point, images of stripping her of those small pieces of material.

"Patrick..." Luke's voice died off as Patrick ran his hand up Clarissa's thigh. "Sorry, I'll come back."

"It's okay, Luke." She told him without turning around to see him.

"She told me you found something." Patrick tossed the piece of sandwich that was in his hand back onto the plate. "It better be good news."

"Actually, it is." Luke stepped forward and held out a disk to Patrick. "I have confirmation that Mallory's daughter is alive."

"Then you've narrowed down her location?" Patrick took hold of the disk, and new hope shot through him.

"No, but it shouldn't be long. I've got a location that she left three weeks ago, so I'm on her trail. That's how I know she has the child with her. Video stills from the security camera at the grocery store are on the disk." Luke shoved his hands in the pocket of his jeans. "The little girl is so young. Maybe a year. All I know for sure is she's small enough for Mallory to carry her."

"A year?" He thought back to Songborn's files. The tests on other subjects had shown an infant who would have never survived the injection with shifter blood. He would have expected the child to be at least two.

"It's impossible for her to be much older than that. You can see for yourself."

"Could…" She paused and looked at Patrick. "I'm going to say what we're both thinking but neither of us wants to voice our concerns."

"What?" Luke asked, completely in the dark.

"Could it have happened during her pregnancy?"

"Shit!" Luke's statement summed up what everyone was thinking. "What does that mean for Mallory?"

"We don't know that's the case," Patrick started, but then stopped and shook his head. "It's the most logical conclusion, especially since Songborn's file on the Barrows goes back longer than a year. As for Mallory, I don't know, only testing will determine the results on her. Do I believe she can now shift? No, it's too much like being bitten."

"Is it possible that her daughter could have gotten it that way?" Luke pressed.

"If introduced at the right time, yes. It would have the same reaction as if the father was a shifter. The blood would have produced the changes within the fetus, but depending on how much blood was introduced, it could speed up the initial transformation that each shifter goes through."

"I just had a horrible thought," Clarissa said. "What if Songborn used a shifter's sperm to impregnate Mallory? Maybe there are more out there like Mallory's daughter."

"Couldn't happen." Luke's voice held a touch of relief.

"Why not?"

"Shifters can only impregnate their mates. We wouldn't be able to get anyone else pregnant no matter how hard we tried," he explained. "The blood, however, could act as the trigger, producing some or all of a shifter's characteristics."

"At least that's one thing we don't have to worry about, and if we can keep a lid on the blood triggering a transition, maybe we can stop this from happening to someone else."

"Have you told President Ashworth about Mallory and her daughter yet? Are you going to?" Luke questioned.

"Not yet, and not until we have her here or things have finalized with him. Right now, we're still negotiating." He glanced back at the computer screen, but there was nothing new waiting for him.

"Right." Luke tipped his head toward the door. "I'll get back to it, then."

"Thanks, Luke, and don't mention anything about what we've discussed to anyone yet. I'm going to go back over the files this evening and see if there's anything that hints to the pregnancy theory. So much of it is in shorthand that even I can't make heads or tails of it yet."

As Luke left, she ran her hand up the inside of his thigh. "I guess our swim will have to wait."

"Not a chance, angel. I'm going to take you to the pool and have my way with you." He needed a little time away from it all to get his thoughts around everything, but more importantly he needed time with his mate. His beast was demanding it. There was nothing he could do until Luke found the Barrows, but he'd make sure Austin was on standby. He'd send Austin to find the Barrows, because he was the one that could be the most convincing. Even if he might scare Mallory at first, he'd be the one who could protect her and her daughter. Patrick would focus on the negotiations, and Austin could worry about bringing Mallory and her daughter back safely. They'd work together, and in the end they'd get more done.

"What about this new development?"

"The only thing that's new is we know for sure she's alive, and we know her age now. There's nothing we can do about how she became infected with our blood, and even if I found something in the files, we can't do anything for her until she's here." He stood and placed his hands on either side of her waist. "With you, there's a lot of things I can do."

"I'm going to keep you occupied for every minute you'll stay away from this office. We deserve it."

"Then let's get started, love. I've got a few hours to burn and there's no one else I'd rather spend it with. My beautiful angel, I love you."

He leaned down, closing the distance between them, and pressed his lips to hers. Desire and need coursed through him. Since she had come into his life, she had given him a reason to fight for what was right. The Forever Creek pride would always fight for what was most important—love and family—until they could fight no more.

Furever Mated

Complete Crimson Hollow Box Set

Romancing the Fox

Sinopa refuses to live among the tribe and produce cubs, but to appease her family she agrees to Garret Fox posing as her fiancé for a week. The ploy backfires when an undeniable attraction manifests between her and the predator. Is he meant to be her mate, or is her life in danger?

Loving the Bears

Ari and Kaden always knew they'd share one mate who would complete their unique bond, but when they find Camellia—the right woman to satisfy them *and* their bears—they must help her overcome her past before she can accept the truth.

A Lion's Chance

After a near death experience, Ginger Fox takes off to visit her brother, who recently mated with the Deputy of the Crimson Hollow Tribe. Meanwhile, Liam O'Neil catches Ginger's scent and he can't stop himself. With the help of a little boy who needs them, Ginger soon realizes there's more to life than touring the country, but is she ready to settle down with a lion?

Swift Move

When the tribe sends Brett Oaks to bring home the runaway Swift, he has no idea she is his mate. Now he has to overcome her terror and need for revenge before he can claim her as his own.

Purrable Lion

When Captain Noah Jones, is sent to investigate recent attack near the tribe he expects to find carnage—just like with previous attacks. What he doesn't expect is to find *her*, his mate. Karri Mallory not only finds herself in the wrong place at the wrong time, but if she wants to stay alive she must put her trust in the very people The Saviors are hunting.

Bearly Alive

Jase, Chief of the Crimson Hollow Tribe, has stood aside, watching Becky deal with the demons of her past while and open her heart to shifters—but when his bear alerts him to the peril she's in, it's time to intervene and protect his mate. He must claim her now or risk his bear going rogue to eliminate the threats to her and her son.

Saved by a Lion

With a bounty on her head Arlene Mallory wants revenge but before she can get it The Saviors find her. Chained in a cellar she vows to take the information she has to her grave and it will be a painful journey. Roger is tasked with finding her, but he's doing it for more than his tribe—she's his mate. Will he find her before it's too late?

Different Sides

Murder? One call is all it takes to shatter Elise Dalton's heart. Her father's been murdered and the accused is none other than the man she had given her heart to. Though he'd cut himself out of her life years earlier, being the daughter to the chief of police, she has heard enough gossip to let her know that the choices he's made have lead him down a path of self-destruction. He isn't the same man she'd fallen in love with but a part of her doesn't want to believe he could kill her father in cold blood.

Gun carrying, motorcycle riding, bad boy Flash Arquette has done some terrible shit in his life. He's even taken the fall for someone, and every time he's done the time for his crimes. This time, though, he's innocent and no one's listening to him. He doesn't care what anyone thinks of him except Elise. She had to know the truth. He's hurt her enough in the past, but he would never have done this to her. The only problem is the convincing evidence against him and his inability to give them proof of his innocence without breaking the contract he signed.

Their lives have taken opposing paths, but as the steel bars close around Flash, Elise realizes she's lost him for good. The small ray of hope that he could change dies and the grief doubles. When those around Flash come forth with information that he's been set up, she's not sure she believes them, but she has to find out the truth. Nothing will bring her father back but she might be able to save Flash from death row.

Marissa Dobson

Born and raised in the Pittsburgh, Pennsylvania area, Marissa Dobson now resides about an hour from Washington, D.C. She's a lady who likes to keep busy, and is always busy doing something. With two different college degrees, she believes you're never done learning.

Being the first daughter to an avid reader, this gave her the advantage of learning to read at a young age. Since learning to read she has always had her nose in a book. It wasn't until she was a teenager that she started writing down the stories she came up with.

Marissa is blessed with a wonderful supportive husband, Thomas. He's her other half and allows her to stay home and pursue her writing. He puts up with all her quirks and listens to her brainstorm in the middle of the night.

Her writing buddy Pup Cameron, a cocker spaniel, is always around to listen to her bounce ideas off him. He might not be able to answer, but he's helpful in his own ways.

She loves to hear from readers so send her an email at marissa@marissadobson.com or visit her online at http://www.marissadobson.com.

Other Books by Marissa Dobson

Alaskan Tigers:

Tiger Time

The Tiger's Heart

Tigress for Two

Night with a Tiger

Trusting a Tiger

Alaskan Tigers Box Set Vol. 1

Jinx's Mate

Two for Protection

Bearing Secrets

Tiger Tracks

Healing the Clan

Alaskan Tigers Box Set Vol. 2

Her Black Tiger

Tiger Trouble

Alpha Claimed

Forever Creek Shifters:

Forever Fight

Protecting Forever

Crimson Hollow:

Romancing the Fox

Loving the Bears

A Lion's Chance

Swift Move

Purrable Lion

Bearly Alive

Saved by a Lion

Furever Mated Box Set

Stormkin:

Storm Queen

Reaper:

A Touch of Death

SEALed for You:

Ace in the Hole

Explosive Passion

Operation Family

Marine for You:

Lucky Chance

Back from Hell

A Marines Second Chance

Tanner Cycles:

Until Sydney

Beyond Monogamy:

Theirs to Treasure

Cedar Grove Medical:

Hope's Toy Chest

Destiny's Wish

Leena's Dream

Fate:

Snowy Fate

Sarah's Fate

Mason's Fate

As Fate Would Have It

Half Moon Harbor Resort:

Learning to Live

Learning What Love Is

Her Cowboy's Heart

Half Moon Harbor Resort Vol. 1

United Homefront Ranch:

Destination Heaven

Phantom Security

Different Sides

Undercover Agent

Clearwater:

Winterbloom

Unexpected Forever

Losing to Win

Christmas Countdown

The Surrogate

Clearwater Romance Volume

One

Small Town Doctor

Stand Alone:

SEALed Rescue

SEALed in Texas

Through Smoke

Through Fire

Starting Over

Secret Valentine

Restoring Love

www.ingramcontent.com/pod-product-compliance
Lightning Source LLC
Chambersburg PA
CBHW020905200626
46814CB00001BA/191